"He's in it!" Crowder's eyes licked over me like a blowtorch.

"Show me proof," Commodore Grayson said. "Then we'll talk about it."

"Turn him over to me for an hour and I'll have all the proof you want!"

I kept my eyes on the commodore's face. "Answer his questions," he said. His lips barely moved.

"Now then, Tarleton," Crowder said in a saw-edged tone, "when was the last time you saw Danton?"

"I didn't know it was the last time," I said. A sick feeling was growing under my ribs. *Paul, what have they done to you . . . ?*

PLUS THREE BONUS STORIES

KEITH LAUMER

THE STAR TREASURE

BAEN BOOKS

THE STAR TREASURE

A Baen Book

Baen Publishing Enterprises
260 Fifth Avenue
New York, N.Y. 10001

First Baen printing, October 1986

ISBN: 0-671-65596-5

Acknowledgments: The three bonus stories published with this novel have previously appeared and are copyright as follows: "In the Queue," *Orbit* 7, © 1970 by Damon Knight; "A Relic of War," *Analog*, © 1969 by The Condé Nast Publications Inc.; "Test to Destruction," *Dangerous Visions*, © 1967 by Harlan Ellison.

Cover art by Vincent Di Fate

Printed in the United States of America

Distributed by
SIMON & SCHUSTER
TRADE PUBLISHING GROUP
1230 Avenue of the Americas
New York, N.Y. 10020

PROLOGUE

The wide doors swung open; the elderly man, tall and straight-backed in a braid- and decoration-heavy uniform advanced across the room, halted, executed a formal salute.

"Good morning, Admiral," said the man who sat behind the immense, mirror-polished desk. "How pleasant to see you. It's been some time; not since your retirement, I believe." He smiled faintly, the intricate network of fine wrinkles around his eyes almost invisible against his dark skin. His small, round skull was entirely hairless. One large, pink-palmed hand toyed with a silver writing instrument. Except for that and a folded paper the desk was totally bare.

"I requested an interview two weeks ago," the old man said. His voice had lost its resonance, but still carried force. His face, hollow and sagging with advanced age, was set in a grim expression.

"Ah," the seated man said easily. "Unfortunately, I've been much occupied lately—"

"I know," his visitor said. "That's the reason for my coming here today."

The black man's smile faded by an almost imperceptible degree. "To be sure, Admiral. I've read your note; I understand your concern—"

"You're making a serious mistake, Lord Imbolo. I don't know the reasons for what's been happening—but whatever they are, they're in error."

The seated man placed the pen on the desk carefully, as if handling a rare and fragile object. He sighed.

"There's no error, Admiral," he started—

"The charges are fantastic!" the old man cut him off. "They're lying to you, Imbolo!"

"I think not, Admiral—"

"You have to call a halt to this pogrom, Imbolo. It can't go on!" The old man's voice shook, but his eyes glared with the fierceness of a trapped falcon.

"Admiral, you've served the Public long and well; you find it difficult to believe that changes are taking place—"

"I know all about the changes, Imbolo. I've heard the Hateniks ranting. I've seen the underground papers. I have nothing to do with that. It's the Navy I'm thinking of. Over three hundred years of tradition are being destroyed by this sneaking corps of informers, weasels, worming their way into every level of command—"

"You're not in possession of all the facts, Admiral. Rest assured—"

"I'll not rest at all until I've heard your assurance that these cases will be reopened, your informers called off, and these men restored to duty!"

"Impossible," Imbolo said flatly.

The old man's hand slipped inside his silver-buttoned tunic, came out gripping a flat, snub-barreled power gun. Without a word he raised it, took aim at the still faintly smiling face before him, pressed the firing stud.

For a long moment he stood, his arm extended, sighting along the weapon, before his face reflected the realization that nothing had happened. Slowly his arm fell. He seemed to shrink; the rigidity went out of his face, his shoulders. Abruptly he was merely a withered figure in an ill-fitting costume. Languidly, Lord Imbolo tapped a spot on the desktop. Instantly, a pair of immaculately uniformed Marine guards were in the room.

"The Admiral is unwell," he said softly. "See that he's cared for."

The gun dropped to the floor with a soft thump as the impassive men took the would-be assassin's arms, turned him, walked him from the room. Lord Imbolo watched them go, then he sighed, and resumed his interrupted perusal of the latest list of officers and men suspected of unreliability and other crimes against the Companies and the Public.

PART ONE

One

Midshipman Blane was cashiered at 0800 hours on Sarday, Ma 35, 2190, on the parade deck of the ship of the line *Tyrant*, fifty million tons, on station off Callisto, nine months out of Terra on the Trans-Jovian cruise.

Blane was a slim, sandy-haired lad only a year out of the Academy. He stood obediently at attention while the commodore read the findings of the court: guilty of attempted sabotage in that he did willfully place and attempt to detonate an explosive device with the intention of destroying a capital Fleet vessel on active patrol in Deep Space.

"In an earlier age," the commodore went on, "a terrible vengeance would have been extracted from a man who undertook, however ineffectively, the destruction of his ship and the murder of eighteen thousand shipmates. Today the law holds that society may legitimately exact only those punishments commensurate with its ability to confer benefits.

"Charles Yates Blane, society has reposed confidence in your abilities and integrity; that confidence is now withdrawn. Society has conferred on you rank and responsibility; of that rank and those responsibilities you are now relieved. Society has endowed you with citizenship and the privileges of participating in her benefits; those privileges are now revoked. You are no longer a member of the United Planetary Navy, nor have you the right to wear the uniform."

At a command the drummers started the roll. The commodore grasped the insignia on the Midshipman's collar and ripped it away. He stripped the single gold stripe from his cuffs. He snapped off the ornamental silver buttons with the Fleet eagle, one by one, and dropped them at his feet.

Blane didn't move, except to sway a little at each jerk, but tears were running down his face.

The drums halted. In the aching silence, the vice-Commodore said, "Charles Blane, ex-officer, ex-citizen, you will now be removed to a place of security and held there until the arrival of a Fleet picket boat which will transport you to a designated location where you will be free to work out your destiny unassisted, and unimpeded, by the society which you have forfeited."

For the first time a trace of emotion showed on the Commodore's face: the faintest of sneers—all that was left to a civilized man of the bared fangs of the ancestral carnivore.

"Take him away," he said. The drummers resumed the roll; the guard closed in, fore and aft, and walked him down the gauntlet of the men and women he'd tried to kill, and out of our lives.

2

Afterwards, Paul Danton—Commander Danton during duty hours—stopped to talk to me.

"What did you think of the ceremony, Ban?" he asked.

"Anachronistic," I said. "Somewhat self-consciously so. But effective. I gave up my plans for blowing up the ship when those buttons hit the deck."

"Why do you suppose he did it?"

"I can't conceive. He seems to have gone about it rather badly."

"I wonder if he really intended to succeed?"

"I assume so—unless it was all a trick to get himself marooned on a Class I world." I smiled at this whimsy, but Paul looked thoughtful, as if he were considering the possibility.

"Could he have had any legitimate motivation, Ban?"

"For killing us all off? We may not be the best company in the world, but that hardly justifies such sweeping measures."

"For a gesture of rebellion," Paul corrected.

"Paul, you haven't been reading Hatenik pamphlets, have you?" I said it jokingly, but somehow it didn't ring as humorously as I had intended.

"Perhaps even the Hateniks have their points," he said mildly.

" 'We hate hate, and we'll kill any dirty son of a slime culture who doesn't agree with us'?" I suggested.

"They're fanatics, of course," Paul said. "But can we afford to ignore any voice of our times?"

"Are you trying to tell me something, Paul?"

"On the contrary," he said, "I'm looking for answers."

* * *

The routine of the ship went on. We moved on out to the vicinity of Saturn. There were four hours of watch to stand each day; there were dances and banquets and lectures and concerts and games. Among the ten thousand female crew members there was an adequate number of young and beautiful ones to make life entertaining. The weeks passed. I saw Paul now and then; we didn't discuss Hateniks and the basis of civilization. In fact I had almost forgotten our talk, until the night of my arrest.

3

It was just after oh three hundred hours when the deck police rapped at my door. They were very polite about it: The captain's compliments, and would Mr. Tarleton report to the bridge as soon as convenient. Their hands never strayed near the guns at their hips, but I got the idea just the same.

I hadn't turned in yet. They stood by while I wiped the whiskers off my chin and pulled on my deck jacket. Only one of them fell in beside me for the walk upstairs; the other man posted himself beside my door at parade rest and watched us go. I appreciated his delicacy: frisking an officer's room with him watching would be bad for morale.

It was a long walk back to the A deck lift, a long ride up to G territory. *Tyrant* wasn't one of those modern cybernetic jobs, manned by ten men and a switchboard. She had over a hundred miles of corridor in her. We couldn't have covered over one percent of that, all in a dead silence like the one before the casket slides into the converter.

Armed guards let us through a big armored door

marked *Command Deck—Auth Pers Only.* Inside, a warrant with a face like a clenched fist looked me over and jabbed buttons on a panel. An inner door opened and I went through and the door closed softly behind me. I was standing on fine gray carpet, smelling a faint odor of Havana leaf and old brandy. Beyond a big curved quartz window that filled the far end of the room Saturn hung, half a million miles away, big enough to light the room like a stage. It was a view that almost, but not quite took the show away from the man behind the desk.

He was all the things a Fleet Commodore ought to be: big, wide-shouldered, square-jawed, with recruiting-poster features and iron-gray temples, his shirt open at the neck to show the hair on his chest. The big Annapolis ring glinted on his finger in the dim light from the desk lamp that was set at just the proper angle to glare in the customer's eyes when he sat in the big leather chair. I saluted and he motioned with a finger and I sat. He looked at me and the silence stretched out like a cable under test.

"You enjoy Navy life, Lieutenant?" His voice was like a boulder rolling over a deckplate.

"Well enough, sir," I said. I was feeling more baffled than worried.

He nodded as if I had made an illuminating remark. Perhaps I had.

"You come from a Navy family," he went on. "Admiral Tarleton was a distinguished officer. I had the honor of serving under him on more than one occasion. His death was a great loss to us all."

I didn't comment on that. Most of the Navy had served under my father at one time or another.

"We live in troubled times, Lieutenant," the Commodore said, brisk now. "A time of conflicting loyalties." I had the feeling he wasn't talking just to me. There was a soft sound from the corner of the room behind me and I looked that way and saw the other man, standing with his arms folded, beside a glass-doored bookcase. His name was Crowder; he was short, soft-necked, with a broad rump and a face to match. I knew him slightly as a civilian advisor on the commodore's staff. I wondered why he was here. He made a smile with his wide lips and looked at my chin. To my surprise he spoke:

"What Commodore Grayson means is that certain misguided individuals appear to see such a dichotomy," he said. "In actuality, of course, the interests of the companies and the Navy are identical." He had a strange, uneven voice that seemed to be about to break into a falsetto.

I stood by and waited for the lightning bolt that would destroy the poor fellow who had been so naive as to interrupt the commodore—with a remark that was 180 degrees out of phase with what he'd been saying.

But the commodore only frowned a little, in a well-bred way. "A junior officer is at a disadvantage in assessing what he might call the subjective aspects of a complex situation," he said. "Academy life is sheltered; fleet patrol duty keeps a man jumping." He smiled at me in comradely fashion, bridging the gap in years and rank. Or almost bridging it. Under the surface charm I caught the glitter of something ominous, like water in the hold.

"You knew Commander Danton quite well—?" Crowder threw the question from behind me, cut it off suddenly, as if he'd said too much. I turned slowly and tried to see into his face.

"What do you mean, 'knew'?" I said. It came out

sounding a little harsher than was quite appropriate for a junior officer addressing an FS-24.

" 'Know him' I meant, of course." His voice was still as bland as his kind of voice could be.

"I've known the commander since I was a small boy," I said.

"What are Commander Danton's views on the matter of, ah, divided loyalties?" His tone was a few degrees crisper now.

"Commander Danton is the best man I know," I said. "Why do you ask?"

"Just answer my questions, Lieutenant," Crowder said.

"That'll do, Crowder," Grayson growled. But instead of fading back, Crowder pushed away from the wall and walked over into the light. He frowned at me, at the big man behind the desk.

"Perhaps you don't quite grasp the situation, Commodore," he said in a tone like a torn fingernail. "This is a security matter."

I looked at the little man's doughy face, at the fat neck where his collar had rubbed it pink. I looked at the commodore and waited for him to squash this underling like a bug under his boot. The big man looked at the plump civilian and some of the color went out of his outdoor-man tan. He cleared his throat and stared past me. His eyes looked blind. The silence was like an explosion.

"Now then, Tarleton," Crowder said in a saw-edged tone, "when was the last time you saw Danton?"

I kept my eyes on Grayson's face. His eyes stirred and moved to me. "Answer his questions," he said. His lips barely moved.

"I don't know," I said.

"What do you mean, you don't know?" Crowder rapped.

"I mean I didn't know it was the last time," I said, and pried into his face with my eyes, trying to dig some meaning out of it. A sick feeling was growing somewhere down under my ribs. *Paul, Paul, what have they done to you . . . ?*

"Are you being tricky, boy?" Crowder snarled, showing his teeth.

I tried to catch Grayson's eye, but he wasn't there any more. He was somewhere far away, where rank still lived in its high tower, above all contention. I was on my own—and Crowder was still waiting, rocking on his heels.

I stood up and faced him. "I'm not a boy, Mr. Crowder," I said. "I'm a line officer of the Navy. And if this is line-of-duty, I suggest we have it on tape." I reached for the record button on the commodore's desk, and Crowder shot out a hand and covered it.

"Mr. Tarleton, I suggest you start realizing the position you're in and begin giving me the kind of cooperation I expect." He let his eyes slide to Grayson. "That the commodore and I expect."

"Tell me what you want to hear," I said. "I'll see if I can say it."

"Has Danton spoken to you of anything—any, ah, discovery he fancied he'd made, perhaps? Some supposed secret he pretended to have uncovered?"

I looked thoughtful. "He did comment . . ."

"Yes, yes?" Crowder glanced at Grayson triumphantly.

". . . that the Chambertin '78 in the Deck Officers' mess was a trifle tannic," I said. "But I don't suppose that's any secret."

Crowder's undershot jaw dropped. His little pig eyes almost disappeared.

"A jokester, eh?" He spat out the words like a cockroach in the soup and reached for a desk button. Grayson moved then. He stood, looming over the security man like a djinn over Aladdin.

"That's enough," he said as softly as steel slicing cheese. "Nobody brigs my officers without a charge that sticks!"

"He's in it!" Crowder grunted, but he pulled his hand back.

"Show me proof," Grayson said. "Then we'll talk about it."

"Turn him over to me for an hour and I'll have all the proof you want!" Crowder's eyes licked over me like a blowtorch.

"Get out, Crowder," Grayson whispered. The civilian opened and closed his mouth, but he knew when to stand on a pat hand.

He stalked to the door, looked back from there, looked around at the rug and the paneled walls and the view behind the big desk. Then he looked at Grayson and smiled a knowing little smile.

"We'll see, Commodore," he said. His grin made it an insult.

When the door had closed behind him, Grayson looked at me. I had the feeling there were things he wanted to say, but he didn't say them. It was just as well. I wouldn't have believed him.

"That will be all, Mr. Tarleton," he said in a dull voice. "Consider yourself under arrest in quarters until further notice." He sat back of the desk, just as he had when I came in; but it was different now. He didn't look like a symbol anymore; just an old man in a trap.

Back in my suite, I called Paul's apartment, but there was no answer.

Two

I stripped and stepped into the sonospray and then used the tingler, but I still felt soiled. As I pulled on fresh clothing, something crackled in the breast pocket.

It was a note on thin blue paper, folded and sealed with a blob of red contact-wax. It was brief and to the point:

> Ban: This is ninety second paper, so don't linger over it. I may be on the trail of something very disturbing. If I should drop out of sight, it will mean I was right. I don't want to involve you in this; but I ask you to convey a message to Trilia: *Confirmed.* Will you do this for your friend,
>
> Paul

I read it three times, looking for the meaning that seemed to be eluding me, but it became no clearer. Then the paper turned to gray ash in my fingers and powdered into dust.

I wiped my hands and looked at the blur that the

wall had turned into, for as long as it takes for hope to wither and die. Then the desk phone buzzed. I pressed the button.

"Lieutenant," a cautious voice said. I recognized it as MacDonald, boat deck NCOIC. "Look, maybe I'm out of line, sir," he said, "but—I just got a prelim code 78."

"So?"

"That's the change-station alert code, Lieutenant. *Tyrant*'s going to pull out in a few hours—and we've got a couple boats ex-hull."

"Go on."

"Commander Danton logged out at twenty hundred hours, ETR oh four thirty."

"Destination?"

"Phoebe Station."

I thought that over; there was nothing on Phoebe but a nav beacon and some standard emergency gear. Nothing to take a Section Commander out on a lone mission on off-watch time.

"You said 'boats,' MacDonald."

"Hatcher took a cutter out half an hour behind the commander. A G-boat, one of the ones with the paired 20 mm's. And she carried full charges; the son of a bitch checked."

I chewed my lip and thought about that. I didn't like what I was thinking. Hatcher was a subordinate of Crowder's—a stupid brutal man, capable of anything.

"Very well," I said. "Warm up nine-two. I'll be along in a few minutes."

I dialed myself a drink and swallowed half of it, finished dressing. I eased the door open; the corridor was clear. I stepped out and started toward Y deck, with the feeling that I was walking in an evil dream.

2

MacDonald met me in the launch bay. He was a short, well-muscled man with red hair that grew flat to a round skull, and burn scars along his jaw from a boat deck explosion in '88.

"She's topped off, sir, full reserves," he said. "Not that that'll help much if the execute order comes through before you dock back in." His eyes asked questions, but I went past him, down the row of sleek-hulled boats waiting for any hands that would use them—or misuse them. He followed, stood by as I climbed in.

"The last time the commander came in from one of these ring-runs, it took me half a watch to buff the rock burns off his boat," he said. "What's he doing out there, Lieutenant?"

"Worried about the equipment, MacDonald?" I showed him a grin that didn't quite make it.

"The equipment—and maybe some other things."

I nodded as if that was the answer I'd expected. "I'm on a special run, in case anybody asks. That's all you know, Mac, understand?"

"I guess you know what you're doing, Lieutenant." His expression said he doubted it. His look slid along the line to the two-man G-boat at the end.

"How's if I side you, Lieutenant?" his voice was a little hoarse. It had a right to be: he was laying twenty-eight years and his neck on the line.

"Negative. You stay here, in the clear. I need a good man behind me."

I buttoned up and thought some thoughts while the relays clicked and the tube pressure built. And then I stopped thinking them, because there was nothing among them that made my future look bright, or very long, even. I stuck with just the one idea: that Paul Danton was out there alone somewhere; and the G-boat that had followed him was the Navy's latest hunter-killer, with all guns loaded, and manned by a sadist.

Then the GO light flashed and I closed the lever and they poured a concrete dam in my lap; when I could see again I was twenty miles out, with the mile-long city of lights that was *Tyrant* dwindling behind me and the diamond blaze of the Rings arching across the screen ahead.

3

Almost at once I picked up the characteristic residuals from a fleet scout. It took a few moments for the course computer to take readings, analyze the data and produce an extrapolation that I liked no better than the other aspects of the situation.

Paul hadn't made for Phoebe station after all. His track headed straight for the Rings; to be precise, for a point at the edge of Cassini's Division. The fact that the spot in question was over the Interdict line and twelve thousand miles into off-limits territory was only a part of my aversion to it: a few million cubic miles of dust and ice scattered across a few billion cubic miles of space constituted a difficult obstacle course through which to take a boat, roughly equivalent to strolling across the sighting-in range at Carswell on a busy afternoon. I was still contemplating that thought when the panel speaker came to life:

"Carousel nine-two, code forty. Code forty. AK, nine-two!"

The voice was that of Walters, another of the civilian advisory staff. Code forty meant "abort mission soonest."

"In case you've forgotten your manual, Tarleton, that's a recall order," he went on. *"You have exactly ten seconds to comply!"*

I had no adequate answer for that. I listened to the star static and watched the rings grow on the screen, resolving into individual points of light and clots and streamers of dust, looming over me like an impending storm. Or possibly it was just my guilty conscience that made it look that way. It wasn't every day that a line officer of the Navy mutinied—even me.

An hour later my proximity alarms began emitting warning bursts: the garbage density ahead was reaching the limits of my D and D gear to handle. I punched in a deceleration and switched my forward screen to high magnification but saw nothing to explain what Paul had been doing here. The plane of the rings was about ten thousand miles ahead now, the Division a stark black swatch through the brightness that filled the screen. The boat bucked and yawed as the automatics made course corrections to avoid the occasional high velocity particle orbiting here.

I tuned up and down the band, searching for a transmission on the Section frequencies, to no effect. By that time I was looking across a dazzle like sheet ice at the globe of Saturn, spreading over sixty degrees of sky. My speed was down to nine hundred kilometers per hour, a snail's crawl but still too fast for the amount of gravel pinging on my hull.

Paul had thought there was something here that was worth throwing away a career—and possibly a life—for. Something Crowder had sent a G-boat to prevent him from reaching. What difference my being here would make, I didn't really know; but as long as there was a chance that Paul needed my help I had to try. I had gotten that far with my inspirational talk when the matter was taken out of my hands by a blast from the alarms an instant before the panel swung up and smashed the world into rubble.

4

I floated somewhere, a mote among the swarm of fragments circling a dead star. A few eons went past in their leisurely fashion, and some of the bigger pieces bumped together and stuck. The resultant mass hurtled on through space, sweeping up the dust that rained in, generating heat and light—

The light hurt my eyes. I fetched a groan up from somewhere down around the planetary core and managed to raise an eyelid. The panel before me was atwinkle with pretty flashing colors, all signalling emergency. Beyond that the DV screen framed a golden glow that faded to cherry red and dimmed out. I dragged myself upright in the harness and swallowed a taste of blood and made an effort to focus in on the dials. What I saw was not encouraging. The cryston hull of the boat was intact, of course; but what was inside it hadn't fared so well: life support system inoperative, main drive inoperative, oxy tanks broached and leaking. I was still alive, but that was a mere detail, subject to change.

The boat was still moving along at a good clip, tumbling slowly. The braking tubes responded at about half power when I tried them. I had managed to reduce speed to 30 KPH relative before a long slab came sailing out of the dark at me, end over end, and caromed off my hull aft, putting a nice spin on her to go with the tumble. Two more solid impacts and half a dozen minor ones later I had averaged out to a matched course with the rest of the junk. I had time then to notice a cut on my jaw and a swollen eye and register a cabin pressure of .9 PSI at a temperature of -56 K before I saw Paul Danton's boat drifting a thousand yards away with the hatch open.

5

My suit was still tight, of course, which accounted for my continued survival. I managed to open the hatch in spite of its battered condition and climbed out under all those stars. I spent a few seconds reacquainting myself with the size of infinity before kicking off toward Paul's boat.

It was standing on end, slowly falling over backward. At a hundred yards I could see that it was empty. There were no signs of external damage, which meant that Paul had come in more cautiously than I, under full control; which indicated in turn that this was indeed his chosen destination. And unless he had headed off into the haze in history's most elaborate suicide, he had to be within a few hundred yards of his boat. The only hiding places in sight were two boulders, one the size of a condominium apartment, dead ahead, the other smaller and off to the left. I picked the more distant one on a hunch and headed for it.

I had covered about half the distance when my headset came to life and a voice said, "Hold it right where you are." It wasn't Paul's voice, which meant it was Hatcher.

Then I saw the stern of the G-boat peeping from behind the rock I had decided to bypass. I was about a hundred feet from the other slab, closing fast. I didn't brake, didn't answer, didn't do anything.

"My cross-hairs are on you," Hatcher warned; but I was fifty feet from the rock now, and he hadn't fired yet. It came to me that he would hesitate to shoot. Crowder would prefer me alive so that he could dig my secrets from me with a blunt instrument. That thought helped me across the last few yards. Then I saw rock melt and spatter dead ahead. He fired again as I slammed the boulder hard enough to give me a view of constellations that didn't show on the charts. But I grabbed and held on, clawed my way up and over—and was looking at a dead man.

Paul was drifting a few feet from the rock, his hands stretched out as if he were reaching for it. His faceplate was open, and a strange, crystalline flower grew out of his helmet, a branched spray of red-black frozen blood. The face behind it was swollen, the eyeballs bulged from their sockets. I held on and looked at what was left of my friend and the cold inside me spread until it filled me like fire fills a burning house.

"I was warned about you," Hatcher's voice grated at me like gravel in the gears. "Your being here tells us what we need to know, Tarleton. Now, come out of there with your hands back of your helmet."

I hugged the rock and pulled my eyes away from the corpse and pictured the situation: the position of my boat—smashed and useless; of Paul's boat, of the G-boat, the two rocks. As for Hatcher: I couldn't be sure. He might be in his boat, or he could be somewhere else, possibly miles away; the shot could have been telescopically sighted.

"I'm warning you for the last time, Tarleton, if I have to come out—" he cut himself off, but he'd said enough. Or perhaps he was trickier than I thought, and the slip had been intentional.

I moved up the rock far enough to allow me a glimpse of my boat. It was drifting slowly toward me. From his vantage point, Hatcher would be unaware of that. I wondered how I could make use of the fact.

I made an effort to clear my mind and think analytically. It was difficult to understand Paul's death. Crowder would have wanted him alive, that seemed clear. Hatcher had blundered. He would be in an agitated state of mind, hoping to salvage something from the situation.

Quite suddenly I was certain that he intended to kill me. My interference could supply the excuse he needed—provided I weren't alive to testify. That was why he had waited here; to perfect his alibi.

I spoke for the first time: "You're an idiot, Hatcher," I said. "Why did you kill him? He wasn't armed. Or did he outwit you, open his faceplate before you could stop him?"

Hatcher swore in a manner suggesting my guesses were accurate. I laughed, a hearty chuckle, full of the rich amusement of life.

"I daresay you haven't yet gotten around to reporting your little slip, eh, Hatcher? You may even have given Crowder the impression you had him neatly bagged, ready for questioning."

"Shut up, damn you, Tarleton!"

"Crowder couldn't have monitored your intercom transmissions out here: too far, too much particle noise. So he didn't hear you hail Danton, and he can't hear us now. The fact is, he doesn't know what's happened out here, right, Hatcher? You're still working on your story, eh? And you've an idea I can help you."

"I'll save your neck for you, Tarleton," Hatcher whispered, as if he was afraid Crowder could hear him after all. "You back my play, and I'll get you out of this alive, I swear it!"

I laughed some more. By this time, it was beginning to seem a little funny, even to me. Or maybe it was the fine, feverish edge of hysteria showing through.

"Tarleton—listen to me!" Hatcher sounded rather desperate now. "You know what Danton was up to; give me the answers, and we can both be in the clear."

"Don't be a fool," I said. "Commander Danton wouldn't involve himself in anything illegal—and if he had, he wouldn't involve a friend in it."

This time Hatcher just made noises. He was a man with a great deal of fury in him. While he raved I moved Paul's body into position.

"Hatcher, you poor simpleton," I cut into the tirade, "all I have to do is wait until the boat that's no doubt following me arrives; it will be my pleasure to tell Crowder how you had Danton in your fingers and let him slip away—and the secret with him."

"That cuts it, Tarleton!" Hatcher's voice slashed at me. "You just blew your only chance! You're dead, Tarleton! You're—"

The boat was close enough—and I had him mad enough. The time was now.

"You'll have to catch me first, butterfingers!" I gripped the frozen body by the ankles, turned it, and gave it a hearty shove away from me. The corpse sailed out in a flat glide, arms outstretched. A quarter of a mile away, Hatcher scrambled into view, coming up over the curve of his rock, a blast rifle in his hands. Flame winked and molten rock flashed a few feet from me; Hatcher had fired at the decoy, but the rock was partially blocking his field of fire.

"Hatcher, wait!" I shouted. "I didn't think you'd really shoot! I'll talk! I'll tell you everything you need to know!"

I hugged the rock and waited to see if Hatcher was taking the bait. He didn't fire again. Through the phones I heard a sharp hissing; he had activated his back-pack: he was giving chase. I risked another peek and saw him coming fast, heading to intersect the body he thought was me. His course would bring him within a few yards of my shelter. I faded back and waited.

Suddenly he was there, sliding past ten feet away. I set myself to launch myself at his back just as he abruptly swore and braked, in the same motion twisting to face me. He fired from the hip and missed as I dived backwards.

"Clever," he said. "But not quite clever enough." I moved farther back, with the idea of keeping the rock between us. Beyond that, I had no more plans. The difficulty was in guessing just where he was.

I heard the back-pack again, briefly. Then silence. On instinct, I shifted position, keeping flat. I could hear his breathing in my ears.

"Look behind you," he said suddenly. I looked. He was there, hanging in space about twenty feet away, the gun aimed squarely at my face. There was something else there, too, something he hadn't noticed.

"If you have any last words," he said. "you'd better say them now."

"You want to know all about Danton and the big plot, don't you?" I said quickly. "I—"

"You're bluffing," he cut me off. He moved the gun from my face down to my chest; drifting slowly closer. "You don't know anything, Tarleton. You're a fool, mixing in matters that don't concern you."

"Yes, but—"

At the last instant he sensed the silent boat sliding up so smoothly behind him. He half-turned as the battered prow struck him, held him spread-eagled across its scarred curve as it closed the last few feet and rammed the rock beside me with all the inertia of a hundred tons of metal.

6

Clipped to Paul's suit I found a small torch, set to a proper intensity for rock cutting. It took me half an hour to find the place where Paul had been working: there was a neat, wedge-shaped cut in a surface of the type that represented a former crustal layer. The exposed rock was grayish, straited, indicating that once, long ago, the slab I was riding had been part of a sea bottom.

I searched Paul for the piece that had been cut away, without success. But of course Hatcher had been there before me. I disliked touching what remained of him, but I overcame my aversion and found the wedge of rock tucked into a belt pouch.

It was smooth on the cut faces, rough on the other. There was a depression in the latter, as if an oversized thumb had been pressed into soft clay.

"What is it, Paul?" I asked the empty space around

me. "What was it you died to protect?" I pushed Paul's body ahead of me back to his boat and maneuvered it inside. I was envisioning the expression on Crowder's face when I accused him of murder by proxy, when another thought intruded itself.

Crowder might quite logically accuse *me* of killing Hatcher.

And why stop there? If I had killed Hatcher, I might also have killed Paul Danton. And how could I prove I hadn't?

"Nonsense," I told myself. "What possible motive. . . ?"

But what motive had Hatcher had—or Crowder? What had they been trying to conceal? What was it that Paul had discovered, that he had hinted at in his note?

Abruptly, I understood.

Mutiny.

Unthinkable though it was, the ship was in the hands of Crowder and company. Everything fell into place at once: Paul's oblique hints, Crowder's strange ascendancy over the Commodore, Hatcher's incredible arrogance, Paul's murder.

It was still unclear what Paul's errand had been in the Rings, what significance the bit of stone had; perhaps it had been nothing more than a red herring, a distraction for Hatcher to puzzle over.

I realized then that I could not return to the ship. If a man of Commodore Grayson's rank and experience had been unable to resist the mutiny—if Paul Danton had failed—what could a junior lieutenant hope to accomplish on board?

But I was not aboard. I was here, free, and with a boat at my disposal.

Two boats. Hatcher's G-boat was much the more spaceworthy.

I realized then what it was I had to do.

It was a long run from Saturn's rings to Terra; a lonely ride for a man to make in a hundred-ton side-boat. There wasn't enough food, air, or water aboard—not enough of anything. But Captain Bligh had sailed the *Bounty*'s longboat from Tahiti to the Thames with nothing but a bad temper and a compass. I could try to do as well.

"Goodbye, Paul," I said to the corpse. "I'll do my best." I left him there and crossed to the G-boat. Using minimal power, I maneuvered it away from the scene, lost it in the mist of the rings twenty miles from the two derelicts.

It was a nine hour wait before a point of light glowed suddenly, far away through the misty rings, like a lamp behind a curtain. It grew, became a blue-white dazzle that moved slowly upward, angling away, dwindling.

I watched the ship out of sight, while my mind tried, and failed, and tried again to grasp the reality that I was marooned, on my own, a light hour from the nearest friendly face.

Then I punched an in-system course into the panel and settled down for the long run home.

Three

Adventure has been defined as somebody else having a difficult time, a long way away. But this was me, and I was here. A hundred and eighteen days isn't forever; hardly long enough for a seed to sprout, grow into a plant, and give birth to a ripe tomato. Long enough for the bare branches of winter to turn to the leafy green of spring. Long enough for half an inch of beard to grow, for the air to thicken and foul, for the water recycler to form a rime of green mould, for the last food canister from the last case to be scraped bare and then split open and licked clean. Long enough for the last paper garment to shred away to tatters to show the bones poking through skin a dirty shade of gray-green. Long enough for the brain to run a million circuits of the skull, like a squirrel in a treadmill, and end up a small, scared huddle of thwarted instincts, crouched in the farthest corner with blank eyes.

What is there to say? Even the fall of Rome only took three volumes. The time passed.

I came in past Luna at full interplanetary velocity,

skimmed atmosphere a thousand miles out and watched the cryston hull glow cherry red. Something about that got through to me, wherever I had gone. I tried for a long time before I sat up and poked keys, setting up an approach ellipse. I was cackling while I did it, about something that was very funny, but which I had temporarily mislaid. There was more waiting after that; and after a time the buffeting began. It was hot where I was, and the buffeting got worse, and then I was working hard, unstrapping, crawling forward into the small, dark space with the lid that closed down and left me just room enough to pull the lever that was nestled in my hand. That was hard to do, and once or twice I forgot it and almost went to sleep; but part of me seemed to think it was important. I got it pulled and heard sounds that might have been relays closing and automatics starting up. Or maybe it was just the caretaker, trimming the lawn over my grave. Thinking about graves made me think of Earth, and for a second something almost popped into my mind. And then the big twenty ton roller hit me and spread me out so thin the red sunlight shone through me until it faded out into a roaring darkness.

2

I came to consciousness with salt water the temperature of blood slapping at my face. I breathed some of the water and coughed, which helped. By the time I had cleared my lungs, I was sitting up looking over the side of a Mark XXI survival raft at a glassy green hill down the side of which I was sliding. I rode up the next one and caught just a glimpse of more of the same before another faceful of spume hit me. I was busy with that for a while, and afterwards was too weak to do anything but lie the way the fit had left me, on my back, looking up at a sky the color of beaten lead. At about that time I noticed I was cold, but it was just a passing observation. The sky darkened, not gradually but in abrupt jumps. Suddenly it was twilight, and some innocent, maidenly little stars were peeping out, like the first flowers of April. That was a nice thought. I liked it. I held onto it and tried to build it into something, but nothing came, and it faded, and . . .

It was full dark and cold. I hurt all over. My skin was stretched tight, scraped and salted and nailed to a frame to cure. I moved, and the nails tore my flesh and I made some small noises which were all I could manage at the time. Someone had lined my throat with dusty parchment, and driven spikes into my eye sockets, and red ants were crawling over me, taking bites and spitting them out. I tried to lick my lips, but it was someone else's tongue, three sizes too large.

Need water, I told myself clearly, but no sound came out. The old Tarleton brain was ticking over now. *Need water,* it said again. *Dehydration. Can't drink much salt water, but skin can soak it up. . . .*

That seemed to mean something; something difficult and unpleasant that had to be done, that I had to do. It was a project that all the world was waiting for, counting on me for. The least I could do was try. I reached down somewhere inside me for that hidden well of strength, tapped it with an effort like Samson bringing down the temple, like Hercules pinning Eupton, like Atlas clean-and-jerking the world. I sat up, and fell over on my side. That put my head against the gunwale.

There was a line stretched around the perimeter of the raft, a slack end trailing. I got it around my arm and used some more of the sort of willpower that builds pyramids, and rolled myself over and down into the water. The cold sting of it brought me part of the way out of the fog, far enough to clutch the rope two-handed and hold on with my chin clear of the water. I rode her that way for what seemed a long time, and by then the chill had blanked off the minor aches and itches, leaving just the major agony of living. My brain kept coming back to the idea of letting go—so easy—and sinking down into all that soft and eternal forgetfulness. But my hands wouldn't cooperate. They held on, pulled me closer to the side of the raft that went up, down, up, down. . . .

I caught it on the down-stroke, heaved hard and kicked, and succeeded in bumping my nose hard enough to make the bright lights dance.

I lunged again, scissored the legs I was using at the time, got an elbow over the edge, swore at the ocean that tried to pull me back, and flopped into the bilge-water at the bottom of the raft. Then it was nap time again.

After a while it was daylight; watery gray, but the wind felt a little warmer. I remembered the emergency ration kit that all Mark XXI's carried. It was somewhere only a few miles away at the other end of the raft. I used a lot of very precious energy crawling there, got the flap open, pulled out the plastic box, and got the lid open.

It contained a card stating that it had been inspected 10/7/89, and found unsatisfactory.

I went along with that.

The sun had jumped to zenith while I wasn't looking. It gave about as much heat as a forty watt glare strip.

The thought occurred to me that it was time to do a little reconnaissance: note my position, the wind direction and strength, the water temperature, respiration, and pulse. . . .

I was sitting up, looking across restless water at a misty shore line. It was too far away to make out any detail, but somehow it looked to me like the shore of Africa. Or possibly New Jersey.

I lay down to think about it, and was doing rather well until the shelling got noisy. It was coming closer; the ground heaved with every detonation. The barrage had been going on for a long time, and pretty soon they'd be coming over the top and charging with fixed bayonets, but I wasn't ready, not nearly ready, and I couldn't find my rifle, and anyway, I was already wounded or possibly dead and where were the aid men, and—

The last burst picked me up and threw me a thousand miles into an open grave and the mud showered down on me and a giant tombstone fell out of the sky to mark the place, but I didn't care anymore, because I was far away, in that place where the heroes and the cowards lie together with a fine impartiality, waiting for eternity to pass, slowly, like a procession of snails creeping across an endless desert toward a distant line of mountains.

3

The first sensation I became aware of was the stink. Then the heat. Then the flies on my face and the buzz of the other ones, looking for a landing place. The pain ran a poor fourth until I moved. I managed a groan, which is a form of communication. Nobody answered, so I groaned louder. Still no response. So much for that. No more groans. Try something else.

What, for example?

Well, perhaps you could sit up.

Good idea. I'll try it.

Someone hit me over the head with a pillowcase full of sand.

Any other ideas?

Certainly. Later. At the moment I need my rest.

Sorry, sir. Won't do. Move the dogs. Tarleton. Shake a leg, rustle the bones, lift the frame, baste well and bake in a medium oven.

Hot out here. Sun shining in my face. Got to get in out of the sun. Yesterday cold as hell, today hot as the same. Trouble enough without second degree radiation burns.

One eye open, looking at dirty sand, clots of seaweed, tired-looking bushes, sickly trees full of vines, blue-white sky.

Try the other eye. Same thing, except for difference in viewpoint. Eyes three inches apart, producing stereoscopic effect. Depth perception. Been to the depths, what did I perceive?

Move head. Something ugly in field of view. Dead animal. Correction, dead hand. Hand of corpse, fingers like claws, tendons standing out. Wonder who's dead? Tried to move to get away from corpse, and hand twitched.

That scared me, and I rolled over on my face. That was a better position. From there I could see a flat stretch of beach, calm blue water on one side, woods on the other. No houses in sight, no boats, no people, no grazing cows, not even any seagulls.

Just me, all alone in the world.

It was a pitiful thought. I wanted to cry. But first I

had to fell trees, build a shelter, gather nuts and berries, make a bow and arrows, hunt game, prepare stew, and dine, before retiring to my couch of aromatic balsam boughs for a well-earned nap.

On second thought, I'd start with the nap.

The sun jumped down the sky and cold water sluiced across my chin. The tide had come in rather suddenly, disturbing me just as I was getting comfy. On top of my other problems, this seemed rather unfair.

I got a good grip on the sand and pulled myself forward. Or almost. Actually, I pulled a palmful of sand backward.

Exposing a perfectly white sphere about the size of a golf ball, but without the little dimples.

I didn't know what it was, but some monkey perched far back in the ancestral tree did. He knew what was good. He jammed the turtle egg in my mouth, shell and sand and all, and crushed it and felt the pain like injections of acid as the salivary glands went to work on something besides daydreams for the first time in too many days to count.

There were seven more eggs in the clutch. I ate all of them.

After that I vomited. That was hard work. It made me hungry.

I found myself crawling, scratching at the sand for more eggs. There didn't seem to be any more eggs. Another wave came sluicing across the tidal flat and almost bowled me over. That made me steer inland. After a while I was among bushes. They had bitter leaves.

There were some little white berries on a bush. I tried them. They tasted like varnish.

When it was too dark to see, I curled up in a tight

ball and contained the pain inside me, which would otherwise have burst out like a ruptured appendix and crawled away, leaving nothing behind but my empty shell, like a cast snakehide, or a katydid husk.

Voices woke me.

I lay for a while and listened to them. They jabbered in a language that was all gobbles and grunts, like Hawaiian song lyrics. It was a novel kind of delusion; I held onto it; it was almost like company.

Something hard dug into my ribs. I opened my eyes and was looking up at the dirtiest human being on Earth. He was short, brown-skinned, wrinkled. He wore ragged khaki shorts, a felt hat that had once had a shape and color, tennis shoes with burst seams through which bony brown toes protruded. He was the best looking man I'd ever seen.

I tried to tell him so; the words were a little garbled perhaps, because of the excitement of the moment, and my voice wasn't quite its usual rich, well-modulated self. But I told him how glad I was to see him, how long it had been since my last full meal, and supplied other data of interest to heroic rescuers of deserving hardship cases like myself. Then I flopped back and waited for the nourishing soup and soothing balm that the script called for.

He brought a big knobbed stick out from behind him and hit me over the head with it.

Indignation has never been listed as one of the basic survival mechanisms, but I can't think of a better name for the fine, warm emotion that sent me up off the ground like the last kernel in the popper. I made a lunge for him, missed, and dived face-first into the dirt. He turned around and ran as if he'd just remembered his toast was burning.

In two minutes he was back, with friends. It took them thirty seconds to flush me out of the pile of dead leaves I'd burrowed into. There weren't any sticks this time. Two of them grabbed my arms and two more my legs, giving me a nice view of a pair of knobby knees, upside down, and off we went down the trail.

4

The quaint native village they took me to was built of brush, rusty oil drums, and wooden slats with words like *Akak* and *Coco* stenciled on them. They put me on the floor in a hut with a native beauty who might have been any age from thirty-five to sixty. She had two teeth strategically placed in a mouth that reminded me of an amateur short-stop I used to know, named Bad Bounce Feldman. But she gave me fish—fried whole—fruit, bread of a sort, and canned peaches. That made her beautiful.

Nobody in the village spoke English, French, German, Russian, or Cantonese. Nobody bothered me; nobody except old Gertie paid any attention to me.

I spent a week in the hut before I discovered I could crawl outside and sit in the sun.

I tried speaking sign language to Gertie, signaling "your pardon, ma'am, but would you be so good as to inform me of the name of this charming region, and its approximate location?" The only answer I got was a snicker. I drew a map of the world in the dirt and offered her my stylus, which she smelled and threw away.

There was no radio in the village, no power transport other than half a dozen much-battered boats rotting on the beach, none of which appeared capable of navigating across a reflecting pool.

When I was strong enough, I explored the island; it was about nine miles long by four wide. There were other islands visible from the low peak from which I did my exploring. None of them seemed any more densely inhabited than mine.

I was filled with a fine fervor to rush to Washington and report mutiny and murder to the Chief of Naval Operations—as well as to receive official congratulations on my epoch-making navigational feat. But the days passed and nothing happened.

It was almost three weeks before company arrived.

5

The whole tribe—if they were a tribe—were gathered on the beach to watch the boat come in. It was a down-at-heels air cushion launch, painted a milky gray and flying a Company ensign. It rode up on the beach—a stretch of gray sand like industrial waste—and squatted there in a cloud of dust while the spinners ran down. Two Polynesian-looking men in neat Company uniforms jumped down, then a brown-skinned, blue-eyed, bow-legged man in gray shorts and jacket with Principal Officer shoulder tabs. He mopped at his forehead with a big blue and white bandanna and came up the sand to where my crowd was waiting. No one rushed forward to exchange bananas for transistor trideos. They waited, with a certain amount of yawning and shifting from foot to foot. I was making my way forward when the bow-legged man called something in the native dialect. The old boy in the sneakers—the one who had greeted me that first day—his name was something like

Tmbelee—edged forward a few feet. He wasn't carrying his stick today. I waited while they talked. I got the impression the bow-legged man was asking questions. Tmbelee pointed in my direction once, which seemed to irritate the visitor. After a while he turned away, still looking irritated, and started toward the boat.

I called after him. He halted and waited until I overtook him.

"I need transport to the mainland," I said "Ah—you *do* speak English?"

"Um," he grunted. "Tumbela say you were Englishman." He looked me up and down like a tailor disapproving of my clothes. I could hardly blame him; I was wearing nothing but a pair of flowered shorts Gertie must have salvaged from the local dump.

"I sail for Lahad Datu," he said. I had never heard of Lahad Datu.

"That's fine," I said. "Anywhere. I'm a Naval officer, and— "

"Damn goose chase," he said, talking to himself. "Couple million square miles bloody ocean to search. Bloody nonsense." He jerked a thumb at the villagers, who were wandering off now.

"I ask if they see man I'm looking for. Bloody fools."

I felt a stab of emotion. "You're looking for someone?"

"Naval deserter. Bad man. Orders to shoot to kill. Describe him to them: young fellow, twenty-five year, black hair, six-one, strong." He laughed sourly, rolled a small blue eye at me. "They say you might be chap I want." He frowned again.

"What's civilized man doing here among aboriginees?" He snorted that as if no matter what I said he wouldn't approve.

"Research," I said quickly, hoping the shock he'd given me didn't show. "In the beginning, anyway. Seem to have lost my drive somewhere along the way." I smiled a self-forgiving smile, soliciting his understanding of my human failings. "I got to drinking; and there was a woman. Usual story. But that's behind me now. Have to get back, pull myself together. Never too late."

"Very well. You get kit and come 'long."

"My kit's already in my pocket," I said. I went back to my hut long enough to give my issue folding knife to Gertie with a little speech of gratitude. She looked at it and made noises like a Neapolitan helicab driver demanding a larger tip.

Back on the beach my benefactor looked at me and shook his head and laughed his sour laugh again.

I didn't understand the joke until I got a look in the mirror in the spare cabin he gave me.

Four

I tried to analyze the situation in the light of the latest development. I realized that I had been assuming that Crowder would cover up my absence from my post of duty if only to avoid having to make explanations. I had also assumed he'd assume I was dead. But he was ahead of me; he'd allowed for the off-chance that I would try for Terra in the G-boat, and prepared a story. There had probably been a cordon looking for me all the way in; only the needle-in-the-haystack principle had let me get through undetected—at least until the last few thousand miles, when the ground and satellite stations would have picked me up.

They'd no doubt tracked the boat in through atmosphere, and then lost me. A life raft on the Pacific, contrary to Search-and-Rescue propaganda, is a hard target to spot. But they were still trying. Only the handy disguise that starvation had given me had saved me from walking into the net head-first.

Very well; my plan to report in to the first Naval Station or Public installation I could find would have to be modified. I'd have to remain inconspicuous, travel quietly, and turn myself into one of my influential contacts in Washington with my side of the story. It shouldn't be too difficult. There were no national borders, no passports, no travel restrictions, no reason for anyone to look at me twice—provided I didn't call attention to myself. On that note, I turned in and slept in my first bed in over four months.

2

Lahad Datu was a concrete and aluminum port surrounded by basha huts and palm trees, on the north side of Darvel Bay in North Borneo. My friendly Company man—Superintendent Otaka—dropped me there with an old set of ducks and a hundred credit chit as reward for my help with the navigation through seven hundred miles of tricky currents. I used it to buy myself a steak, a haircut, a suit of clothes, and a hotel room, in that order. The launch's salt-water shower had kept me clean, but there was nothing like plenty of hot, soapy *fresh* water for restoring the sizing to my soul—that and twelve hours' sleep in a good bed on solid land.

I had optimistically bought clothes a few sizes too large; they hung on me like Jack Pumpkinhead's vest. My skin was getting some color back in it, and my teeth were tightening up in their sockets, and my hair had pretty well stopped falling out; but I wouldn't have any trouble with anybody looking for a husky youngster. I looked like a fifty-year old invalid, and felt much the same. Climbing a flight of stairs winded me; I couldn't carry a cafeteria tray without spilling my coffee. I was safe from any casual lookers—but my fingerprints and retinal patterns hadn't changed.

Once the beady official eye zeroed in on me, the game would be up.

There were jobs available in Lahad for an old beachcomber with an education, and few questions asked. I gave the name John Bann and took a post as a bookkeeper for a taro plantation and settled down to building up my health and a getaway stake. It was going to call for some nice calculating: the pleasure of eating balanced against the disguising emaciation that was fading more every day under my new regimen of food, sunshine, and a half mile walk every morning and evening from the bungalow to the office. The pay wasn't big—the bossboy was taking advantage of me—but my expenses were even smaller. Food is never a problem out in the islands, if you're willing to settle for fish and fowl and fruit and native bread. My housing was provided; and two sets of white drills were my total wardrobe requirement.

In two weeks I had saved the price of a jet ticket to the other side of the world, and had gained another ten pounds. That put my weight at one-fifty and took ten years off my age, making me a tall, skinny middle-aged man with a permanent stoop.

There were a few decent restaurants in the town, which I visited in the company of a girl named Lacy, a rather pretty little thirty-year-old brunette of mixed French and Chinese ancestry. She confided that she preferred the company of an older man. I didn't ask her what older man. She meant me.

My bungalow was two doors from hers. It wasn't long before she was dusting and straightening and putting flowers on the table. After dinner we would sit out on the raised verandah and drink tea and watch the spectacular sunsets and talk and listen to the taped symphonies from Radio Borneo at Brunei.

When darkness fell and the stars came out I would sometimes find myself searching along the zodiac for the little point of light that was Saturn; but that part of life all seemed very remote and far away. It hadn't been me who had spent seven years in space, deserted my ship, killed a man in the dazzle-plain of the rings, rode a side-boat back four hundred million miles to a miracle splash-down in the sea. That had been another fellow entirely, a hearty young daredevil full of inexperience and the fine and righteous fire of revenge. Later, when I was feeling better, when things had had time to blow over, I'd look into picking up some of the threads of that identity. But right now, life was sweet enough—and I'd earned the right to a little convalescent leave.

I went on feeling that way until the night the Constabulary killed Lacy.

3

I had stayed an hour later at the office, running down a two-credit shortage in the LP account. Afterwards, instead of walking directly home, I had taken a stroll the long way around, up by the reservoir for a view of the valley and a little fresh air to drive the eyestrain headache away. I got back to the compound just at dusk, approaching along the jungle road instead of coming in via the University Avenue gate.

I felt no alarm when I saw the two gray-painted cars parked across from my place, only wondered in an absentminded way who was having trouble with their house energy-unit; the only time we saw a Company car here was on a service call. A stranger in slightly out-of-place looking clothes gave me a sharp look as I ambled past. I was almost at my gate when I heard the sounds; scuffling, a slammed door, running feet, a terse masculine shout. Lacy whirled through the gate ten feet from me, a lock of hair curled down over her eye. She looked at me and opened her mouth and behind her someone hit a piece of iron with a hammer, hard, twice. The left side of Lacy's blouse jumped, as if a finger had poked it from the inside, and threads flew, and there was a blot of brilliantly crimson blood as big as my hand, as big as a plate, then covering her whole side—

"Johnny—they . . . waiting . . ." she said, quite clearly, and crumpled as if someone had cut the string that was holding her up. She fell to the sidewalk, her neat little legs curled under her. I saw the entry holes on her right side—just tiny burn marks against the white nylon—from the high-velocity needles that had gone clear through her. Her face looked perfectly composed, as if she were playing a little game of possum on the quiet street in the twilight. All this in the timeless half-second before feet pounded on the walk Lacy had come along a moment before.

Then I had turned and was running, straight-arming the stranger who had been just an instant late in getting his gun out, skidding in through Fan Shu's gate and sprinting across his garden patch and over the hedge and around the pond and through the trees and into the jungle, as if I'd planned the routine in advance, learned it by heart, waiting for this moment.

4

By dawn I was twenty miles form Lahad, hidden out under a hibiscus hedge beside a vast pineapple field. I ate a pineapple and dozed. I could hear traffic passing along a road half a mile away; copters criss-crossed the sky, none very close. When it was dark I went on, keeping away from roads.

My feet blistered and swelled. My legs ached. Once an hour I stopped to rest. I saw no searching parties on foot, no packs of trained dogs. But why should they bother beating the brush for me? I would have to try to leave the island eventually. That was where they would be watching and waiting. How I would elude them I didn't know—but that was a problem I would consider later. At the moment it was sufficient that I was still alive and free.

I didn't understand their killing Lacy. It had been a brutal, senseless act, totally out of keeping with the tenor of the modern world. There was little crime on the planet, little need for cadres of efficient police.

Perhaps that was the explanation. Lacy had died because an over-excited amateur had panicked. Somehow it didn't make her death any more endurable. I hadn't loved her, but she had been my friend. She had died because of me.

There had been too many deaths. Something was very wrong with my peaceful world. I couldn't afford to be caught and shot—not until I had seen the people I had to see. There was more at stake than my life, or my career, or justice for Paul Danton, or revenge for Lacy. I wondered what it was.

The next dawn found me on a coconut farm. No one came near me. I tried to open a coconut, but couldn't. I slept, listening to the breeze sighing through the fronds overhead.

The next six days were like the first two. I walked, avoided towns, stole enough fruit to keep the pangs at bay. For all its intensive cultivation, Borneo was sparsely populated. It was like a deserted world, except for the air traffic: the high jets, the low-flying copters, none of which seemed to be looking for a man on foot. My feet stopped hurting. I caught a fish in a canal and built a fire and cooked it. My shoes began to come apart. I threw them away and went on barefooted.

On the morning of the eighth day I came up on a stand of imported cottonwoods the landscape designers had placed on a knoll as a backdrop to an Area Superintendent's villa. The Super—a little man, probably a Japanese—came out of the house for a pre-breakfast stroll in the garden. It was a very nice garden; green lawn, paths, a fountain, flowerbeds as neat as a jeweler's display window, and as colorful. The villa was well-designed, sturdily built, with a fine view down across a long slope to the highway that bisected the geometrically precise plantation. On the hillsides in the distance were terraced vegetable farms, patterns of soft color in the dawn.

It was an orderly, productive world, with a place for everything and everything in its place—except me. I had gotten out of step with the system—and suddenly I wanted back in. I was a commissioned officer of the Navy, a superior human being. Why was I tired, dirty, dressed in rags, peeking out from the bushes at normal human life, envying the lucky ones who lived in houses, slept in beds, strolled in gardens? It was still a world of justice and order; all I had to do was make contact with the authorities, tell them what I knew and what I suspected, tear away the blindfold and let the light in.

There would be a phone in the house below; in seconds I could be face to face via screen with Admiral Harlowe or Senator Taine. They'd listen—and act.

I got to my feet and walked openly down to the house. At my ring, the door opened and I was looking at a man with a gun in his hands.

5

It was a twin-bore power gun, aimed at my chest. He held it very steadily, with a cool expression on his face as if he were lining up on an aphid with a spray-projector. I stood very still and wondered what a power bolt through the lungs would feel like.

He let me wonder for a while. Then he spoke sharply over his shoulder in Japanese. I understood enough to know he was telling someone to search me. A short, wide woman emerged from behind him and patted me from chest to ankles in a businesslike way, as if she frisked suspects before breakfast every morning. She told the man I was clean. Without lowering the gun he motioned me inside, closed the door behind me.

"Who are you?" he asked me. His voice was as light and crisp as dry toast, and about as emotional.

"I'm looking for work," I said. "I just—"

"Your name," he interrupted.

"John Lacy," I said, not very smoothly. "Sorry if I startled you, but—"

"You're the man known as John Bann," he cut me off. "The Constabulary seem most eager to find you. They've visited my farm twice in the past five days."

"You're crazy," I said in a voice that sounded as weak in my ears as a re-used tea-bag.

"Why do they want you?" he asked.

"They didn't say."

"Let me see your wrists."

I held my hands out; he told me to turn them over and I did.

"Who told you to come here?"

"Nobody. I was tired of walking."

"How did you intend to get out of Borneo?"

"I don't know. I hadn't gotten that far."

"What about your friends?"

"What friends?"

"The ones who delivered you from the police trap."

"Nobody delivered me from anything. I was warned in time to make a break for the woods, that's all."

"How did you get here? The roads are patrolled."

"I stayed off the roads."

"You walked one hundred and eighty miles?"

"I didn't know I'd come that far."

"We are eight miles from Tarakan." He looked at me as if he was waiting for me to say something. "The port is under surveillance, of course."

"What are you going to do?" I asked him.

Instead of answering, he spoke to the woman again; he was telling her to notify someone to come at once. Then he walked me through the house to the kitchen, a bright room, full of sunshine.

"Why not let me go?" I said. "I'm not guilty of any crime."

"You would soon be apprehended," he said. "Kindly be seated and remain silent."

He sat with the gun held steadily on me, not moving, not talking, not even blinking. It was ten minutes before I heard a vehicle outside; I started to get up and he motioned me back.

"Please, Mr. Bann. Be patient."

The opening of a door; low voices; footsteps. Four men came into the room. They were not Constabulary.

One was a big, blunt-handed fellow with a heavy, sagging face set in a permanent scowl. Another was small, too thin, chestless, with arms like sticks of wood. The third was plump and pale, dead-faced, gray-skinned. The last of the quartet was a foxy fellow with a nose that looked as if it would drip. All were dressed in light coveralls, none too clean; they seemed to be field hands. A faint odor of fertilizer followed them in.

My host said something and they all stared at me, spreading out for a better view. The woman was back, standing with arms folded, lips pushed out.

The foxy man said something in Japanese that seemed to be. "Is it certain?"

I didn't understand the reply. I listened hard to the conversation, picking up about half the words:

". . . be sure?"

". . . dangerous . . . live . . ."

"Why . . . purpose . . . long time."

"Who else . . . here . . . afoot."

". . . trap . . . death . . ."

"you . . . waiting [with contempt]."

"Not . . . decision . . ."

They stopped talking and looked at me.

"Would you mind telling me what's going on?" I said. "Who are these men?"

"My colleagues," my host said. "Shik . . . Freddy . . . Ba Way . . . Sharnhorst. My name, by the way, is Joto. And of course, Mrs. MacReady."

They looked at me. I looked back at them, trying to read something in their faces. All I seemed to see was a kind of dull animal curiosity, as if I were a mangled body.

"Fine," I said. "Have you decided what to do about me?"

"Indeed, yes," Mr. Joto said, and almost smiled. "First Mrs. MacReady will give you breakfast. Then we will smuggle you out of Borneo."

Five

The breakfast Mrs. MacReady put before me was magnificent. I hadn't realized how hungry I was until I smelled it cooking. While I ate, the men talked. I didn't try to follow their conversation; I had a feeling that I wouldn't have understood it even if I had known the words.

"Very well, you leave tonight," Mr. Joto announced.

"How?"

"You will be transported with the day's consignment of produce and loaded aboard an outward-bound ship."

"Won't anyone get curious when they see me riding down the conveyor belt among the pineapples?"

"You'll be quite hidden from view inside a ten-pack case."

"What about things like breathing and eating?"

"No difficulty at all. The cases are not air-tight. It will be delicately handled, of course, fruit being delicate cargo. It will be stowed in open stacks. Once underway you can emerge. You'll have the freedom of the barge, of course. It's unmanned."

"How far will it take me?"

"What destination do you have in mind?"

"Washington. Northamerica."

He looked thoughtful. "Let me see . . . Flotilla 9, Convoy 344 . . . Tomorrow is Wednesday. Excellent. 344 it is. I can put you in a Barge coded for Philadelphia and Norfolk."

"Close enough," I said.

"The barges are unmanned, of course," he went on. "In the event of any problem, a maintenance crew may come aboard, but you'll have no difficulty in eluding observation if that should be the case."

"How long will the trip take?"

"In this season—seventy-two hours."

"What happens when I arrive?"

"You will be met."

"May I ask by whom?"

"By reliable persons."

"One more question," I said. "Why are you doing this?"

"I think you can guess the answer to that, Mr. Bann."

"I'm a total stranger to you. You don't even know why the Constabulary are chasing me."

He smiled a slight smile. "You killed two of the swine. That is sufficient credentials, Mr. Bann."

I opened my mouth, but changed what I was going to say in time.

"You approve of killing policemen?"

Mr. Joto made a spitting sound.

"You could turn me in and collect a handsome reward, I imagine," I pursued the point.

"You think I would take the money of the black-souled tyrants who grind the free spirit of man into the dust?" he hissed. "That I would abet the schemes of the jackals who have robbed us of all that gives life value?"

I looked around at his cheerful house with its sunny garden and the peaceful acres spreading away to the horizon and wondered what he was talking about.

"They think they are secure in their high seats of power," he orated. "But the spark of rebellion still lives. They have not yet stamped out the spirit of defiance."

"Defiance of what?" I asked him.

His head jerked as if I had hit him. Then he nodded; his long lips twitched.

"Yes," he said. "You're wise. Keep your own counsel. An excellent habit. What I know nothing of, I cannot betray under torture."

He seemed to be speaking English, but on the wrong wave length. I let it go at that and turned in to get as much sleep as possible before fruit-packing time.

2

They woke me in pitch darkness, led me down to the kitchen, issued me a ceremonial cup of hot coffee, and gave me a coverall very similar to a shipsuit that Mr. Joto said would keep me warm, dry, and vermin-free. It was a poor fit and smelled like stale crackers, but was still an improvement over what was left of my office suit after a week out of doors. Mrs. MacReady was very brisk and efficient about handing over a false ID, showing the name John Bann and registering a substantial credit balance. She added an aid kit, compass, pocket knife, hand light, and ball of twine. She didn't say what I should use them for. I stowed them solemnly in the pockets of my suit, like a Space Scout preparing for his first hike. Freddy and Ba Way hovered in the background looking tense and worried. There was a feeling of petty furtiveness about the proceedings, an adolescent solemnity; I had the feeling that at any moment someone would produce a dirty pocket knife and propose a blood-oath ceremony.

We left the house via the back door, crossed the rose garden, took a bricked foot-path back to a big equipment garage. A man I hadn't seen before was there, warming up a personnel carrier. We climbed aboard and drove off down one of the neat, tree-lined roads in the pre-dawn mist, turned off after half a mile, pulled up in front of one of a row of open-sided, metal-roofed packing sheds. Big green-painted cargo carriers as shiny as limousines were backed up the ramp. There was a sweet odor of rotten fruit in the air. Joto and his minions hopped down and went briskly to work shifting the big six-sided anodized cases, using a monorail power hoist. It was all done by the numbers, like something long rehearsed.

"Right, in you go," Mr. Joto said, and waved a hand at a case that looked like all the others except that a hinged panel in one end was standing open. I went over and looked in. There was a cylindrical nest in the center of the honeycomb that held the pineapples. It was big enough to lie down and turn over in, not much more.

"When you are ready to emerge, you simply depress the release with your toe," Mr. Joto told me, pointing out a small lever at the bottom of the door. Nobody else said anything; they stood there in the early morning gloom and looked at me, expressions of anxious expectation on their faces. They had spent a lot of time and effort on their invention, and now they were waiting for me to find out whether it would fly, or crunch in on the test-hop.

I had a sudden, graphic sense of the absurdity of the situation: I, Lieutenant Banastre Tarleton, an officer of the Regular Navy, shivering in a smelly costume of cast-offs, about to be entombed alive by a gang of half-baked revolutionaries, dedicated to the overthrow of everything I believed in, assisting me in the misguided belief that I was a murderer.

But perhaps they had tricked me. Perhaps they meant to seal me in and call the Constabulary, who would pull me out, blinking sheepishly and scratching my flea-bites, having fouled my nest in the meantime. I had my mouth open to tell them I'd changed my mind, that I'd take my chances on my own, that the whole thing had gotten out of hand and that I'd decided to walk out to the highway and give myself up, explain that it was all a mistake . . .

But somehow it seemed to require too much effort. It was all so remote, so unreal.

"Goodbye, Mr. Bann, and good luck," Joto said, his voice echoing, and offered his hand. Automatically, I shook it, then Freddy's and Ba Way's. Mrs. MacReady sniffled and wiped at her eyes—as surprising as seeing a stone lion meow. Then I was crawling head-first into an overpowering odor of pineapples, turning over on the thin padding, looking back past my feet at the narrowing patch of watery daylight. The last thing I saw as the door closed was Joto's strained features staring in at me like the first arrival at the scene of an accident, peering into the wreckage, afraid of what he'll see but secretly hoping for the worst.

3

I lay on my back in the darkness, wondering vaguely if the ventilators worked, if the release lever would work, remembering all the questions I should have asked and hadn't. But it didn't really seem important. There were metallic clatterings, faint jarrings, a sensation of movement, dizzying, dreamlike. Deep vibrations started up, became a steady thrumming, accompanied by a swaying first to one side and then the other.

I found my thoughts flitting back over everything that had happened to me in the five months since my life had slipped out from under me like a roller-skate on a stair. Incidents jostled each other, searching for a pattern, a scale: the weeks in the foul-smelling cockpit of the sideboat, fingering the piece of rock I had taken from Paul's body, wondering at its meaning; the Commodore's look in the hooded light as Crowder rocked on his heels and smiled; Gertie, staring in dismay at my parting gift; Lacy's soft hands, soft lips; the stark clarity of the moment when I thought Mr. Joto would fire the power gun into my chest. But no pattern came, no meaning. This wasn't me; this was the kind of feckless, chaotic tangle that other, lesser people let their aimless lives fall into. I had an honorable place in a meaningful world, a framework of order that delineated the parameters of existence. My being here was a ghastly mistake, a fantastic mesalliance of bad luck and foolish error.

But they wouldn't listen. I heard the door closing, one by one, heard the keys clattering in the locks, locking me in—or locking me out?

The voice of the President of the Court echoed

down through the hole they had drilled into my tomb:

"Guilty or not guilty?"

I tried to shout "Not guilty," but my voice caught in my throat. It was barely a whisper. No one could hear me.

"Guilty—or not guilty?"

I took a deep breath to try again and choked instead.

"Guilty—or not guilty of plotting to overthrow the Public?"

I had to answer, had to say something. Anything. Perhaps if I confessed—

"Guilty!" I shouted. But that was a whisper too. No one was listening, no one cared. . . .

4

The vibration had changed tone, was shifting downscale. I tried to sit up and banged my head on the padded ceiling above me. The sound of the engine groaned down to an idle. More thumps and jarrings; a sharp jolt, then pressure under me, a sense of swooping, soaring, then dropping suddenly, braking with a jerk that snapped my head against the floor, another heavy shock, clattering, then stillness. No sound, no motion. Faint and far away a soft whirr started up. That would be the air pumps cycling. But they weren't working properly; it was stifling hot. I was suffocating, I needed air and light; there had been a mistake, and my case was stacked at the bottom of a solid heap of cases, end to end, and I was trapped! I tried to find the lever with my toe, but my foot was made of lead, my leg was paralyzed. I was tied hand and foot on a runaway flatcar rolling down a hill, in a boat rushing toward a falls. I had lost my lifeline and was falling away from the hull of the ship, falling toward the sun, and it would be a hundred years before my frozen body plunged into the photosphere, but already I could feel the searing heat, slowly beginning to boil me in my own juices. . . .

5

I woke up tasting a bitter coffee taste.

"Doped," I said aloud. "Joto's method of keeping me quiet and cooperative. Clever fellow, Mr. Joto." My voice sounded muffled. I groped with my foot and the panel sprung open. I hitched myself out and was standing in the hold of a freight barge, on a catwalk. Strips of glare lighting showed me thousands of cases like the one I had crawled out of, stacked solidly in long ranks, aisle after aisle, tier after tier.

I found a ladder and went up, out through a narrow door into cold wind and white sunlight. A narrow strip of deck ran beside the three hatches. The ship was double-hulled, shallow-draft, designed to run on the surface, or submerged in rough weather. Half a dozen other barges were in sight on either side, far away, gray blurs on the horizon. I was in the clear, on my way. Mr. Joto's crazy plan had worked. For a moment I envisioned the kind of organization that seemed to imply, but I pushed the thought away.

"Just luck," I told myself. "Crackpot luck."

I went forward, found the emergency personnel facility they had told me about. There was a bunk, a radio sender, a tiny galley-bar with a supply of frozen rations. I made a sandwich and sat on deck and watched the gray ocean slide past. When I tired of that, I did a few turns around the deck. I took a nap. I woke up and ate again, walked more laps, watched the sun set. Saturn was an evening star, a faint glimmer in the dusty rose sky. I wondered if I had really been there. It seemed less real than the dope-dream about the grave.

In the dream I had denied my guilt, and no one had heard me. Then I had confessed, and still no one was listening. Words were just words, not the substance of reality. My guilt or lack of it had no relation to what I happened to say on the subject. I realized with a sudden harsh insight that I had done what I had done—was doing what I was doing—in a moral and intellectual vacuum. I had simply reacted. The crunch had come, and I had run.

Now I was on my way to Naval SHQ to make my report. But was I actually fighting for a great ideal or merely drifting downstream? Had I betrayed my dead friend's trust in me, or risked all to vindicate it? Was I a traitor, or a noble victim of unkind circumstance? A hero—or coward? Had I murdered Hatcher, or had he died by accident? Had I made an epic voyage, or merely fled from danger like a whipped dog? Was I bound now on a mission of loyalty, determined to risk all in the cause of duty—or was I only scuttling for cover? And when I arrived—what?

Joto had said I'd be met, but had supplied no details.

I pictured a party of grubby anarchists coming alongside in a small boat, spiriting me away to a candle-lit cellar to join in a discussion of how to plant a bomb under the Metropolitan Library, and found myself wondering what sort of reward I'd get if I made contact with them and then turned them in to the Constabulary.

"Treachery?" I asked myself. "Or my duty as a citizen?"

I had an adequate supply of questions, but not enough answers. Not nearly enough answers.

Six

The third nightfall came on the open sea. For another hour the barge ploughed steadily on to the northwest. Then quite suddenly there was a light off the port bow, then three lights, then an entire array of lights, spreading along the horizon. They closed in on each side; the barge slowed. We were entering a deep bay; whether New York harbor, Delaware Bay, Chesapeake or another I had no idea. I saw other barges lying at anchor on the black water; mine maneuvered along a channel among them. It halted; the sound of the engine dwindled away and died.

Waves slapped the hull and ran back along the side like miniature surf. I could dimly make out the shore, about a mile distant on either side—too far to swim in icy water.

A tug appeared, maneuvering between barges, coming alongside. I made a tentative move toward it, and saw a man standing on its deck. I backed quickly to the starboard scuppers, lay flat.

The tug bumped the side of the barge; the man appeared over the rail, tall and wide in tight-fitting dark clothing. He climbed up on deck, stood looking around, then walked across to the cabin hatch. With no more warning than that, my mind was made up. I rolled my leg over the thick curve of the gunwale, lowered myself down the smooth, out-bulging side to arm's length, and let go.

2

I made very little splash going in; the water was bitter cold, but I felt it only on my hands and face; the suit's automatic seals snugged against my throat and wrists at the first pressure. I pushed away and swam forward past the barge's blunt bows. When I was clear, I looked back and saw the man on deck, silhouetted against the light, staring around him. He walked aft, out of sight. He'd know I'd been there, of course. I had made no effort to conceal the evidences of my stay. That seemed suddenly to be a serious error. I turned over and swam hard until I was well away from the barges, floated long enough to catch my breath, then settled down for the long haul to shore.

Forty-five minutes later I waded out on a stony beach below dark, weed-topped dunes. I crossed them and walked quickly along in their shelter toward the lights of a town. There was a small pavilion above high tide; a bricked path led from it across a lawn, past free-form flower beds full of flowers that looked black in the moonlight, through an open gate into a circular plaza softly lit by shop windows where displays of resort wear and sports equipment and cameras floated in pooled light. There were no people in sight. I caught my reflection in a window. My hair was wet and rumpled, but the waterproof suit still held its creases. I hoped I looked like any other waterfront roustabout out for an early morning walk.

A tube stop entry glowed halfway around the walk. Inside, I checked the big wall map with its glowing lines and moving points of light, and deduced that I was on the outskirts of Baltimore, and that the next Washington car would be along in six minutes. I spent the time drinking a cup of cofty and eating a vitabun from a dispenser shaped like a miniature rose-covered cottage, listening to the airlocks thudding. There was a louder thud and the gate slid back on a cosy interior. I stepped inside. There were no other passengers in the car. The seats were soft. I coded instructions into mine and gave it my counterfeit card to nibble and leaned back and dozed off. I opened one eye the first time the chair was shunted forward and sideways into another car. It seemed only a few moments later I was waking from a rosy dream with a soft voice in my ear telling me I would arrive at Washington Twenty-five in thirty seconds.

The deceleration pressure against my back ended, the door slid back and I stepped out into a silvery-green room full of the bustle of early commuters, but no commuters. The sound was canned.

A lone Constable gave me a sleepy look as I went past him up the passage and out into crisp morning air. Above the trees the Washington Monument thrust up, snowy white, newly resurfaced. Farther away, across the river toward the towers of Arlington, the Kennedy Memorial floated on mist—and beyond it The Pentagon loomed like a gray prison.

There was a cab stop across the way. I got in the first in line, gave it the address, sat back and looked out the window as it scooted along the empty streets, over the trac bridge, boosting around a wide curve to the south, all alone in the early morning.

The Gonspart Tower was a two-thousand foot cylinder, pale blue, standing on a silver stem in the center of a circle of garden, not quite crowded by the other towers that spread out over the Virginia hills. I had been there before, in happier times. The cab whirled in under the overhang and waited while two plump, important-looking men in gray clothes got into a car with the Great Seal blazoned in gold on its side. One of them looked vaguely familiar. He was talking into a phone as they pulled away. They hadn't looked at me.

I went in through the curved glass doors, studied the menu-board, found Trilia Danton listed as residing on the 118th level, Corridor 17, Apartment 61. I walked along the curve of the silver wall until I found lift 27, rode it up alone. The corridor where it deposited me was empty. I walked along the deep-pile passage to a driftwood-gray door with a gold number 61 on it.

I poked the ID end of my card in the slot and waited. Nothing happened for a minute or more; then the door slid back and I walked into a room full of dark fabrics and muted colors and complicated reflections from polished wood and metal furnishings and bric-a-brac. There was a window—not a DV, but one of the kind which pipes in the live view from the roof via fiber optics—but the heavy drapes were drawn almost closed.

"Ban—I'm so excited you're here," Trilia's voice said from the air, sounding brash and tinny. "I'll be out in a moment."

I said "fine" and stood by the window and watched the few cabs that were out crawling along the loops of road that were flung across the landscape. The sun was above the horizon, making miles-long shadows behind the towers. Something clicked behind me and I turned and Trilia was there, tall, golden-haired, elegantly groomed, closing the door behind her. She smiled, came across toward me, but instead of coming up to me slid aside and sat on a long, soft-cushioned couch, with the window at her back, patted the seat beside her.

"Ban, sit down, you look—you look fine," she changed whatever it was she had been about to say. "I haven't quite recovered from my astonishment yet," she went on, talking rapidly. "How in the world do you happen to be here in Washington? I thought *Tyrant* was still on the trans-Jovian. When did she get back? Why hasn't Paul called?" All this with the strained brightness of a hostess in an official reception line.

"*Tyrant* isn't back, Trilia," I said. "Just me."

She looked puzzled—or perhaps it was a look of sudden fright. I could see her trying to decide which question to ask first.

"I have a message from Paul for you," I said.

"Y . . . yes?"

He said . . . '*confirmed.*' "

Her face went as pale as the slice of sky behind her. Her hands tightened and moved together.

"Why, what a . . . a curious message," she said in a voice that sounded like the original Edison recording. Her smile was a jumble of tensed facial muscles.

"He seemed to think you'd understand," I said.

"Just . . . one of his little jokes, I suppose," she said. "You know how Paul was always joking."

I thought about it, but I couldn't remember Paul Danton in the role of prankster.

"But where *is* Paul?" she said. The question hung in the air like an echo.

"Paul is dead, Trilia. Didn't they tell you?"

She made a sound as if I had hit her in the stomach.

"Four months ago," I said. "It was painless, instantaneous. Are you saying the Navy hasn't notified you?"

Her hand clawed at her throat. I sat beside her and caught her hands, held them.

"What does the message mean, Trilia?"

"Nothing," she whispered. "It's a meaningless message. A joke, as I said."

"Trilia, I have to know. What connection does it have with Paul's death?"

She snatched her hands away. "Nonsense! Paul's not dead! He can't be!"

"I saw the body, Trilia. He was murdered. If you'd tell me what 'confirmed' means, I may be able to find out why he was murdered."

"You're insane! I don't believe any of it! You're trying to drag Paul down with you, but you can't! You won't!"

I caught her by the shoulders, not quite shaking her. "Listen to me, Trilia: I came a long way with that message. Paul wasn't playing tricks when he gave it to me. I want to know what's going on, what he meant, what he was involved in—"

"Nothing! Paul was involved in nothing! He was—he *is* a dedicated career officer—"

"He took a scoutboat out into the Rings, alone. He was looking for something, Trilia. What?"

"It's all lies—or your imagination!" Her voice was weak, without conviction.

"Paul knew something a man named Hatcher didn't

want known. And Hatcher never moved without orders from Crowder. Paul was onto something—"

"No! I won't listen to any more!" She leaned toward me as she shrilled this. When her face was an inch from mine she hissed: "Ban—get out quickly! They're . . ." her voice died away. She was looking at something behind me. I looked that way; the door she had entered through was opening. A man slid through it, holding a gun in his hand. He was a tall man, dressed in black.

"Lieutenant Tarleton," he said in a voice as flat as a millstone. "Sorry I missed you at the barge."

3

He looked at Trilia. Trilia looked at him. I looked at both of them. He put the gun away and smiled a rather cold smile. He went across to a chair and seated himself, making himself at home.

"Pleasant crossing?" he asked.

"Who's this?" I asked Trilia.

"He said . . . that he had news of Paul."

The man crossed his legs. It was an attitude of relaxation, but he did not appear relaxed. His eyes were sharp and restless.

"You were wise to come here," he said to me. "It might have been difficult to re-establish contact if you hadn't."

Trilia was staring at me. "Ban—is what he told me true?"

"What did he tell you?"

"That—that you were being sought as a deserter. That you're a part of—"

"Thats enough, Mrs. Danton," the stranger said

sharply. His smile took none of the edge from his tone. He shifted his look back to me.

"Lieutenant, our organization has gone to no little trouble and expense to assist you in eluding arrest. I would now like to have a full report from you."

"A report of what?"

He seemed to think that over. "Of Commander Danton's findings," he said carefully.

"His findings with regard to what?"

"You may speak freely, Tarleton," he said. "I've checked the apartment thoroughly; we're not under surveillance."

"Maybe you'd better tell me who you are," I said.

"My knowing you is sufficient credential, I think."

"I don't agree with you." I stood. "What is it you expect from me? I know nothing about Commander Danton's affairs."

"That doesn't agree with my information."

"Then your information is in error. Maybe you'd better go now."

He stood, faced me squarely. "Let's make the position quite clear, Tarleton. We've helped you. We expect help in return."

"Who is 'we'?"

"You're making a mistake, Tarleton. You can't turn your back on us now. That should be obvious to you."

"Is that a threat?"

"Take it as you will."

Trilia was beside me, touching my arm. "Ban—is it true? Did they bring you here?"

"A little man named Joto put me aboard a barge," I said. "That's all I know."

Trilia made a distressed sound. "Ban—you have to . . ." her voice faltered.

"I have to what, Trilia?"

"Perhaps you're right," the man said. "We'd better be going. We're distressing Mrs. Danton.

"Go where?"

He pointed upward. "I have a cab waiting."

"All right," I said. "Let's go."

"No," Trilia said suddenly harshly. "Don't go with him, Ban. It's time to put an end to this . . . farce."

The man narrowed his eyes at her. Before he could speak she forestalled him.

"You have a gun," she told him flatly. "You can shoot both of us. Then you may as well shoot yourself. You can't leave this building without my cooperation."

"I can make it very painful for you—"

"Don't waste time bluffing. I have to be here—alive—holding down the lock release for you to pass out through any exterior door. A burglar precaution, you understand. The professional burglars are aware of the system. Perhaps you should have researched matters more completely before you came here."

"Tell me what's going on, Trilia," I said.

"This man is a member of an underground Hatenik organization. Their avowed objective is to overthrow the Companies."

"What connection does a crank organization have with you—or me?"

"Paul was . . . on communication with them. As his wife, I . . . went along. Now Paul's dead. *They* told me—weeks ago. I said I didn't believe them, but I was fooling myself." Her voice broke on the last word.

"Mrs. Danton, you are doing a very foolish thing," the man in black said.

"Oh, no. I'm doing what I should have done long

ago. Now get out! I won't inform on you—out of respect for Paul's word, not from any compunction I might have about seeing you fanatics transported!"

"This can end in only one way," the man said in an ominous tone.

"I've told you—"

"Wait, Trilia," I said. I turned to catch her eye; I winked. "I think we're safe in trusting him; it's not a trap." I turned back to him. "You can't blame us for wanting to be sure," I said. "This is a dangerous game we're playing. You *could* have been OSI."

"Very sensible," the man in black said tonelessly.

"Ban—don't! You don't have to! He can't force you—"

"No question of force," I said. "It's all right. I *want* to go with him."

"Let's be going," he said.

"Push the button, Trilia," I said. "Everything's going to be all right."

Her eyes searched mine; they looked desperate, haunted. "All right, Ban—if that's what you want."

I followed my guide out into the silent corridor. We rode the lift in silence to the top, stepped out in a chilly vestibule. He pressed the door-release.

"Ban—are you all right?" Trilia's voice said from the grill above the door.

"I'm fine."

"It's not too late, Ban."

"I'm on my way, Trilia. You'll hear from me."

The lock clicked and we stepped out onto the windy terrace of the roof. The sun was up now, a platinum disk through the haze. The world looked big and very far below.

"You were wise, Lieutenant," the man in black

said. "You saved the lady a great deal of unpleasantness."

"Leave her alone," I said. "She won't betray you—but you got her husband killed. You can't expect her to love you."

"She won't be molested—unless she sees fit to reinvolve herself."

We stepped into the waiting copter and lifted off into the low traffic lane.

4

The place to which he took me was an old-fashioned apartment building in the Alexandria section, shabby evidence of the fact that slum-dwellers make slums. We walked down concrete stairs, were met by a man of an indefinable scruffiness who stared and jerked his thumb along the passage.

We ended in a room that had once been painted brown; it was furnished with a long table lined with straight chairs; other chairs were against the walls. There was no carpeting, no curtains at the painted-out window, no decoration on the wall. Light came from a glare panel roughly bolted to the ceiling. There was an odor of dust and stale food. The man in black told me to sit, posted two sullen-looking ex-youths to watch me, and went away.

It was half an hour before the door rattled and swung in to admit a large, dark-haired man with small, pointed features, a massive belly which he seemed to guide ahead of him as he walked. Four other men and a woman followed him into the room, giving me quick sharp looks before taking chairs behind the table. All of them seemed to vary from the norm in some manner: too fat, too thin, too tall, too short. Their clothes were badly fitted, none too clean. Their expressions ranged from frowns to glowers. They looked like very unhappy people.

The big man took the center chair. He settled himself and moved a finger and another man noisily placed a chair across the table from him.

"Please sit there, Mr. Tarleton," the big man said. His voice surprised me: it was almost a squeak. I took the chair. He looked at me.

"So you're a deserter," he said.

"I suppose that's the way it was reported."

"You have another version?"

"No."

"Now you're wondering why we made the pick-up on you. Not here: at the Borneo end."

I waited.

"You were down in our records as a close acquaintance of Danton," he said. "We know Danton. Then we got the news you'd gone over the hill. We alerted our people. We've got lots of people. Joto got you before the Stabs. Clear?"

"Clear enough. But who do you mean by 'we'? Just who are you?"

"We're an organization, Mr. Tarleton. Individual names wouldn't interest you."

"What kind of organization?"

The big man had a disconcerting habit of looking at me as if waiting for the fatuousness of my own remarks to dawn on me. I countered it as well as I could by looking expectant.

"An organization that's not content with the scraps, Lieutenant," he said at last. "An organization that intends to do something about it."

I went on looking expectant.

"Some of us," he said carefully, "had an idea a man like you might be thinking along the same lines."

I wanted to shift position in my chair. I didn't. I thought of several things to say, and didn't say them.

"We could use an ex-Naval officer, Lieutenant. If he was anti-regime, that is."

That was the first time I'd heard the expression "ex-officer" used in reference to me. I didn't like the sound of it.

"Use him in what way?"

The big man breathed in and exhaled slowly, not quite a sigh.

"But you're pretty well pleased with things in general, aren't you, Lieutenant?" he said at last. "Oh, I don't mean this little mess you've gotten yourself into; you're pretty sure you can square that, I think. I mean the overall picture: the Companies running the world in the name of the Public, the Navy enforcing their policies of Closed Space, private property, no trespassers. The well-fed, mindless mob at the bottom, the Starlords at the top."

"I wouldn't put it that way," I said.

"The Starlords." The big man used the nickname with a snicker, a sinister lift of his delicately shaped lip, two sizes too small for his head. "Lord Imbolo. Lord Catrice." He pronounced the words as if they were obscenities. "Lord Anse. Lord Banshire. Lord Uhlan. Benevolent despots of the world."

"I suppose you have a right to your opinion—"

"You *suppose*; don't you know damned well we have a right?"

"Very well; you have a right; and so do I, of course."

"Sure you do." He nodded rather sadly. "Even if your opinion is just what they programmed into you. That's all right."

He looked down at his fingers. I had a feeling they would need washing. "What I *don't* like too well," he said slowly, "is your skipping out on Tancey." He raised his chin far enough to stare at me. "What was the idea, Tarleton?"

"I never heard of Tancey," I said. "When the barge dropped anchor I went over the side, that's all."

"You claim you didn't see him?"

"I saw a man. It might have been anyone."

"Going to the Danton woman was all right too," he said slowly. "Except that I understand she's gone sour."

"Mrs. Danton just lost her husband," I said. "All she wants is to be left alone."

"Uh-huh." He nodded and carefully picked at his left nostril. "What was it Danton turned up?" he asked casually.

"Nothing that I know of."

"Oh?" He nodded, pulled the corners of his mouth down. "You gave the Danton woman a message."

"Yes."

He hunched toward me, his hands folded on the tabletop. "Tell me about that message, Mr. Tarleton."

"The message was addressed to Mrs. Danton," I said.

He looked bleakly at me. They were all looking at me.

"Maybe we'll have to have another talk with the lady after all," the big man said.

"Leave Mrs. Danton out of this," I said. "She wants nothing to do with you, as I think you're aware. In any event, your man Tancey must have heard what I said."

The big man looked aslant at the man on his right, then those on the left. In the silence I heard a copter beating across the sky, sounding very far away, in another world.

"What did the message mean?" a thin man asked in a quiet voice.

"It meant that his suspicions were confirmed," I said.

"Suspicions of what?"

"Mutiny."

No one moved. No one spoke. I was still on stage, with my piece still to speak. It didn't seem to be going over well.

"The ringleader is a man named Crowder," I plowed on, "a member of the Commodore's civilian staff. They were working through Grayson. I suppose they threatened to take reprisals against the ship's company if he didn't cooperate."

The big man's tongue came out and touched his upper lip and went back in.

"Danton managed to leave the ship; he was trying to hide a message when they caught him and killed him." I paused, but no one clapped.

"I discovered he was ex-hull and followed. I was too late: I found his body. One of Crowder's men was killed. I knew I couldn't go back. By luck there was a late-model G-boat on hand. I took it and made the run in."

"Is no surveillance maintained over the planetary approaches, Lieutenant?" a pale little man with uncombed, colorless hair asked, in a crisp voice.

"Certainly; but an object as small as an auxiliary boat is difficult to detect, even if you know where to look."

"So you just waltzed right through and soft-landed

in the water, swam ashore, and walked in on Joto," the woman said in a soft voice.

"There was a little more to it than that, Ma'am," I said.

"I'll bet there was, Lieutenant. I'll bet there was." The small man smiled a bright, tight smile.

The big man had tilted his head sideways, was studying me solemnly.

"Mutiny, you say," he said.

"That's right."

"With what object, Lieutenant?" He sounded genuinely puzzled.

"I'm afraid you'll have to ask the mutineers," I said.

"Your contention is that Commander Danton knew of this planned mutiny a year and more ago, before the vessel set out on the cruise?" the woman queried. "And rather than initiating an official investigation, he confided his suspicions in his wife?"

"So it appears."

"And having had his fears confirmed, he entrusted you with the information, consigned again to the lady."

"All I can tell you is what happened. I leave the interpretation to you."

"It appears Commander Danton relied rather heavily on the element of luck, eh, Lieutenant?"

"I doubt if he planned for matters to turn out as they did. Crowder must have become suspicious of him and forced his hand. He did what he could under the circumstances."

"And on the strength of these conjectures, you deserted your post, and undertook what some might regard as an impossible voyage."

"At the time it seemed a logical decision," I said with less confidence than I felt.

The big man leaned back and put his plump, pale hands flat on the table.

"A man like you would like to be a hero, eh, Mr. Tarleton?"

"I was trying to save my skin, among other things," I said.

There were several moments of silence then. They looked at me and I looked back.

"Tell me, Mr. Tarleton," the big man said. "Just where would you have us believe you stand?"

"I should think that would be clear enough. I'm a Naval officer."

"You don't wish to make common cause with our organization?" the little man asked, raising his eyebrows.

"I'm afraid our interests don't coincide."

"Strange. A mutineer, arriving with exciting news of the seizure of a major Naval vessel by forces presumably inimicable to the regime: there seem to be several opportunities there for an ingenious man who wished to ingratiate himself . . ."

"I'm not interested in ingratiating myself," I said, and pushed back my chair and stood. "I'm grateful to you for your help," I said. "I'm sorry if you got the wrong impression."

The big man steepled his fingers. "What are your plans now, Mr. Tarleton?"

"To turn the matter over to the Chief of Naval Operations."

"Including yourself?"

"I hope that under the circumstances my actions will be vindicated. In any event I'm making a full report." I took a breath and said my next line: "Now, if you don't mind, I think I'd better be going."

"Oh," someone said inanely.

"And what do you intend to tell them about us, Lieutenant?"

"I don't think it will be necessary for me to mention you."

"How will you explain how you reached Washington?"

"I could have stowed away on the barge unassisted."

The big man's eyes lingered on me, then turned away. "Tancey," he spoke sharply across the room. The man in black rose and looked at me lazily.

"You can't simply walk out of here, of course," the big man said to me. "Tancey will drop you in a safe place."

Everyone was getting to his feet. Two of the men behind the table fell in behind me as I followed Tancey out into the hall.

5

The copter dropped in to a landing among trees in a hollow a few miles out in the green Virginia countryside. The four of us climbed out. Tancey licked his lips and reached inside his coat and took out the gun he carried there.

"What's that for?" I asked, and discovered my mouth was dry as a blotter.

"Just how stupid do you think we are, Tarleton?" one of the other men spoke up. I turned and looked at him. He was pointing a gun at me. So was the third man.

"The thing I can't figure," the same man said, "is why anybody thought we'd go for it." He was a rabbit-faced fellow with big, bony wrists and too much Adam's apple.

"Why'd you back out, fella?" the third man said. He was small and soft-looking, with nervous features. "The story start to sound too fishy even to you?"

"Why don't we ask him a few questions?" the rabbity one said. "I want to know how much he knows, what they were after."

"Waste of time," Tancey said. "He's conditioned; he can't talk if he wants to, right, Lieutenant?"

To my disgust, I discovered that I was shaking. My stomach felt light and fluttery, my knees wobbly. The sky seemed to glare down like massed searchlights. I had the feeling that time was rushing at me like a juggernaut, narrowing down, focusing in to an unbearable tension. In seconds, I'd be dead. It seemed so wrong, so ridiculously wrong, after I had been through so much, come so far. . . .

"Walk over there, Lieutenant," Tancey said, and motioned toward a dense growth of brush. I backed a step. My legs didn't seem to be working properly. I wanted to say something, but there was no breath in my lungs. The three of them stood watching me, Tancey on the left, and a little apart, the other two, close together. I watched the guns in the way I imagine a mouse watches a rattlesnake.

"Hell," the rabbity man said, "he's—"

He had gotten that far when Tancey pivoted smoothly at the waist and fired once, twice, two soft *chut!s*. The rabbity man and the soft man fell down like empty bundles of clothes. Tancey lowered the gun.

"Sorry to have put you through all this, Lieutenant," he said in an entirely different voice. "Krupp,

Naval Intelligence. Too bad you ducked me at the barge; it could have saved us a great deal of melodramatics."

6

I sat in another chair, looking across another table. This time the men behind it wore the gold-braided blue of senior Naval officers. Two of them were strangers to me, but the other three were men I had known since childhood—not that their expressions reflected the fact. They listened in grave silence as I gave a full account of my activities from the moment of my interview with Commodore Grayson to my arrival at the Danton apartment.

"I hoped that Trilia Danton would be able to shed light on the situation," I finished. "Unfortunately, she wasn't able to tell me anything."

Admiral Stane made a note on the paper before him and looked at me with a neutral expression.

"It was your impression that Commander Danton had taken the boat into the Rings in order to secrete a message there?"

"That was just something I told the Hatenik council, sir. I don't know why he went there."

"You say he had cut a specimen from a fragment of crystal rock," Admiral Lightner said. "Where is this piece of material now?"

"I'm afraid I lost it somewhere along the way, sir."

"The man Hatcher was killed accidentally, according to your testimony, Tarleton," Admiral Wentworth said. "Crushed by your boat which was drifting in a derelict condition after being fired on by Hatcher."

"That's correct, sir."

"That strikes me as a rather curious accident, Lieutenant."

"Yes, sir."

"You were aware that the area into which you took your boat was off-limits."

"Under the circumstances, sir, it seemed to me that I was justified in following Commander Danton."

"Just what were those circumstances, Lieutenant?"

"The circumstances that the Commodore seemed to be acting under Crowder's orders, that Commander Danton was missing and Crowder seemed to be very eager to find him, and that the commander was in danger of being left behind when the ship changed station."

"If Crowder was, ah, in charge of the ship as you suggest, why did he permit you to leave the vessel?"

"I don't think he expected me to take any such action, sir. And possibly he had his hands full consolidating his position; he hadn't yet taken over complete control."

"What motive do you attribute to these alleged mutineers?"

"Sir, I haven't the faintest idea—unless they're in some way linked with the Hatenik movement, which seems unlikely."

Admiral Stane hunched forward on his elbows, frowning. "Lieutenant, you paint a rather lurid picture of mutiny, treachery, murder and God knows what else. You tell us a story made up of wild conjectures, coincidences, inexplicable actions on the part of men of tested reliability. And as evidence, you offer—what?"

"It should be easy enough to check out my story," I said. "The major points, at least."

"Wouldn't it be better, Lieutenant, if you simply made a clean breast of it?"

"You think I'm lying to you, sir?"

"Isn't it true, Lieutenant," Admiral Lightner spoke up in a harsh voice, "that you were apprehended in a sabotage attempt by Mr. Hatcher—a Special Intelligence officer—and that you killed him? That you then fled the ship, were overtaken in the Rings, where you attempted to hide, by Commander Danton—who mistakenly believed you to be innocent and hoped to convince you of the folly of desertion—and that you killed him there? That you then managed to return to Earth, either in the G-boat or with the help of the revolutionary group known as the Hateniks, and—"

"No, sir," I cut in. "That's fantastic."

"More fantastic than this fabric of fantasies you've had the gall to present to this Board?" Wentworth barked.

"Gentlemen, I respectfully suggest you contact *Tyrant* at once; Commodore Grayson will confirm what I've told you—if he's still alive."

"Oh?" Wentworth said. It was hard to believe that stony face was the same one I remembered smiling over the problems I was having assembling my first model spaceship, twenty years earlier. He spoke into the whisperphone. A few silent seconds ticked by. The door opened and Commodore Grayson walked in, cool and immaculate.

"You've monitored the conversation, Grayson," Wentworth said. "Any comments?"

Grayson looked at me in the way one might look at something adhering to the sole of one's shoe.

"If a mutiny occurred aboard my command," he said, "it was never called to my attention."

7

The court-martial was a modest affair. The charge of murdering Paul Danton wasn't pressed; the prosecution confined the indictment to the contention that I had killed Hatcher, stolen his G-boat, and deserted my station. Inasmuch as the charges were entirely true—with the exception of a slight technical quibble in my mind as to the first point—my assigned defense counsel had very little to say. He made a half-hearted suggestion that I plead insanity, which I declined.

I raised the point of Paul's death. But without my mutiny theory, which had died without a murmur, I had nothing to offer in explanation of my accusation that Hatcher had killed him on Crowder's orders. My testimony sounded wild even to me. I requested that Crowder be called, but since even I couldn't make the claim that he had a direct connection with Hatcher's death or my subsequent actions, the request was denied.

Commodore Grayson testified that I had served competently until the moment of my desertion; he sounded rather sad as he declined to suggest any explanation of my behavior.

The court declined to find me guilty of Hatcher's murder, which left only the charges of grand larceny of Fleet property, and desertion.

Of those offenses I was found guilty as charged.

Admiral Hatch, the president of the court, called me forward and asked if I had anything to say before sentencing. He looked bewildered, as if things were happening a trifle too fast. I felt the same way.

It seemed to me that there were a great many

things that needed saying about Paul's message, his death, the shot Hatcher had fired at me, about Crowder's behavior during the interview in Grayson's office, about whatever it was Paul had been seeking in the Rings.

But I had already said all that.

I wanted to say that I was a dedicated career officer, that the interests of the Navy were my interests, that it was all a huge mistake, and that my only wish now was to return to duty and forget the whole thing.

I said, "No, sir."

I stood at attention, feeling as unreal as a photograph pasted on a cardboard cutout while the sentence was read. The words seemed to apply to someone else, not to me:

". . . dismissed from the service . . . forfeiture of pay and allowances . . . abrogation of citizenship . . . transportation for life. . . ."

There was no colorful ceremony; no one plucked off my buttons or broke my sword over his knee. They drove me in a closed car to a large, gray building and led me along a bright-lit corridor to a neat little room with a bed, a desk, a private toilet, but no window. They gave me a physical examination, a variety of inoculations, and a plain gray suit, which I put on.

After that, time passed slowly.

There were meals, served in my room. I was allowed to watch trideo, except that certain channels were blacked out from time to time; news broadcasts, I deduced. I slept, requested exercise equipment, which was supplied. Lights out; lights on.

I estimated that nine days had passed when I was taken from the cell, driven to Andrews, placed aboard a shuttle, and flown west, accompanied by two armed Petty Officers who didn't talk much, even to each other.

At the staging base, I was told that I might have visitors. Since I lacked living relatives, I declined the opportunity, but was advised that a caller was waiting. They ushered Admiral Hence in, and left us alone together in a small room as cosy as a gas chamber.

He had a little trouble getting to the point; but eventually he came out with it plainly enough: in return for all I knew about the Hatenik organization, a high-level pitch for a reduction of sentence.

I told him I knew nothing about the Hatenik organization that Tancey/Krupp didn't already know. He had to let it go at that, of course. Navy anti-interrogation conditioning was as effective against official inquiries as against anyone else.

Before he left, he paused long enough to give me a searching look and ask me the burning question:

"Why, Ban?"

I didn't have an answer that didn't sound like the ravings of a lunatic.

The next day they loaded me aboard a stripped-down transport with twenty-one other prisoners, outward bound for a planet called Roseworld.

PART TWO

Seven

My first sight of my new home was at dawn: pink light on a pink desert stretching to a line of pink mountains in the pink distance. We filed out of the ship into heat and dryness and a pervasive odor of hot iron, lined up in two ranks as directed, were counted off, right-faced and marched under armed guard across to a long, low shed flying a Fleet Station ensign.

Inside, a small, neat, tired looking man in a plain coverall told us that we were free men. We would not be confined or coerced in any way. If we wished, we could walk out of the station and never come back.

He paused to let that sink in.

"However," he went on, "those of you who wish to remain here—for as long as you remain here—will abide by the rules set up for the conduct of this station. These rules are arbitrary and absolute. There is no appeal from them. The penalty for any infraction is forcible ejection from the station area, with no return."

There was a certain amount of throat-clearing and foot shuffling among my twenty-one fellow convicts, but no one spoke. I think we were all picturing the expanse of pink desert that surrounded the station.

"Nothing is free here," the lecturer went on. "If you choose to make use of the facilities of the station, you'll pay for what you use. The one exception is air. We make no attempt to control the use of air. This is not out of a spirit of generosity. The air is not supplied by the station, and thus is the property of all." He didn't say it as if it were a joke. No one took it as one, so far as I could see.

A middle-aged man with a narrow, lined face raised a hand. The lecturer nodded.

"Does that include, ah, food and so on?"

"It includes everything supplied by the station, including answers to redundant questions. You now have a one-credit charge against you."

"Well, how does one go about paying? You know we have no credit balances—"

"Two credits; that point is to be covered in my standard presentation. You work. How much you work is up to you. How much you're paid is up to your overseer."

"That's not really much of a choice, is it?" a tall, rangy, leathery fellow spoke up in a grating voice. "We can go out and starve in the desert, or stay here and work—on your terms."

"You're free to accept the terms, or reject them."

"What if I decide to reject them?" the rangy man stood suddenly and took a step forward. "What if I—" That was as far as he got. There was a sharp click and a door slid open and two armed men in gray came through it.

"If you reject them, you leave the station—now."

The rangy man sat down.

"The choice of work is yours," the lecturer went on. The two guards stationed themselves against the wall, folded their arms, and looked at the rangy man.

"There's plenty of work for every man, here and elsewhere on-planet. If you choose you can leave this station for a contract at one of the outstations."

"What are these outstations?" the man who had asked about the food inquired.

"Three credits. They're industrial installations: mines, factories, processing plants and so on."

"What if you go to one of these places and find you don't like it? Are you free to leave again?"

"When you depart this station you're no longer under station jurisdiction. Enforcement of outstation rules is the responsibility of the individual overseer."

"Could you come back here if you don't like it out there?"

"Five credits. What you do after you leave this station is entirely your affair. So long as you break no rules of this station you may enter it and remain here."

"What kind of jobs are available?"

"Six credits. Manual labor requiring varying degrees of skill."

"Manual labor? I'm a . . . I was a . . . That is, my training . . ." He ran down and subsided. I was wondering what use Roseworld would find for the kind of training I had.

"We waste nothing on this station, including time," the lecturer said. "You're free to go now. Those desiring job assignment may report to the employment office in the next bay. Outstation recruiters will be on-station from time to time." He pointed to the man who had asked the questions.

"You. You'll report to employment at once for six days' compulsory non-compensated labor."

"Eh? Six days—"

"Food and shelter will be provided during the work-off period. I suggest you learn to remain silent and listen. You'll be told as much as you need to know. No charge for that information."

2

At the employment office I was offered a choice of three jobs: cook's helper, vehicle maintenance helper, or common labor. I took the latter, on a day to day basis. That way the pay was lower—one credit per six hour day—but there was no obligation to stay if one received a better offer.

The work I was assigned to consisted of raking gravel, shoveling sand, breaking stones and loading them, scrubbing the station windows, floors, and kitchen. The work was heavy, and quotas were assigned, but they were fairly light. I did my best, but I had never recovered my strength after the starvation ordeal. I ate well enough at the mess, and slept adequately in the dormitory. On off-duty hours, there were taped trideo shows available—at a price—and books. Or one could stroll around the station and admire the sand gardens. Aside from a few ornamental Terrestrial cacti planted near the admin building, there was no living thing in sight.

There were ninety-four inmates at the station, a dozen administrative personnel, some of whom were exiles, and twenty well-armed guards. None of us spoke to anyone unnecessarily. The station rules turned out to be mild and reasonable. It would have been an idyllic existence for a lobotomy case.

A week passed. I seemed to be waiting for something to happen. I was neither depressed or elated. I worked, slept, ate, walked. I raked pale pink gravel and placed rose-pink stones and hosed the magenta dust from the buildings, making blood-colored mud. None of it seemed real.

On the tenth day—or possibly the eleventh: I had begun to lose count of the days—a recruiter arrived from a place called Llywarch Hen.

It was after the evening meal. I was on my bunk, reading a history of the Peloponnesian Wars when he came in, accompanied by two guards. They stood by looking watchful and bored as he posted himself in the center of the long room and started his speil: his name was Cymraeg, he stated, and he was here to give us an opportunity at something a little more stimulating than Station life. He was a big fellow with bushy brown hair turning gray above the ears, a big, powerful body, thickening a little at the waist. There were a dozen or more small, puckered scars on his face and the backs of his hands. His voice was rasping, harsh as metal rubbing on stone; but his diction was that of an educated man.

"We conduct a mining operation at Llywarch," he said. "Your pay will be based on performance. You work long hours or short, as you elect. A four-hour day will cover your subsistence. Any time above that will buy a variety of items not available here, including alcoholic beverages, fresh beef, tailored clothing, private quarters, manufactured articles of many kinds, and so on.

"In addition to the pay—one credit per hour after basic—bonuses are paid for certain classes of find, including gem stones, fossils, indications of various rare minerals, and other items."

He told us that Llywarch Hen was one hundred and twenty miles from Base station, that it was one of the oldest Outstations on the planet, having been established in 2103 by the original discovery party who had been in need of tungsten to carry out repairs to their ship. Any prospective employees would sign a five year contract, cancellable by the contractor, but not by the employee. In the event of cancellation, transport back to Base would be supplied free.

No one had any questions to ask. When he called for candidates, seventeen of the twenty-one men in the barracks stepped forward.

Mr. Cymraeg went along the line, carefully scrutinizing each man. He paused before a big fellow with pale, shifty eyes. He looked him up and down. He reached out to prod him in the ribs and the big man knocked his hand aside.

Mr. Crymraeg's mouth twitched at the corners. He nodded.

"You," he said. He stopped again before a wide, thick-shouldered man with coal black hair and gray-blue jaws.

"Turn your head," he said. The man turned his head.

"The other way."

He turned it the other way.

Mr. Cymraeg said, "You," and passed on.

He looked over a tall, narrow fellow with a face like a prematurely aged teenager. As they stared at each other, tears started to run down the prospect's face. Cymraeg went on.

He didn't stop again until he reached me. He looked at me carefully. I looked back at him. At close range his skin was coarse, pocked with tiny scars.

His eyes were yellowish green, slightly bloodshot, rheumy. His lips were faintly crooked, lumped with old scars. He was a man who had endured much battering.

"What's your name?" he said. His breath had a faint odor of rusted metal. It was the first time since I had arrived on Roseworld that anyone had asked me that question. I had almost forgotten I had a name.

"Jones," I said. "Jonah for short."

He hesitated and I thought he was about to turn away. Then he nodded and said, "You."

3

Cymraeg had selected five men from the other barracks, all well above average in size though by no means the best physical specimens available. It was apparent that most if not all of the men were basically of strong physique, although a number of us had deteriorated to a greater or lesser extent, some before arrival on Roseworld, others after.

We eight recruits signed contracts under the watchful eye of the little man who had given us our first orientation; his name was never mentioned, then or later. Cymraeg loaded us in a squat, dust-covered personnel carrier, started up what seemed to be an antique turbine engine, and without ceremony drove along the station street to the end and headed out across the desert.

4

It was a five hour run to Llywarch Hen across sand and rock, through ranges of dusty-rose hills, without a sight of life or water. In spite of the closed body of the vehicle, dust filtered in, coated everything including the lining of my throat. Cymraeg stopped every hour and allowed us to stretch our legs in the shimmering heat. We were issued water and food, not enough of either.

It was late afternoon when we came down a winding track through eroded red hills into a hollow which by comparison with Base Station looked almost civilized. There were houses in neat rows, surrounded by gardens of an impossible, vivid green, walks lined with growing things, a shopping area, and beyond that a complex of large gray-painted buildings with tall stacks from which black smoke wisped.

Unfortunately, our vehicle didn't stop there. It swung off on a perimeter road, passed a factory surrounded by a high wire fence, followed a twisting track up into broken country cut by arroyos and canyons, emerged in a level area blasted from the rock. There were low sheds in sight, a rank of dust-coated vehicles, pieces of heavy rolling rock. A dozen or so men in shapeless coveralls stood watching as we pulled to a stop.

Cymraeg ordered us out of the carrier and turned us over to a big bald neckless man with a round head and a seamed dark face, who led us off to a small open space between huts. He lined us up in a row and walked past the row, came back behind us, then posted himself front and center.

"Is there a man here who thinks he can run this squad?" he asked. His voice seemed to come from somewhere down around his ankles.

A lean, sandy-haired man with a tight mouth and quick eyes, standing on my left, stepped forward. The bald man sauntered over to him.

"What makes you think you can run a squad?" he asked softly

The lean man's mouth twitched. "I'm accustomed to command," he said, not very loudly. "I'm a, ah, former—"

A large black hand caught the front of the lean man's coverall, lead him to his toes.

"You're a former nothing," he said. "You've got no past and damned little future. Get me?"

The thin man made sounds. The bald man dropped him; he staggered and recovered his footing.

"Still think you can run this squad?" the bald man asked him.

The thin man shook his head, backed into line. He stood there, staring at the bald man.

"You have no right," he said quickly as the bald man turned away.

The bald man turned back.

"Grab my shirt," he said. The lean man stared at him.

"Grab it," the bald man said softly. "Right here." He pointed to his chest, just below his throat.

The lean man reached out cautiously and gripped the cloth.

"Now pick me up."

The lean man swallowed hard. He crouched a little, and his shoulder went down. His face turned red; he grimaced; his arm tensed, trembling. He let his breath out explosively and dropped his hand. The bald man hadn't budged.

"Still think you can run my squad?" he said.

"I . . . I," the lean man said.

The bald man walked back to his front and center position.

"Count off," he said.

We counted off.

"Ones, left face; twos, right face."

I was facing the lean man. The corner of his eye was twitching with a fine tremor. He looked past my left ear.

"You've heard of the buddy system," the bald man said.

The lean man's eyes flicked to my chin, flicked away again.

"Well, we don't use it here," the bald man said, sounding savage. "The man you're looking at is your enemy. He's your opposition. He's the fellow that can keep you from collecting the bonuses; he's the one that runs the quota up. Anything he gets comes out of your hide, understand me?"

No one answered the question.

"All right—fight," the bald man said.

The man facing me frowned and stole another glimpse at my chin. I heard a meaty impact and a grunt and from the corner of my eye saw a man fall out of ranks.

"Hit him, damn you!" the bald man yelled. The lean man gave a jump and brought his fists up; he feinted a left jab at my face and crossed with a right that grazed my chin as I leaned back. I hit him in the stomach; he leaned on me and I pushed him away and he went to his knees. There was scuffling all round. A man staggered back and fell over my man.

"All right!" Baldy barked. "Your four pair off."

I found myself facing the wide, thick man who had been recruited from my barracks. His eyes were glassy; blood was running from the corner of his mouth. He swung a wobbly left hook that missed, and went to his knees. I hadn't touched him. Another man fell. There was one other man on his feet, a barrel-chested chap with hair like brass wire. He looked around, saw me, shot a fist out—

The sun exploded. I was sitting on the ground, with a throbbing head, tasting blood in my mouth. The blond bruiser was rubbing his fist and looking pleased with himself. The bald man was yelling an order. The other men were getting to their feet. I found mine and stood on them.

"Anybody want to challenge the winner?" Baldy said. No takers. Baldy turned and casually slammed a right into Blondie's midriff, uppercut him as he doubled over, caught him with a roundhouse right as he toppled backward.

Baldy flexed his pink-palmed hands.

"Anybody else think they can run my squad?" he asked.

He listened to a few seconds of silence, then jerked a thumb at the man at his feet.

"Get him on his feet," he said. "We're moving out now."

It was a twenty-minute hike over rough ground to a big pit like a meteor crater, wreathed in dust. Three openings were visible in the sides near the bottom, shored up with steel bracing. Tracks ran from each to a platform at the center of the excavation, from which a conveyor belt rattled endlessly upward to a loading platform at the opposite side. Men in coveralls moved in the dust clouds like a disaster crew at a fire.

Four of us were ordered into number two shaft, four into number three. I was in the latter group with the lean man, Blondie, and a young fellow who hardly looked old enough to have died and gone to Hell. We followed a man in a coverall and mask along the passage; a glare strip hung along the ceiling shed enough light to follow the twists and turns.

He halted us in a hollowed out chamber with branching tunnels, a turntable at the center. Men appeared from the side branches trundling loaded barrows which they upended into the waiting ore cars. The air was clearer here; water sprayed at intervals from a pipe running around the walls. There was mud and rock underfoot. A steady rumbling filled the air.

Another man appeared, detailed a man to pick up spilled ore, which was loaded in a special car; another was assigned to manhandle cars onto the turntable. He motioned to the lean man and me to follow him into a side tunnel.

There was no glare strip here; our guide led the way with a torch. The passage ended against a broken rockface. In the artificial light, dark strata in the rock glistened like black glass. An empty ore car waited.

It was quieter here; the lean man was having trouble with his breathing. My neck ached from bending under the low ceiling.

"You birds ever operated a rock cutter?" the miner asked. We hadn't. He swore a little and picked up a heavy apparatus from the floor, slung a strap over his shoulder, thumbed a lever. A clatter started up. He held the chisel-end of the jack-hammer against the rock and cut a horizontal groove an inch wide and four feet long, at waist height. He cut another groove a foot lower, shut down the tool. He picked up a short, thick chisel and a rock hammer, set the chisel in the upper groove, and gave it a blow with the hammer. A flat slab of rock fell. He picked it up and tossed it into the car.

"That's the way we do it," he said. "One little chip at a time. If you see anything—*anything* except red rock and black glass, hold it as you were and fetch me. Clear?"

"Look here," the lean man said, "you mean we're expected to just . . . just take over, without instruction?"

"I just instructed you, you poor crot. You better get hustling: you got a quota to make."

"But we—haven't eaten or rested—"

"You eat when you earn it; you rest when you can pay for a bed. At the rate you're going that might be awhile."

"How . . . how do we know when we've met the quota?"

"I'll be sure and tell you. So long, smart guys. Long live the revolution."

Eight

The lean man and I experimented with the power hammer, threw a lot of chips, eventually made a wavering cut of uneven depth. We took turns pounding at it, managed to knock off a double handful of small fragments.

"There seems to be a knack to it," my partner said.

"There is to most things," I agreed. We kept at it. The material was a kind of hard chalk, apparently identical with the hundred and twenty miles of surface we had driven across to reach Llywarch Hen. I wondered why we were digging fifty feet underground for more of the same, but my curiosity was a mild and transient thing, soon forgotten in the absorbing business of pounding rock. After an hour both of us were bleeding from half a dozen small cuts from flying chips. It was hot and stuffy in the dead-end passage. In the light of the torch that had been left to illuminate our labors everything looked gray now; the rods and cones had tired of registering pink.

After a while the bottom of the car was covered. The lean man asked me how long I thought we'd been at it. I didn't know. We gave ourselves a break, sat on the stone floor in the dusty heat and looked at nothing. After a while we went back to work. The level in the cart rose slowly.

The light startled me, flashing on the rockface and glinting on the glassy black striations. A man came up, looked at the scene of our labors, flashed the light in the ore car.

"Shift's over," he said. "Let's go," and turned away. The lean man dropped the hammer and started after him.

"What about the cart?" I said. "Are we supposed to bring it along?"

"Forget it. I'll take care of it."

"We don't want to impose," I said. "Come on, partner, let's push it."

"Why? He said—"

"Let's get in the habit of doing things for ourselves. Nothing's free, remember?"

The man with the light snorted and went on ahead.

Back in the main cavern, a man with a clipboard watched as we maneuvered the cart onto the scale. He punched a dispenser at his belt and handed each of us a chip of blue plastic. The lean man took his and scurried for daylight.

"This covers the time, I take it," I said. "I'd like a receipt for the rock, too."

The tally-man stared at me. "A receipt, he says."

"How else do I have proof of what I've dug?"

"You put in your time, you get your bed and a meal. What more you want, Greenie?"

"I heard something about quotas."

He lifted his face mask and wiped his face with his hand and spat. "You get no chits for anything less than a full cart, Greenie. Now beat it—"

"Suppose I fill it next shift."

He looked at the cart disparagingly. "You haven't got enough there to cover demurrage."

"What does that mean?"

"You tie up a cart, you pay for it. You dig hard for four hours and have a little luck and you can load enough to cover tool and cart rent and enough over for a couple chits. Ten chits make a credit. You drag your feet and make half a load and you get basic time: bed and breakfast. That's you, Greenie. Now beat it before—"

"What happens to my rock?"

"It'll get taken care of."

"I see." I went around the cart and started pushing it back up the track. He acted as though he would block my way but at the last moment he stepped aside.

"A wise one, eh?" he said as I went past. "OK, brother, I got ways of evening up."

I dug for a few more hours. I filled the cart level, then added a few more chunks just to be on the safe side. I had to lie on the floor and rest for a few minutes before I felt equal to pushing the cart back up the tunnel.

There was a different man on duty with the clipboard. When I was six feet from him, a ten pound piece of rock fell from the cart. I stooped for it and a man was there, grabbing it, shoving me back. His eyes were wild.

"That's mine, you," he growled like a grizzly with his paw in a beehive.

I had trouble swallowing. I doubled my fists; my

hands felt as big as catchers' mitts, hot as bunions. Other men were gathering around. All of them were looking at me in an unfriendly way.

"Put it back," I said.

The man who had pushed me looked around at the others. "I got scavenger detail," he said. "You saw it fall."

"Break it up," the clipboard man said. "You lose, Greenie," he said to me. "Better learn how to load." He turned suddenly and backhanded a man who had come up beside my cart, causing him to drop a fist-sized chunk of stone he was in the act of lifting from my load.

"Pick it up," the clipboard man ordered. The man he had hit picked up the rock and tossed it back on the cart.

"Thanks," I said.

"Don't thank me, Greenie," the tally-man grunted. "If I let him get away with that once, he'd try it again and get clobbered. Trouble slows down production. I don't earn my chits slowing down production. Now let's get that cart on the scales."

"Your predecessor didn't seem so interested in production."

"If he could con you out of a half-load he'd come out ahead." He pulled a lever; there was a clickety-clack and four pale yellow rectangular plastic tabs clattered from a dispenser on the scale into a cup. He scooped them up, handed me three.

"What are you waiting for?" he barked. "Shove off, you."

"I'm waiting for my other chit."

He looked outraged. "You think I work for free, Cull?"

He was a big man, healthier than I, not nearly so

tired as I. It depressed me to look at him. I started toward him; he palmed me off.

"Wise up, Greenie; it's a fair shake."

I swung and missed and almost fell down. He grabbed my sleeves below the elbows and rammed my funny bones together.

"I don't need trouble," he said in a conversational tone. "You be nice and I'll give you a tip: those tabs are seven-day board—and they've got two days on 'em already." He pushed me away. "I leave it to you, Greenie: is it worth a chit?"

I thought about the ache in my empty stomach and the drought in my throat and decided it was.

2

I found my own way back out of the pit and along the path to the camp. A sign on one of the sheds indicated that it was the mess hall. I was surprised. No one gave away information for nothing around here.

Inside, there were tables, an eating ledge along one wall under the windows for those who preferred to eat standing up, a stainless steel serving line at the far end. A dozen or so men sat at the tables, no two at the same table. I saw Cymraeg over by the windows, brooding over a cup of something that steamed. A sign on the wall said: *Take All You Want—Eat All You Take.*

As I reached for a tray, a man appeared out of nowhere, gave me a distasteful look and punched a hole in my blue ticket, after which I was free to take my choice from eight items ranging from cold hotcakes to something that appeared to be oatmeal with chopped mushrooms. Another man was waiting at the far end of the line. He held out a large, callused hand. Like everybody else I met here, he seemed to be bigger, stronger, and in better shape than I was.

"A chit, sport," he said cheerfully. I walked through him and took a table near Cymraeg. The hotcakes weren't bad, if you like yeast. The oatmeal was disappointing. When I finished, I dumped the tray in a slot as I had seen others do, and left the building. The fellow with the outstretched hand was waiting. This time the hand was in the shape of a fist like a knuckly sledge hammer.

"A chit for what?" I said before he could speak.

"Tax," he said.

"Is this supposed to be official, or are you in business for yourself?" I asked, backing away.

"What's official?" He looked reproachful. "Look, pal, why make it tough? Pay up and eat in peace. I keep the scroungers off, right?"

I tried a dodge around the right end, but he caught my arm, stopped short of breaking it. I kicked him in the left shin. He frowned and didn't break the other arm.

"You guys," he said sadly. "You got to have it the hard way."

He was wearing a nicely fitted, new looking coverall, cut from a soft tan material. It had ducky little tabs on the shoulders, and flaps on the pockets with shiny brass buttons. He bent my arms back into shape and released me.

"Come on, give," he said.

I feinted a move toward my pocket and instead swung at him, on the theory that the best way to discourage bullying was to make it more trouble than it's worth. I missed, snagged his pocket flap and ripped it half off. The button went flying. He staggered back, clapped a hand to his chest, swore, and began scanning the ground. He saw the button and put a foot on it, said, "Hold it!" as I slid toward the corner of the building.

I held it.

"You're one of them kind, hah?" He sounded more disappointed than angry. "You know what this outfit cost me? Nine creds. Yeah. Nine creds. And you tore it. All for a lousy chit."

"Hardly worth it, eh?" I said, and made a yard sideways. "Maybe you'd better forget this particular chit."

"Hey, listen," he said. "Let's don't go lousing up my deal, OK?"

"I never did like paying taxes," I said. "Even legal ones."

"Look, forget that legal stuff, hey? Here legal don't mean anything. Nothing at all. Only what works counts, is all. And my racket has been working nice. Up to now."

"Just strike me off the tax rolls, that's all," I said.

"What you figure—you can make it solo?" He looked me over. "Forget it, chum. You ain't got the build for it."

"I plan to live by my wits."

He rubbed his chin. It looked like a boulder weathering out of a cliff. "Look, sport, you need protection, see?"

"They need me to dig," I said. "They won't let you kill me."

"Right." He stabbed a finger at me. "Or maim you—that means break you up to where you can't load rock—or lose you too much sleep or eats so you get sick. But that still leaves me plenty of operating space. You like having your arm bent? How's about half an hour a day of it, guaranteed no sprains? Just for openers."

"Have you got half an hour a day to put on it?"

He looked disgusted. "That's the weak point," he said. "But you're the first to spot it."

"How long have you been operating your tax service, Heavy?"

"Six days. It just come to me. I bought the suit yesterday out of the take." He frowned, creasing a forehead like a shed roof. "Look, a deal: you walk behind me—and I give you full protection on the chow line. How's it sound?"

"How far behind you?"

"You know—just for show. A few high-signs, like, to let the rubes know we got a arrangement. That way nobody won't start to get ideas when they see you don't cough up."

"Count me out, Heavy. I don't think we'd get along."

He frowned and moved toward me, stopped dead as the door of the mess hall opened: Cymraeg stepped out, holding a smoking cigar between his thick fingers. He looked at Heavy.

"I've been watching you operate your tax service," he said. "I've decided I don't like it." He jammed the cigar in his mouth and walked on.

When he was gone, Heavy looked at me unhappily. "There goes the tax business," he said. "Well, it was soft while it lasted."

"Just how does Cymraeg fit into the picture here?" I asked. "A Company man?"

Heavy looked at me with mild disgust. "He's a con, Slim, just like the rest of us. No Company man ever puts a foot outside Base Station. If he does, he's had it. He stays. Anyway that's what they say."

"You could take him," I said.

"Yeah—but I can't take the Syndicate."

"Wait a minute," I said as he turned away. "What's the Syndicate?"

"Nothing," he said.

"Maybe I'd better ask Cymraeg," I said.

He stood there looking over his shoulder at me. He looked around as if checking for eavesdroppers, hitched up his belt, moved closer to me.

"Look, Greenie," he said earnestly. "Just cut your rock and pay your tabs and keep breathing, OK?"

"Oh, that," I said, a trifle more loudly than was strictly necessary.

He nodded, almost eagerly. "Sure. You're pretty low. You just got here. A couple months ago you were a gung ho Navy type, honor and duty and a fat retirement plan. Officer, maybe a light commander. All of a sudden here you are: eating pink dirt." His finger poked me in the chest. "Listen," he said. "Eating dirt's better'n not eating at all, right? You got a long time to be dead in. And what the hell: a guy might even have a few laughs before then, who knows?"

"I'm laughing all the time, Heavy," I said.

"I guess you're one o' them linen cases," he said. "Them are the worst. They keep asking why, and there ain't no answer. But look at it like this: a guy can cop it anytime, anyplace. A accident in the Power Room; a little flaw in the LS system; hell, a busted flitter fan back home on leave. So what happened to you was like that. It don't mean nothing. It's like a rock falls out of the sky and hits you. But you're still alive, see? You can still smell and taste and breathe. You can get a few kicks, even. I mean, it ain't all over. Not yet."

"What's your interest in the matter?"

"Nothing, Slim. Just . . ." He held out a hand and looked up as if he were checking for rain. He closed his fist. "A guy got to fight back, some way. You know?"

"You know something, Heavy?" I said. "I have a hunch you're a linen case too—whatever that is."

He looked at me, a rather wild look. "Get yourself a breather, Greenie," he snarled. "You look lousy. And slow down. You can't do it all in a day." He walked away slowly, rubbing his knuckles. I went into the nearest barracks and gave the blue tab to a fellow who sneered and pointed to an empty bunk. I don't remember lying down on it.

3

I worked alone the next shift. The cutting seemed to go a little faster. No rocks fell from my cart. The tally-man paid off in full with no argument other than a resentful look. I passed Heavy leaving the mess hall. He grinned and wagged his head ruefully.

At the end of five days I had collected thirteen chits which were redeemed by an official in the camp at the rate of eleven for a one credit chip. The latter was stamped from one-year plastic to discourage hoarding. I used it to buy a second-hand breathing rig from a tally-man.

After three weeks as a rock chipper, I demanded and received my turn at scavenging. It was easier than rock-cutting. The rules—tacit, but rigid—permitted me not only to collect anything that fell off a cart, but also to sweep up around the various cutting faces, collect chips from the loading area, and in general scrounge whatever I could. In addition to loading two carts a day on a four hour shift, it served to keep the mine remarkably clean of debris.

I didn't form any friendships. Heavy was the only man at Llywarch Hen who knew how to smile, but we never talked. Occasionally I saw one or another of the men who had arrived with me, but they didn't appear eager to form an alumni association. Little by little I came to know the system of bribes and fees, learned when and how to resist the squeeze, when to pay up docilely. The system was administered by self-appointed beadles, old timers with the muscle to make argument painful, but it was made possible only by a common disinclination to let anyone get by with anything.

I went from scavenging to cart-maintenance, which was paid by contributions from the membership, collection being the business of the receiver. With my slightly enlarged earnings, I bought my own hammer and chisel and went back to rock cutting. That was where the bonuses were. My skill improved. I learned the precise angle at which to hold the chisel, the precise force of the blow required to scale away a ten-pound flake of stone. I searched diligently for signs of some substance other than pink chalk and black glass.

And one day I made my find.

4

It was a lumpy, porous chunk of blackish metal about the size of an inch-thick dinner plate. I cut it free and cleaned the adhering chalk away. It had the general appearance of meteoric iron, but was much heavier and harder than iron. I left my half-filled cart and carried my trophy back out to the tally-man.

He saw me coming from fifty feet away and whirled and poked a button I hadn't seen poked before. A whooping siren went into action. Men came swarming out of the side passages, were immediately shunted out the mine entrance by the shapers-up who posted themselves in strategic positions, fending the crowd away from the weighing-table. Two of them took up stances flanking the tunnel I had been working in.

I dumped my trophy down on the scale and watched the tally-man make notes in a pad. He twiddled his change-maker and handed over a black bonus tab as if he hated to part with it. It was stamped with numbers which established its value. I had been around long enough now to know this wasn't an item he could chance cheating me on. He handed over a blue tab as well, although I had not completed four hours.

"The find covers shift credit," he said. "Report to Admin on the double."

As I went out, a squad of four inside workers passed me, headed for my work-site.

In the Admin hut, a solemn, clerkly little man clucked over my tab and made entries in a computer-input console, then played a tune on a coding panel which caused a small package to drop into a hopper with a pleasantly heavy *thunk*. He handed it over the counter to me.

"One hundred credits," he said in an envious tone. "Thumbprint here." He pushed a form toward me. I opened the packet and counted the chips: one hundred of them, all of a healthy golden color. I tucked them away in a pocket.

"What makes a piece of metal so valuable?" I asked.

He gave me a severe look. "Take your bonus and

move along," he ordered. I had an urge to reach across and squeeze his neck a trifle, but I knew the rules about man-handling office personnel. I left quietly.

Four men were waiting in the space between huts. They moved out to surround me.

"You got lucky, eh, Greenie?" one of them said. He was a long-faced, chinless, sallow-looking fellow, six-six, wide and bony. His three friends were equally wholesome types.

"It's all in knowing where to look," I said.

Their heads jerked as if they were all attached to the same rope. Two of them said, "Hah?"

"Don't talk smart, Greenie," the chinless man said. "That kind of talk can get a man a trip." He looked at me from under his tangled eyebrows, a quizzical look. "We had an idea you might be planning to drop down to Hen, is all," he went on. "A Greenie like you won't know the ropes. You'll want somebody to keep you out of the hot fat."

"I'll manage, thanks," I started around them and the spokesman put out a hand.

"Do yourself a favor," he said softly. "We walk behind you. No trouble, no pay. Fair?"

"It's your turn to be smart," I said, and started on; I was counting on the fact that I hadn't seen open robbery committed. It seemed to be about to work; but apparently the sight of all those credits walking away was too much for the small-headed fat-necked member of the quartet. He muttered, "Cover me," and moved in. I side-stepped with the idea of beating a hasty retreat to the Admin building, and someone wrapped his arms around me from behind. I tramped on his instep and yelled—the loudest sound I'd heard in weeks. It jarred them; the man behind me loosed his grip far enough for me to ram an elbow into him, but before I could pursue the advantage the others had grabbed me and were hustling me into the nook they had emerged from.

There was a sound like a boot kicking a ripe melon and suddenly my arms were free. I turned in time to see the man I called Heavy step in close to the chinless man and sink a fist into his stomach. The chap with the chins was in an awkward position against the building, having difficulty with his breathing. The remaining members of the quartet were backing away. Heavy made a shooing motion and they turned and darted off. He gave me a broad wink.

"Maybe it's time to re-open our business discussion, Slim," he said. "Before you fall in with evil companions."

I worked the kinks out of my shoulder. "I was thinking of paying a visit to town," I said. "If you'd like to come along, possibly we could work out something."

Nine

Preparations for my first venture away from camp were simple: my blue tab gave me barracks-entry; I stripped, and tossed the suit into the vibrator which cleaned it of foreign particles while the sonospray booth performed the same service for my body. I donned the same garment and we walked out of camp along the road by which I had arrived three weeks earlier. There was no signing in or out, no guard, no password. I was as free as a bird—except that I didn't eat or sleep until I had put in my shift time. Even my new-won wealth wouldn't change that; only the perishable, non-transferable blue tabs were negotiable in the barracks and the mess. It was a system that insured steady production.

It was late in the afternoon. The pink sun glared on the dusty road. Pink dust motes danced in the air.

"Tell me a few things, Heavy," I said when we were a hundred yards past the last hut. "If Cymraeg is a prisoner like the rest of us, who really runs the camp?"

"Why ask me? Nobody told me any more than they told you, Slim."

"How long have you been here?"

"I dunno. A year, maybe a little more. What's it matter?"

"You've had time to find out a few things."

"All I know is what I see. The cons run the camp. The best man appoints himself boss and makes the rules. Guys that break 'em find out about it the hard way and don't break 'em again."

"You're a husky fellow. Why haven't you pounded your way to the top?"

"A smart boss-man like Cymraeg knows enough to discourage any rising young talent. If I got ideas and started pounding too many heads, building up a take-over cadre, his boys would move in."

"How did he establish himself?"

"The last boss got old. He'll get old some day too, and a younger dog will eat him. Meantime, he's in charge."

"Why do they have us mining material that's no different from what's on the surface? Why do they place such a value on a lump of slag?"

"The bonus junk is the money crop. We're not mining rock, Slim. We're just looking for stuff like what you found."

"Why? What's it good for?"

"Dunno."

"All right, we have a loose social order based on prior claim, plus superior ability, plus muscle, held in restraint by the fact that production pays the bills and men make production. But what about the equipment: the huts and the weighing scales and the chit-vendors, and the ground-car—"

"All bought out of production. This place was built by the Company originally, over a hundred years ago; the operation didn't pay. Then Pink Hell was picked as a dumping ground for troublemakers. With convict labor available, the picture changed; the Company offered to pay subsistence for men to work the mines, and bonuses for any finds—such as lumps of fused metal. The men could spend their earnings any way they wanted; they ordered off-planet merchandise and paid good negotiable cash for it. They built the town, stocked it, improved the camp, worked out the chit system. They can't go home again, but there's no reason for them not to live as well as possible."

"You say 'they' as if you weren't one of us," I said.

"Yeah," he said, and laughed, not very humorously. "Maybe I like to kid myself a little, Slim."

"And for a moment, your fo'castle dialect slipped a trifle, Heavy."

He was silent for ten paces. Then he said: "Rule one: don't let your curiosity show, Slim."

"We can talk here," I said. "No one's listening."

"How do you know there's not an induction ear trained on us?" he said softly.

"An ear can't function through solid rock."

He turned and gave me a hard-eyed look that was as different from his usual expression as a rapier is from a banana.

"Safer if you just chip your rock and spend your creds," he said.

I laughed. I shouldn't have started. I couldn't stop. I fell down, and on all fours I laughed until I realized that the line between laughter and sobs is a fine technical distinction, easily lost, and with it the whole careful structure of the defensive shell that had kept me walking and talking, if not thinking and feeling, since the moment I had seen Paul Danton's dead and ruined face.

Heavy saved me. He hauled me to my feet and slapped me across the jaw with a hand like a canoe paddle, backhanded me on the return stroke, shoved me against a looming pink rock slab.

"As you were, Mister," he growled, and suddenly I was seeing a face I remembered from long ago, from my late teens, when I had paid my first visit to the Academy. The face had been younger then, but no prettier, and there had been a captain's braid on the cap that went with it. He had been Commandant of Cadets, and his name was . . .

"Look, Slim," he said, "if you're gonna throw fits, maybe I make Hen solo after all, hey?"

I got my feet under me and pushed his hand away.

"I'm all right," I said. "It was just something I remembered. A joke. An old, old joke."

"Sure," he said. "We're all laughing."

We finished the twenty-minute walk with no conversation.

2

The hamlet called Llywarch Hen consisted of a brick-paved central square lined with small shops, from which radiated a network of crowded streets which spread to the factories at the north, and on the south opened into winding residential avenues adorned with imported trees, flowers, grass. The houses were modest, neat, old-fashioned, with chimneys, glass windows, hinged doors. Except for the pink desert backdrop, it might have been a trideo set for a Twentieth Century suburban drama.

There were people in the streets, no vehicles. Not all the people were male. I saw a middle-aged woman emerge from a food store with a basket of fruit over her arm. Half a block farther on, a thin, youngish woman walked a small dog on a leash.

"All the comforts of home," I said, with startling originality.

"Sure," Heavy said. "Lotsa laughs. How about a couple drinks to loosen up on?" He led the way down one of the narrow avenues to a grog shop under a hanging sign with a sun-faded device of a pink devil with a pointed tail. He took a table in a corner and an old man with gritty, pink-rimmed eyes took our orders for brandy—after I showed him my cash. There were a few other customers in the house, all elderly men, plus a one-legged man.

"Who are they?" I asked. "Why aren't they chipping rock?"

"There's a like retirement plan," Heavy told me. "You buy into it, draw your basic plus a little extra when the medics say you can't dig anymore. Or you can ship back to Base Station. They're supposed to run some kind of old men's home somewhere up north. Only not many take that route, because the story is, you get a fast euthy shot and a cheap funeral."

The brandy was drinkable. We drank two, at a credit a shot. By then the sun was setting. We strolled along to a chop house and dined on real meat and vegetables. That cost another ten credits. Back in the street, a small man with half his face missing hooked his fingers in my sleeve and offered me a chance at gambling, dope, and women.

"How about it, Slim?" Heavy said. "You could maybe run that stack up to double, enough for a real blowout."

"We can spend it fast enough eating and drinking."

"You better come on anyways, you," the shill said

in a damaged voice. "A big man wants a couple words with you."

Heavy and I looked at each other.

"Does this big man have a name?" I asked.

"You'll find out," the runner predicted. "Not him." He jerked a thumb at Heavy. "Just you, is all."

"Maybe you better go at that," Heavy said. "I got stuff to do anyway." He turned and walked away.

"Let's go, you," my new friend gobbled. "He don't like to wait around."

Heavy had told me violence was taboo in town. There seemed to be no reason not to indulge my curiosity.

"Very well," I said. "Lead on."

He slid off along the walk, ducked down a side street, squeezed through a narrow doorway. Steps led down. At the bottom he opened a heavy door onto a bright-lit room where two men sat at a table covered with papers. One of the men was a stranger. The other was Cymraeg.

3

They looked at me, then at each other. Cymraeg raised his eyebrows; the stranger frowned. He started to speak, then jerked his head around and stared at me again. He grunted. Cymraeg seemed to relax a trifle. It seemed to be a rather elaborate conversation conducted without words.

"I've been watching how you handled things, Jonah," Cymraeg said. "You've worked out some answers for yourself. Now you're wondering about some of the less obvious questions." He looked at his thumb. "I wouldn't want to see you go astray; I called you down here to give you the information you'll need to reach the correct conclusions."

"You did say 'give'?"

"No charge this time," he said flatly. "Jonah, you're one of two hundred and twenty-nine men and five women, current census, dumped down in a desert with no laws, police, no courts of justice—or whatever it is courts dispense. Just a mob of condemned criminals and a world that wouldn't support human life for a day without artificial aids. What would you say holds Llywarch Hen together? What makes it work?"

"Government by the consent of the governed," I said. "With the added incentive of death by starvation if you can't fit in."

"Don't overlook the positive side. A clever man who accommodates himself to the system can become wealthy enough to live in luxury, even here."

"In an economy based on an artificial value assigned to a worthless commodity?"

"What do you suppose is behind it, Jonah?"

"It keeps the men busy."

"Why should anyone care whether we're busy or not? Why not let us all kill each other?"

"We were sentenced to exile, not death."

Cymraeg smiled a little. "You got a raw deal, didn't you, Jonah?"

"I was guilty," I said.

Cymraeg's expression indicated that I had departed from the script.

"What was the charge against you?"

"What makes that your business, Mr. Cymraeg?" I heard myself say. I was surprised that I'd said it, and at the sudden quivery sensation in my stomach at the turn the conversation had taken.

Cymraeg leaned back, scanned me from under his scarred eyebrows.

"Desertion," the other man said. He was bone-thin, white-haired; his voice was a husky, penetrating whisper. "Larceny. Murder. Correct, Mr. Tarleton?"

"And you're guilty, you say," Cymraeg grunted.

"Guilty enough." I was looking at the other man, wondering how he knew—and how much more he knew.

"The murder charge was dropped," he said. "The rest was quite sufficient to send him here."

"Why?" Cymraeg said. "Why did you do it—whatever you did?"

"I don't care to discuss it," I said. "Thanks for inviting me down—"

"Don't talk like a damned fool, Jonah," Cymraeg said. "You'll leave when I'm ready for you to leave."

"He testified that a civilian staffer killed an officer and tried to kill *him* when he appeared on the scene," the thin man said. "That the civilian died by misadventure, possibly with a bit of help. That he was convinced a mutiny had occurred, and for this reason he abandoned his ship and returned to Earth. On arrival, he was surprised to learn there had been no mutiny, and that the dead officer was apparently involved in treasonous activities. His defense, was, shall we say, half-hearted."

"You're satisfied with the Navy's handling of the case?" Cymraeg asked me. "You agree you belong here?"

"I believe in an orderly world, Mr. Cymraeg. I broke the rules. I knew the penalty."

"You *thought* you were acting in the best interests of the Navy, didn't you?" he shot back.

"I think so," I said. I was aware of my pulse pounding in my head. My stomach felt queasy. I needed fresh air.

"And how did they repay you? Were you given the benefit of the doubt? Did your old friends rally round? Was any consideration given to your prior service?"

"That wasn't the point—"

"One-way loyalty," Cymraeg growled.

"What sort of medical attention did you receive during the time you were in Naval custody, prior to trial?" the thin man asked.

"I was well cared for."

"Indeed? you came very close to death from starvation, Lieu—Jonah. This is a shock from which the unassisted body recovers slowly and incompletely. Using modern medical techniques, you could have been restored to full health in a matter of weeks. You received no such treatment. Instead you were sent here, assigned to hard labor." He turned to Cymraeg. "How old would you say the L—Jonah appears to be?"

"Late thirties."

He looked back at me. "What's your age, Jonah?"

"Twenty-eight."

Cymraeg grunted.

"They made an old man of you, Jonah," the thin man said. "Now how do you feel about the benignity of the authorities?"

"Come to the point," I said. I was feeling sicker by the minute.

"We were dumped here," Cymraeg said tightly. "Like broken tools that weren't needed anymore. They would have preferred to kill us outright, but this method salves their consciences. But conscience is a luxury they might have done better to manage without." He leaned forward and stared into my face.

"They consider us helpless, Jonah—*but we're not.*"

"I see."

"No, you don't. You think I'm a raving maniac. You think we're so many ants under the heels of the Companies. But they blundered, Jonah. They underestimated us badly. They shipped us here—brought us together, all their enemies in one convenient group. That was stupid, Jonah. But that's not their crowning idiocy. They picked Pink Hell as their dumping ground, their concentration camp. *Pink Hell,* of all the planets in the Sector!"

"Why do you bring the Companies into the matter?" I asked. "It was Navy business."

Cymraeg nodded, looking at me with a pitying expression. "Navy business, Jonah. And who do you suppose gives the Navy its orders?"

"The Public Executive, of course."

"Jonah, you were taught some history at the Academy. It was essentially accurate, as far as it went. But some important items were left out. Have you ever heard of a man named Imbolo?"

"He's a wealthy shipowner, isn't he?"

"Among other things. What about Catrice?"

"Lunar mining," I said. "He donated an opera house to my home town."

"A very generous man, Lord Catrice. Does the name Banshire mean anything to you?"

"There's a building of that name in Boston."

"Lord Uhlan? Lord Anse?"

"I knew the Public Legislature had awarded courtesy titles to a number of important industrialists. I'd forgotten their names. What are you getting at?"

"The five men I named control the Five Companies,

Jonah. And the Five Companies control the world—including the Navy."

"I've heard the theory before, Mr. Cymraeg," I said. "I was never impressed by it."

"Just Cymraeg, forget the Mister. And I'm not discussing theories, Jonah. I'm giving you facts. The Companies hold Earth in a total economic stranglehold. Among them, they control every prime industry and service on the planet—and through the Navy, they control explored Space. The Public is a façade, nothing more. The Executive takes his orders from the Five."

"If you invited me here to hear a political lecture, you're wasting your time, Cymraeg."

"Just listen, Jonah. You doubt what I'm telling you? Consider the facts: what kind of motive power drives a Deepspace Ship of the Line?"

"Is that a rhetorical question? All ships use the bevadrive, regardless of size."

"How are our cities heated and lighted?"

"By tapping the regional powernet."

"And the powernet draws energy from a cyclodyne—which is a modification of the bevadrive."

"I suppose—"

"You haven't heard it all, Jonah. Think about our society, our planetwide culture. Vehicles, appliances, tools, communications system—everything is based on artificially generated power."

"I know all this."

"Jonah, have you ever heard of a device called a Starcore?"

"Never."

"What's the principle behind the bevadrive, Jonah?"

"Nuclear fusion, I suppose."

"You're not sure? You, a Naval officer?"

"I was a communications specialist, not a Powerman."

"Ever know a Powerman?"

"Certainly."

"Did he ever show you his engines? Ever talk about tearing down the drive for overhaul?"

"No, not that I recall—"

"The fact is, the Power section of every vessel in the Fleet is sealed, Jonah. Did you know that?"

"I never had occasion—"

"The same is true of our regional generator stations. Sealed, off-limits to all personnel. You know why?"

"Since I wasn't aware they were sealed—if they are—I can hardly—"

"Because they're empty, Jonah. There's nothing inside. No mighty turbines turning giant shafts. No massively shielded piles pouring out the gigawatts. It's all window dressing, designed to conceal a secret."

"I see."

"You don't see anything. Not yet. As I said, the power chambers are empty—almost. They contain one small item: a Starcore. A thing you could hold in your hand. That's all, Jonah. That's where the power comes from. That's their secret. That's what they're protecting."

"Assuming this is all true—what does it have to do with me?"

"It's the reason you're here, Jonah—instead of back standing watch aboard *Tyrant*."

I stood up. "You seem to be making a great attempt to convince me of something; just what, I'm not sure. I'm afraid you're not meeting with much success. Do you mind if I go on my way now? I still have a few credits to burn."

"Jonah, you know what brainwashing is?" Cymraeg's tone was a whipcrack. He didn't wait for an answer. "Any man can be brainwashed. *Any* man. I want you to consider the possibility that you've been given the treatment."

He seemed quite serious about this. And in a sense it was a legitimate question. I considered it.

"Brainwashed by whom? When? For what purpose?"

"By society," he said. "By the Navy. All your life. For the purpose of making you into an obedient automaton, blindly carrying out your assigned role."

I relaxed. "Very well, if you choose to call the process of acculturation brainwashing, I can't really dispute the point. What would you propose instead? That we allow children to grow up like wild animals?"

He ignored the question. "Our so-called society was designed for the benefit of five men. They've arranged the world for their own pleasures. The rest of us are just house-servants, Jonah, fetching and carrying for them. How do you like that idea?"

"We seem to be quite comfortable in our slavery. The world is a better place than ever before in history."

"Is it?" He wiped his finger on the arm of his chair, showed me the pink dust.

"You weren't sent here because you committed a crime. You were sent here because you were a threat—or a potential threat—to the system."

"I'm afraid that's too obscure for me—"

"Your friend Danton poked his nose in, Jonah. He was getting close to something. That's why he was killed. And they thought you might have known what it was . . ." He was looking at me expectantly.

"So that's what you're after," I said. I almost laughed.

"Jonah, we need that information!"

"You're wasting your time, Cymraeg. Paul told me nothing—"

"You were met by representatives of an organization—"

"Hateniks. They had the same idea you did."

"We don't call them Hateniks, Jonah. That's a loaded term—part of the brainwashing."

"Are you telling me you're tied in with—"

"The organization is a lot bigger than you think, Tarleton— "

"I thought we were calling me Jonah. And how do you know so much about me?"

"As I said—we're a lot bigger than you know. We have members everywhere. And some of us—" he nodded toward the thin man—"can move freely, unlike you and me, Jonah. *They* think they have the cancer isolated, but they're wrong. Information comes in—and goes out. And the information you have could be what we've been waiting for."

"I've told you—"

"I know. You're right to be cagey. But now is the time to use what you know. Danton didn't die with the intention of having his discovery lost."

"What is it you expect me to tell you? You have all the answers, haven't you? The Companies run the world as a private club on this basis of their control of power sources, which you've assured me are not what they seem. The picture seems quite complete. What can I add?"

"Try to get this through your head, Jonah: They're *frightened!* That means they're vulnerable! We know they protect the secret of the Starcore in a way that goes far beyond mere technical secrecy. Why? That's what we need to know! Now speak up, man! Give us what you have!"

"I'm sorry I can't oblige you."

"You're content to let *them* go on holding the world in the palm of their hands? To own you and every other man living, to use them like so many cattle?"

"Put it this way," I said. "*They* invented the Starcore, as you call it. *They* used the product of their ingenuity—their genius—to transform the world into a garden for men to live in. If they also established themselves in comfort—to my way of thinking they deserve it. I haven't the faintest desire to tear them down. I wish them luck."

They stared at me across the table.

"Cymraeg, Paul Danton told me nothing," I said. "And even if he had . . ."

"Go on," Cymraeg grunted.

"Try to grasp something," I said. "I'm not a rebel against society. I liked the world I was born into; I believed in the system. I still do. Certainly, it can be improved. And it's being improved—by evolution, not revolution. I'm not interested in wild eyed saviors who're going to Fix Everything Instantly—mostly by tearing down what five thousand years of cultural evolution have built up. I'm not a Hatenik, Cymraeg. I don't sympathize with the Hatenik mentality."

"Still—by your own admission, you deserted your ship. There must have been a reason."

"I made a mistake—and I'm paying for it. But the continuity of a peaceful, orderly world is of more importance to me than even my own precious comfort. Have I made myself clear?"

"What do you want, Jonah? What is it you're holding out for?"

"You reformers," I said. "You noble do-gooders. You revolutionists who'll remold the sorry scheme of things entire. Don't you sometimes look up into the mirror and feel a certain disgust at what you see? Doesn't all that hate boiling around inside you ever make you feel a trifle sick?" I started toward the door and Cymraeg came up out of his chair and blocked me.

"You're a fool, Jonah! You could be a part of the new power structure, recover all you've lost and more—"

"After you've thrown the rascals out," I said. "I assume a certain Party discipline will be necessary, to maintain order. And for a time the old apparatus of control will have to continue—temporarily, of course. And who better than the Faithful to fill the jobs the blood-suckers were booted out of? And naturally you'll have to tolerate a certain amount of pomp and ceremony about your persons in order to satisfy the public—in their own interest, of course. But even though you'll be living like kings in the palaces formerly occupied by the tyrants, with your police busy day and night rooting out the potential counter-revolutionaries, you'll still be natural democrats at heart, concerned only with the blissful contentment of the peasantry. And what would my reward be? An admiral's star in the New Revolutionary Navy? An empty rank in a meaningless organization made up of party hacks and the politically reliable?"

"You prefer life on Pink Hell?" Cymraeg ground out the words like a rock crusher grinding boulders into gravel.

"That's really all it amounts to with you, isn't it, Cymraeg? Revenge. You want to get your fingers on the necks of the men who sent you here, and you'll tear the world down to accomplish it. Luckily, it's all talk. You're stuck here, Cymraeg. Go ahead with your plots. But count me out."

"You're making a mistake, Jonah," the thin man said.

"Get out of my way, Cymraeg," I said. He didn't move. He looked past me at the thin man. His expression was that of a man facing a disagreeable task—but quite prepared to carry it out. I doubled my fist and swung at his belt buckle. He grunted and grabbed my arms, threw me back against the table. The thin man caught me from behind.

"You're going to tell me what you know, Jonah—" Cymraeg started, and paused, listening. I could hear breaking sounds from outside; there was a thud of feet, a crash of breaking wood as the door burst open. Heavy slammed halfway across the room and came to a halt facing Cymraeg. His sleeve was torn and there was a small cut on his scalp. He licked his lips and looked brightly around the room.

"Come on, Jonah," he said. "I guess it's time you and me was getting back to camp."

"I was just leaving," I said.

Cymraeg and the thin man watched us silently as we departed.

Ten

"It's bad business," Heavy said, after I had told him the gist of my interview with Cymraeg. "I thought he'd just offer you a slot in the local set-up. This other stuff is a surprise to me." He rubbed his chin and frowned at the barracks floor.

"I think 'stir-crazy' is the old term for it," I said. "Forget it."

"He won't let it ride there. He can't. You watch yourself, Jonah."

"You know the rules, Heavy. No violence."

"Don't count on it." He flexed his shoulders and breathed deep as if he were getting ready to come out for the third round. "Well, I got to get back to the rock face," he said. Under his breath, he added, "I got a few ideas; take a day or two to check 'em out."

After he was gone, I lay on my rented bunk and looked at the ceiling and let the thoughts inside my skull bump gently against each other like gas-filled balloons drifting in an empty ballroom. There seemed to be some connections that wanted to be made, but I couldn't seem to make them.

* * *

I gave myself another day off, spent it wandering around the camp. If Cymraeg was in residence, he was keeping to his quarters. Late in the afternoon I climbed up the trail to the crest of the ridge west of camp and sat there for a while, watching the sun set across a zillion miles of rocky desert. It was a big, dull-red star compared with Sol. It sank in a welter of purple and crimson, and the two evening stars came out. One almost showed a disk. There was no moon, but the stars gave enough light to see by. I found myself wondering if Cymraeg and his Action Committee would avail themselves of this opportunity to continue our interrupted conversation. It wasn't a feeling of anxiety; if he intended to follow up, he'd find a time, now or later. The question didn't interest me much. I had no active desire to be put out of my misery—but there was no compulsion to attempt to defer whatever might be going to happen.

The next day I was back to work as usual. The shaft where I had made my find was still under guard. The men on duty were strangers to me, possibly new prisoners. I didn't see Heavy. I brought in my usual load, accepted my chits, dined in the mess hall. The men in the barracks were no more silent than usual. The sonospray cleaned without refreshing, also as usual. I had just composed myself for the night's sleep when they came for me.

2

There were four men, all strangers, all husky, all grim-faced, like men assigned a dirty job but determined to see it through. They switched on the overhead lights and posted themselves in the central aisle.

"On your feet, you men," one of them called down the barracks. I considered ignoring the order, but it would merely have made things less dignified. I got up, along with the rest.

One of the four men made a little speech to the effect that they'd had a report that there'd been some thievery going on, and they were here to check it out.

"The missing items are a rock hammer, fittings for a power chisel, and spare respirator filters," he finished. "The owner is here; he can identify them." He indicated a member of the vigilante quartet.

"I want two men to make the search," another of the men announced. "You, and you." The second you was me.

We started at the far end and worked our way down, bunk by bunk, with the men standing silent and watching, the foursome keeping eagle eyes on the proceedings. There wasn't a great deal to the search: we peeked under the bunks, felt around under the blankets, looked at the bare walls and floor. There was no place to hide anything, but all of us went through the motions of looking just as seriously as if there were. I stooped, patted, gazed around, went on to the next bunk, stooped, patted. . . .

I patted something hard and lumpy jammed between the foot of the bunk and the frame. I pulled back the blanket and saw an almost new rock hammer, a sealed package of filters, and a plastic valve assembly nestled snugly against the mattress.

"All right," the man who seemed to be in charge of the proceedings said. "Who holds bunk number 24?"

I was looking around for a glimpse of the man who had been silly enough to stuff his loot away in such an obvious spot when it dawned on me that *I* had bunk 24.

The rest of the charade was acted out with a minimum of violence. My arm was twisted a little while the "owner" made his identification. To no one's surprise he declared firmly that these items were, indeed, his very own property. The court considered the evidence, and reached the conclusion that someone had taken them and hidden them with the intention of selling them, and the man in whose bunk they were found was the guilty party. Each time I tried to speak, my arm was rotated a little closer to dislocation.

"You all know the punishment for theft," the president of the court stated. He gave me a solemn judicial look. "If you have anything to say, speak up now," he said.

"I suppose I could claim the loot was planted on me," I said. "But the fact is, I sneaked in here early and tucked it away for safe keeping because it never occurred to me you fellows would be shrewd enough to look in such a cleverly selected spot."

The chief executioner looked a bit startled, but not too startled to declare the case solved. He ordered me to get my clothes on; then he and his men formed up around me and walked me out into the dark street. Instead of hitting me over the head, they conducted me to the messhall and called for five days' iron rations and a gallon of water to go. One of them produced a pack and told me to strap it on. The food and water were loaded and paid for out of my remaining credits; oddly enough, the funds just covered my purchases.

They conducted me to a vehicle then—probably the same one in which I had arrived. I sat on the floor in back and braced myself against the swaying and the bumping for a period I estimated at half an hour—long enough to cover perhaps thirty miles, and for cold to seep through my bones—before we bumped to a halt and the turbine whined down to idle. The back doors opened and I was invited to climb out. I did, jumping down into soft sand from which the day's heat was still rising, in spite of the cold. One of the two men who were giving the orders pointed out into the night and said, "Base Station is that way."

The other one said, "Start walking, you."

I started walking. I had covered about fifty feet when the turbines revved up and I turned to watch the car's lights swing around and speed away across the flats. That left just me and all that desert.

"Quite right," I said aloud. "Give the victim a fair chance. It's only a few hundred miles to food and water. Who knows? I might even make it."

3

The days on Pink Hell were about twenty-nine hours long, I had been told, and during the daylight hours the temperature in the lowlands rose to 130°. The sun had been down for a couple of hours, which gave me twelve hours or more of darkness in which to begin my epic trek. If I covered three miles per hour, I'd be thirty-six miles closer to safety by dawn.

Somehow the thought failed to inspire me.

The sand was loose; it slipped back underfoot. The pack was heavy. I quickly discovered that my few weeks of work in the mine hadn't built back the strength and endurance I had lost in three months of enforced inactivity and starvation.

I turned my suit's temperature control up another notch. The shivering didn't stop. A brief investigation revealed the absence of a power unit. It fitted the pattern: they weren't exactly killing me, but they weren't giving me any help either. Curiously, the discovery didn't depress me. I would do the best I could. If I froze, I froze. And if I broke a leg, I would walk on my knees. If they wanted me dead, I'd stay alive just to spite them. I took a bearing on a star and set off again.

In minutes my mouth was dry, tasting of chalk from the unseen dust. In an hour my legs ached and my lungs burned and my mind was beginning to crawl up the sides of its cage, looking for a way out. But there wasn't any way out. I was at the bottom of the trap I had started slipping into so many moons ago, at the moment Commodore Grayson had sent for me, to drop a few hints that would have helped any level-headed young officer to see which way the wind blew . . .

That was a way of looking at it that hadn't occurred to me before.

Suppose the interview had been a warning—or even a plea for help? Suppose that in some obscure way I hadn't yet deduced, he had been trying to tell me something. Something I had failed to understand—and misunderstanding, had gone in precisely the wrong direction. Suppose that Grayson, misunderstanding my misunderstanding, had misinterpreted my actions from that moment on? Not knowing how I had known that Paul was ex-hull, or that I had been tipped that *Tyrant* was about to change station, he might have interpreted what I had done as prima-facie evidence of involvement with the Hateniks. That would explain the ice-cold look he had given me when the suggestion that his command had mutinied had been broached—not that the charge in itself wasn't enough to make any self-respecting commander bristle self-defensively. . . .

I didn't realize I had fallen until I was spitting dusty sand from my mouth. I gave myself a break, sipped some water, got back on my sore feet, and went on. I tried to recapture the line of thought I had been following, but it seemed too hard, too far away, too complicated. It didn't matter. What mattered was going on. One foot after the other, one step at a time, ignoring the pain from the pack straps and the ache in my legs and the flame in my throat. Walking shouldn't be so hard to do. After all, man had been evolving for a million years as a walker. Walking should be as easy as swimming was to a fish. I thought about fish, cool and green and scaled, sliding effortlessly through the deep and silent waters, basking in the shallows, goggling mindlessly at a universe a few feet in diameter. That would be true happiness: to live in health, responding to the primal urges to feed and mate and die, untroubled by the complications arising from excessive electrical activity in the convolutions of a few ounces of gray matter. Never to fear, because fear implies anticipation; never to regret, because without memory the past is nonexistent. Never to yearn for the unattainable, never to question, never to despair. . . .

I was flat on my face again. I had the feeling I'd been there for some time. It occurred to me that somewhere along the way I'd lost something valuable. I began feeling over the sand, looking for it, but there was nothing there but powdery chalk and broken pebbles. And I realized then that what I'd lost was no trinket that could be tucked away in a pocket, something I could replace for a few credits the first time I happened on a shop selling the proper line of merchandise. What I'd left behind in my adventures was youth and health and hope for the future. Those are the treasures that you hold for just a little while at the beginning of life before you lose them once and forever. And mine had gone a bit more quickly than most.

And yet to lie here on my face and wait for my heart to stop seemed even more fantastic than getting up and going on toward a destination I couldn't reach; which, even if I reached it, was as barren and empty as any cell in any dungeon ever cut into the rock of a prison world.

And so I found my feet and stood on them; and I put one before the other. And I walked.

4

I saw the line of the cliff-face as soon as the first faint dawn-glow lightened the sky behind me. Fire glared on the highest rock spires and flowed out to form a burning line that crept down over the sheer face of the old fault; and abruptly heat was searing my back.

A man—even a healthy man—couldn't last an hour exposed to Roseworld's raw sun. The same obscure instinct that had kept me walking through the night sent me tottering for the black refuge of a shallow ravine that cut the plain ahead. It was cooler there, among the tumbled rocks, if not particularly comfortable. I issued myself another ration of water, estimating that at my present rate of consumption the supply would last two days at the most. The question arose then as to whether it would be wiser to drink all I wanted now, thus shortening the process of death by dehydration, or to decrease the ration, thereby extending the torture an extra half day or so. I decided on the former course, then found myself taking only half the usual four swallows. Apparently at some level I intended to fight it out to the end.

For a few hours I slept. The sun woke me, baking my feet. Retreating into the deepest cranny available gave me another hour or two of respite. The sun was almost overhead when I faced the fact that I had made a serious error—if I really intended to keep fighting. From now until late afternoon, my hideaway would be in full sunlight. Long before the sun sank low enough for the slanting rim of the crevice to offer any protection I'd be dead of heatstroke.

The only possibility for me was to reach the cliffs. In another hour there'd be shadow at the foot of the vertical escarpment. It was hard to estimate distance through the heat shimmer, but it couldn't be much more than a mile. I could do a mile in twenty minutes, provided I didn't spend too much time falling down. And the sooner I started, the better. I took another ration of water, crawled up out of what had almost been my grave, and started off.

The night had been bad, but this was ridiculous. I could feel the heat through my boots before I had covered a dozen yards. The high sun seared the top of my head like an arctorch. The air was like poisonous gas. Suddenly it was a joke. They were using a battery of power cannon to kill a fly. Poor little fly, crawling over a red-hot griddle to reach the flames—and someone swats him with a sledge hammer. The whole thing was overdone.

Overdone—like a steak left too long over the charcoal. Did you know that a man can sit on a wooden bench in a room where the temperature is a dry 180° and watch a steak grill on the bench beside him? Clever man. Fry an egg on the sidewalk. Fry an egg on my brain. Fry my brain, calf's brain and scrambled eggs, and a ham steak, and a cold tankard of beer for breakfast. To drown in cold beer. Or even in cold water. You call that death? To fill your lungs with icy sea water and sink down into bottomless green translucence while the light slowly fades through the blue and the violet into utter blackness . . .

The truck came rushing out of nowhere and smashed me flat. I floated for a long time before I drifted aground on a rocky beach under a tropical sun. I was tempted to lie where I was and wait for the next wave to take me away, but instead, I crawled forward. This time I wouldn't be fooled. I'd lie doggo and wait until the boat arrived, and then . . .

They had built a wall in my path. That was unfair. It wasn't in the script. There was a slant of beach, and then the trees, and some sour berries, and shade, black shade, the finest food there was, and I'd find it and slice it and wrap myself in it and this time nothing would tempt me out again.

Not again.

No, not again. I clawed at some of the cobwebs that had accumulated in my mind, and took a fix on reality:

I wasn't on the beach. I was in a desert. I was on my way toward the cliffs, where I could lie in the shade and soak myself in the delectable coolness.

But I couldn't go any farther, because of the wall.

I opened my eyes and looked at rubble, boulders,

a fractured plane of rock, rising up, dazzling in the sunshine.

What do you know? I had made it. The cliffs. But there was a joker. No shade. Not for a while yet.

Well, I'd told myself a man couldn't live an hour in this sunlight. But maybe I was wrong. Maybe what I'd meant was that a man *could* live an hour in this sunlight.

I would soon know.

Soon? Eternity passes so slowly.

But when it's over, it seems so brief in retrospect. The shade lapped at me like cool water. I crept into it and felt the darkness close over me like an anesthetic and I slept.

5

When I woke this time, I lay and looked out at the expanse of black shadow that ended in a dazzle of glare-haze spreading out toward the dusty distances. With no intermediate intellectual exercises, I was remembering the trip out from Base Station, with the early sun casting its black shadow behind the car.

Behind the car.

Llywarch Hen was east of the Station.

I'd been walking east all night.

I may have covered twenty miles or more—getting farther from my destination with every painful step.

A sledge hammer? Nothing so trivial. A hundred ton highway roller. And all for a wounded fly. I laughed and enjoyed the joke for a while, until a question obtruded itself:

What made a single wounded fly so important, worth so much effort?

Admiral Hatch had thought I knew something. So

had the Hateniks. So had Cymraeg. It seemed to be a popular idea.

Perhaps there was something in it.

But if there was, it didn't jump into my mind, full-blown, like Venus from the forehead of Zeus.

But wouldn't it be funny if it did—out here—at the end of the line—too late—too late for me or anyone. . . ?

I slept, and when I woke it was dark.

6

The cliff was steep, but not too steep to climb. I was going in the wrong direction, but the idea of turning back didn't appeal to me. I'd started in this direction; I'd keep on as long as I could. I asked myself why, but I had no answer.

Then I saw the footprint.

It was in loose dust in the shelter of a niche in the rock, deep enough for the light of the two nearby planets to cast a shadow line along the edge where the sole and heel had rested. It looked fresh—but that might mean nothing. Protected from the wind, and with no rain to wash it out, it might have been made a day ago or a week—or longer. Years, possibly.

But the sight of it was curiously comforting. Someone else had made the same trek I was making, had found the same path to the top of the cliff. I was no longer completely alone in an empty world.

I climbed on, looking for more footprints. I found them. They led me to the top, but above, on the exposed sand-drift, the trail disappeared. I paused for a drink—two swallows—a bite of food, and a five minute break, then pressed on.

In half an hour I knew I wouldn't last the night.

Curiously enough, I was quite comfortable. My feet and legs felt numb and swollen, but were no longer painful. I had become accustomed to the rasping and blood-taste of my breath in my throat. I fell often, but softly, stumbling face-forward against the strangely soft ground. Once I got to my feet and was making good time until I realized I was still lying on my face, dreaming I was walking. That frightened me a little. I was careful to be certain I was awake as I got to my hands and knees and tried to stand. But there was no strength left in my legs.

I hadn't broken a leg, but it seemed I'd be walking on my knees in any case.

I thought I was doing quite well until I tasted sand in my mouth. This time my arms wouldn't work. I thought of my water bottle, still half full, but the idea seemed remote and academic, like those ephemeral plans to master obscure languages and take up the violin.

My last clear thought as the darkness swelled, and the little patch of inner light dwindled, was one of relief that I would no longer have to pretend not to grieve for the life I had had, and had lost, and would never know again.

7

I listened to the soft sound of air being inhaled and exhaled for quite some time before I became aware that it was my own breathing I was hearing. That seemed rather odd—as did the comfortable coolness around me, and the sensation of something soft under me. And something else. Sounds. Faint mutterings.

Human voices.

I opened my eyes and saw flickering warm light across a curve of uneven ceiling. By turning my head, I enlarged my field of vision to include a stretch of floor disappearing around a bend in what appeared to be a spacious, water-carved tunnel. The voice and the light were coming from beyond the angle of the cave.

I lay with my face against the softness of what felt like fur and enjoyed the hallucination. I had heard tales of the effect that a freezing man enjoyed a pleasing illusion of warmth in the last moments before his blood crystallized, but it had never been rumored that that class of illusion extended to those who had died of exhaustion.

But possibly I hadn't yet died. It seemed unlikely, and grossly unfair, but the possibility existed. It was a theory that should be tested. I opened my mouth and yelled.

The results were inconclusive. The sound I produced was a weak croak; but it *was* a sound. Further experiments were called for. I was pondering my next move when the hallucination stirred. Shadows moved on the ceiling, falling toward me. A man appeared at the bend, silhouetted against the glow. He came toward me, swelling as he came. He leaned over me, and his face was as big as a melon, as big as a moon, as big as the Universe. . . .

"Feeling better?" a voice said. It echoed and rang down long alleyways of space and time. I made an effort and focused in on it and shaped my mouth and managed a grunt.

"Good," he said. There was another man there then, kneeling beside me, putting a hand on my forehead, pressing a thumb into my wrist. Both men had shaggy hair, bushy beards.

"Dehydration and exhaustion," he said. "Rest and food will fix you up again."

This time I managed words: "I know it's banal—but . . . where am I?"

The first man smiled. "We call our little hideaway the Zephyrs," he said. "A little sanctuary for the outcasts of Hell."

They brought me a bowl of rather slimy, dark brown soup which tasted like water chestnuts, and a not-quite crisp wafer with no taste at all. More men gathered around to watch me. They all looked gaunt, hairy, but healthy. Their clothes were issue suits in various stages of disrepair. After I had eaten, things began to seem a bit realer.

"I'm strong enough to listen now," I said. "My last recollection is of walking and then not walking. I thought it was all over."

"Don't sound so regretful," the man who had first spoken to me said. "You're alive when you weren't supposed to be. That's something."

"How?"

"They're creatures of habit, not very imaginative. The same joke seems to amuse them over and over. We watch the trail, check it at night. Sometimes we're lucky. Last night was one of the times."

"Why?"

"Why not? We have shelter, water, food of a sort, enough to sustain life, plenty for all. The more the merrier, you know."

I looked at them, hollow-eyed, unwashed, half of them in rags, looking avidly at me as though any moment now I'd tell them something astonishing and marvelous. I laughed, a weak snicker.

"The rejects of the rejects," I said. "A select company. It's been a long slide, but I've hit the bottom at last."

"No," my sponsor said. "That was last night. The turning point. From here there's only one way to go: up."

That seemed rather amusing. I was still chuckling over it as sleep returned.

Eleven

The cave was a natural one, so I was told, cut in a dry arroyo by long vanished tides, supplying, against all probability, all life's essentials. The temperature held at a steady seventy-odd near the entrance, dropping as one went deeper into the rock. The water came from a spring: warm water, forced up from far below. The food supply consisted solely of the edible lichens which grew in near total darkness far back in the cave system. They were versatile plants, lending themselves to reasonable facsimiles of salads, soups, nuts, even pseudo-steaks, when prepared by Tank, our cook, a formerly plump little man whose hobby, I suspected, had once been gourmet cookery.

I rested and ate and after a while—hours, days—I felt well enough to get up from my pallet of lichen-like moss and take a few steps. The men of the Zephyrs were friendly enough, if disinterested. Only my first acquaintance—they called him Georgie—seemed to have a sense of high purpose. He gave me an arm to lean on and told me his plans.

"We're under obvious disadvantages, certainly,"

he conceded. "But there are factors operating in our favor, too. First, they don't know we're here. We're a secret force; we represent an element of surprise. Secondly, we have a powerful motivation . . ."

"And thirdly?"

"Our numbers are increasing steadily. We have eleven men now. Twelve, if the other chap survives."

"What other chap?"

"We brought him in two days before you. He'd been badly beaten. But he may make it; he looks tough—or as if he had once been tough."

"Where is he?"

"In the next wing—"

"I want to see him."

"Certainly—but it's not a very pleasant sight."

He led the way across the main cavern and down a smaller side passage. On a pallet by the wall a man lay on his back; his breathing was audible from twenty feet distant. I squatted beside him and looked at a face battered and bruised into a mass of purple welts, swollen to double the size it had been when I saw it last.

"Cymraeg's work," I said.

"You know him?" Georgie asked.

"He was my friend. *Is* my friend."

"Ah. Possibly that's why you're here."

"That—and other things. How badly hurt is he?"

"Tiger—our doctor—says he has broken ribs, possible internal injuries. The smashed nose is rather serious. He's having trouble breathing. It's a wonder he walked thirty miles in his condition."

I felt the first small flicker of what might some day grow up to be a flame stirring down somewhere in the depths where I had buried my emotions.

With George's help, I moved my bedding in beside Heavy's. The effort made me feel sick and dizzy. I lay in the near darkness and listened to his breathing. At times, he would groan, and I would talk to him until he sank back into whatever place it was where he was fighting his lonely fight. As the hours passed, the sound of his breathing changed—not for the better. Tiger came in from time to time to listen, shake his head, and go away.

I woke from a feverish nap to hear a particularly bad groaning fit, cut off suddenly. I looked at Heavy; his eyes were still swollen shut, but I sensed that he was conscious.

"Heavy, how is it?" I whispered.

He made a faint mumbling sound, moved his head from side to side. The swelling was worse than ever. His face looked as though it would burst at any moment. I went into the outer cave looking for Tiger. He was sitting by the fire, patting out lichen wafers to dry on a smooth rock.

"You've got to do something," I said. "He can't go on like this."

"My God, man, do you think I want him to suffer?" his snarl told me how he had earned his name.

"When he's half-conscious he groans; when he's fully awake he suppresses the groaning. That's worse than the groans."

"What do you expect me to do about it?"

"You're a medical doctor, aren't you?"

"Look here, Jonah—I need instruments, equipment—everything I don't have! The man needs surgery, you understand? To remove the bone splinters. What do you expect me to do, operate with my bare hands?"

"There must be a piece of metal here you could use to make a scalpel. Or you can chip one from a stone.

Anything would be better than letting him die in agony."

"And sutures? Forceps? Bandages? Disinfectants? To say nothing of anesthetic!"

"You can improvise something."

Tiger stared at me, threw down the wad of lichen paste and walked past me back into the sickroom. The rest of us followed. Tiger bared his teeth and frowned ferociously at the patient. The other men gathered around and stared.

"The man needs the facilities of a Fleet hospital," Tiger said between his teeth. "If I touch him I'll kill him."

Heavy made a sound. He made it again. It sounded like: "Do something."

Tiger cracked the knuckles of his fist against the palm of his other hand. "The old Navy dictum," he said. "Even if it's wrong—do *some*thing." He turned suddenly.

"Grift, get me an assortment of stone slivers—the hard ones," he barked. "You, Dancer, shred out some lichen fibres. Toad, boil water. Grinchy, you and Tank carry him in beside the fire." He gave me a hot stare. "And if he dies—by God, you can sign the death certificate—Jonah!"

2

Tiger's hand was as steady as a microtome as he made his incision along the line where the bridge of his patient's nose had once been. That was as much as I waited to see. I leaned against the wall at the far side of the room and listened to the sound effects: the surgeon's muttering, interspersed with curt demands for a new blade or more light; the sympathetic grunts of the men watching; Heavy's ragged breathing. It seemed to go on for a very long time.

Then it was over. Tiger went off into a side passage where the wash trough was and made splashing sounds. The others carried Heavy back to his bed. His breathing was easier now. Tiger came back in, came over to me.

"Thanks for getting me off dead-center," he said in a mumble. "Win or lose, I'm glad I went in. Passages plugged with bone splinters and clots. Sinuses blocked. Hell of a mess. Better now, I think. Less pain, at a minimum. It's open now, draining."

The swelling began to reduce at once; by evening he could talk a little. The first thing he said was, "You ought to see the other guy . . ." Pause, ghastly grin. "Not a mark on him. . . ."

3

Heavy mended rapidly; in two days he was sitting up and eating with good appetite. On the fourth day he took a walk, leaning on me, but not very heavily; I still felt very fragile. His face looked terrible; Tiger's improvised stitching was effective but not inconspicuous. The swelling was gone, leaving yellow and black discolorations spread over most of the area below his eyebrows, crossed by raw, livid scars.

"It's not as if I was ever pretty," was his only comment when he studied the effect in the reflecting surface of the wash trough.

I related the story of my conviction for theft. His own was even simpler. They had waylayed him, told him he had flunked out of camp, and invited him to climb aboard the one-way bus to nowhere. Instead he had tackled them.

"I had the naïve idea that the sounds of struggle might bring an aroused citizenry out of the woodwork," he explained. "Camp rules, and all that. But nothing happened, of course. So much for camp rules."

"It doesn't fit," I said. "How can a man who's organizing a rebel underground afford to attract that kind of attention to himself?"

Heavy looked at me in silence for a few seconds. Then he grunted.

"Maybe I have the wrong idea," I said. "I was under the impression the Companies kept a close eye on camp affairs. Those were Company men who appeared on the scene to seal off the tunnel where I found my prize-winning nugget, for example. How does that fit in with a Hatenik running camp discipline?"

"Cymraeg's no rebel, Jonah," Heavy said flatly. "He's a Company spy, of course. He was after information."

"That's not what he said. He told me he was a Hatenik—or a Hatenik sympathizer—"

"He was lying."

"How do you know that?"

"Because *I'm* a Hatenik," Heavy said.

4

"The word," Heavy said, "is an epithet applied by the establishment to anyone suspected of dissatisfaction with the status quo. You're a Hatenik yourself, Jonah—by their definition. That's the real reason you're here, of course." He held up a hand to forestall my contradiction. "I don't deny that technically you're guilty: you deserted your post. But there were circumstances that drove you to take the course you did; and I think you'll agree you were less than satisfied with the situation aboard *Tyrant*."

"What I objected to had nothing to do with the form of government, Heavy—"

"Wrong. You saw this man Crowder in action—a Company man. That got to you. Then you saw a threat to your friend Danton. That was no accident: it was official, Jonah. They meant to kill him. And you took countermeasures. From that moment on, you were finished."

"Try to understand me, Heavy. I didn't like what was happening, true. But I would have sought a remedy within the framework of Naval law. I'm not interested in anarchy."

Heavy touched his battered face gingerly. "What would you call what we have at Llywarch Hen?"

"Hen is a dumping ground, Heavy. It's outside the structure of law and order—"

"But Cymraeg's a Company man, remember? In fact . . ."

"Go ahead."

He studied me thoughtfully, two sombre dark eyes in a Hallowe'en mask.

"I wasn't sent to Hen by accident, Jonah. It was arranged."

"I didn't precisely volunteer myself," I said.

"That's just the point. I *did*."

I looked at him and waited.

"They smelled out our last man, killed him. We needed a replacement. I was it."

"How did you get past the patrol?"

He shook his head. "I didn't. I came in via the court-martial-and-exile route, just as you did. The only difference was that you were railroaded by the Navy and I railroaded myself."

"If this is supposed to be an explanation of anything, it's not working out, Heavy."

"The Companies—the Starlords—have had matters their own way for a long time, Jonah. The end is closer than they think. We're almost ready. We're waiting for . . . something. There's a missing piece, Jonah. As soon as it falls in place, we move."

"You surprise me, Heavy. You're a Navy man. You know where the power is. Aside from a few hand guns issued to the Constabulary, the only weapons systems in existence are the Fleet."

"We have a wide membership in the Fleet. Commander Paul Danton, for one."

"I don't think so. Paul was a man who took an oath seriously. Nothing could have made him betray the trust—"

"But something did, Jonah. Don't you see? If a man like Danton believed in the revolution, there must be something to it, eh?"

"Let me try again, Heavy. It's not really complicated. I believe in peace and order. I believe in laws, regulations, a structure of society—even an imperfect structure. I caught an arm in the gears and the machine chewed me up and spat me out—but that's a personal grievance. It's not a legitimate reason to wreck the machine."

"And if the machine is producing power and luxury for a few Masters—at your expense—"

"I don't resent the fact that the men who built modern technology benefit from it—"

"Doesn't nature's bounty belong to everyone?"

"Nature provides the ocean, Heavy. The fish I catch are mine."

"Suppose someone's robbing your nets? Or scuttling your boat?"

"I haven't seen the evidence of it."

"What if I showed you evidence?"

"I'd look at it, at least."

"Come with me." He led me across the cavern to where Georgie was busy feeding a small fire with briquettes of the ever versatile lichen, over which water was steaming in a stone vessel.

"Georgie, tell him your story," Heavy said. Georgie looked at us in turn and tugged at his tangled beard.

"I was a junior Gunnery Officer aboard a battlewagon," he said. "I took an emergency call one night from my Chief Gunnery Sergeant; a power drop to the static banks. We checked it back to Power Section. I tried to raise a Powerman, but no answer. We went back; there was smoke, high temperatures. A lot of activity. A squad of Special Constabulary was out, staking off the area. One of them spotted my NCO and while he was busy with him I got past the cordon. The smoke was coming from the Transfer Room. A lot of excitement there, powermen running around in the smog, no one seemed to know which end was up. No one paid any attention to me. I was looking for someone to give me orders: whether to pull my battery off the line. I went through an open door—massive damned hatch over a foot thick—and was in an empty room. Or almost empty. There was a squatty looking apparatus in the center of the floor, linked up with a maze of ductwork and piping. Half a dozen men around it. They had pulled a drawer out of the mechanism, and were looking at something inside it, suspended by fine wires. It looked like an egg. A bit long and slender, a glossy white, almost waxy looking. Various color coded leads were attached at one end." Georgie paused to lift off his pot of water and begin splashing it on his face.

"I saw that much before what felt like an entire platoon of 'stabs landed on me. I woke up in sick bay with four guards posted at the corners of my bunk. As soon as I was able to walk, I was conducted to the ballroom, where a ceremony was in progress."

He picked up a sliver of stone from an array laid out beside him, and began scraping at his beard.

"Got the idea when I saw Tiger slicing on you, Heavy," he said. "Painful, but it works."

"Tell the rest," Heavy said.

"Nothing much to tell. I listened to the proceedings and discovered I was in the midst of being cashiered from the Navy. I tried to speak up, but someone had thoughtfully doped me. One of the selective hypnotics, I suppose. I couldn't speak, couldn't move. I tried, I can tell you. All I managed was a few tears of frustration as some old fool popped the buttons off my tunic. They'd been cut off earlier and stitched back with light thread, I realized later. All part of the show. Ouch." Georgie had scraped most of one side of his face. He paused to sluice water over it, and in so doing turned the clean-shaven side toward me. The shock as I recognized him was like a blow with a club.

"I remember, Mr. Midshipman Blane," I said. "I was there."

5

"Our plan is simple enough," Blane said. "We make the march by night, are in position around Hen before dawn, move in on signal and kill or capture Cymraeg and his cadre. The inmates will join us, and in half an hour we'll be in charge."

"I agree it's simple," I said.

"We don't waste any time then, hitting Base Station. It will be a three day march, but we have men who can man communications at Hen. There's no reason for Base to suspect anything's wrong. The car will go in first, and a picked Commando team will take the 'stab barracks; then the rest arrive on foot, and mop up. Again, we'll have the help of the prisoners."

"What about the power gun I seem to recall perched on the roof of the Admin shack?" I asked.

"There'll be casualties—but they can't stop us."

"And after you hold Base Station—then what?"

"We decoy the supply ship down. Then we're off and running."

"Running is right, Georgie," I said. "You amaze me. This scheme would be funny if it weren't so tragic. You haven't a hope in the world."

"We aren't alone, Tarleton," Heavy said. "When word gets out—"

"They'll come with butterfly nets and put everything back where it was," I said. "Except for the men killed in the process. But perhaps you feel they'll be well out of it."

Neither of them spoke for a few moments. Blane sighed and resumed scraping at his chin.

"We know it's a long shot," Heavy said. "But we'll never have a better opportunity than now. We may be discovered at any time; there may be a decision to reinforce the guard garrison at Base, or to increase armaments to keep pace with the rising exile rate. We have to move now, while the population is high and the opposition is still weak."

"That's why your coming along just now is so important," Blane said. "You can give us the extra spark we need—"

Heavy silenced him with a curt sweep of his hand, but the message had been transmitted.

"So that's it," I said. "You, too: you want my Great Secret." I looked at Heavy. "I wondered why you took the chance of befriending me. Thanks for clearing it up—"

"Don't jump to conclusions, Jonah," Heavy said quickly. "It wasn't—"

"Sorry," I said, standing. "I don't know anything that would be useful to you. And if I did, I wouldn't give it to you. I don't agree with you, you see. And if I did agree with you, I'd still consider your plan hopeless." I walked away, feeling their eyes on my back.

6

Lichen, soaked and pounded and formed into a club shape and allowed to dry, made a long-lasting, nearly smokeless torch. I used one to explore the maze of caverns, leaving frequent blaze-marks to lead me back to daylight. Many of the rooms were wide and low, with gullied floors over which I had to pick my way with care. Others, usually cutting the wider chambers at an angle, were mere pot-holed tunnels which twisted and turned, with sudden dips and unexpected reversals and abrupt drops. Only a tiny percentage of the space was in use. I wandered into the grotto where the lichen grew in beds that stretched back and back into darkness. The spring was here, too; the water clucked and gurgled as it gushed from an aperture in the wall to fill a wide basin in the rock before flowing away through a deeply-incised runnel between the lichen beds. I followed it back to a point where the cavern narrowed abruptly, the floor falling away steeply underfoot. The stream made a soft sighing sound as it poured over into the depths.

As I turned to go back, my eye was caught by an illusion of symmetry in the lines of the lichen cavern. I saw the walls as slightly in-slanting planes, their regularity obscured by adhering clumps of stalactite; the floor, except where scored by erosion and stalagmites, seemed almost flat.

Almost artificial.

I studied the lichen beds, realized that rather than growing in irregular patches, they too were essentially rectilinear, camouflaged by barren patches that disguised their outlines.

I blinked hard and the illusion vanished, as illusions will. It was merely a cave where a weed grew wild, nothing more. Man was alone in his corner of the Universe. Two hundred years of space exploration had turned up no life form more complex than the fingersized half-grasshopper, half-salamander creature that was lord of beasts on Rigel IV, a planet of mindless creeping things.

I picked my way back toward the light, ignoring my mind's attempts to trick me into perceiving pattern in the jumble of passages, evidences of intelligent planning in the intersection of tunnel with cavern. And when I reached the main chamber, all pseudo-archaeological musings were driven from my mind by the reception committee that waited for me there.

7

All eleven of my fellow outcasts stood in a group by the fire. They came to the alert and deployed in a loose ring that closed around me as I came up. Blane faced me, looking determined; Heavy stood to the side, wearing what seemed to be a sheepish expression; it was hard to be sure.

"We've discussed your case, Jonah," Blane said. He didn't look like a Georgie now. "We've decided that under the circumstances a man has to be with us—or against us."

"At least you don't bother trying to make it sound noble," I said. I felt quite calm. The disasters I had already been through had exhausted my capacity for excitement.

"Our objective is victory. We'll do what we have to to gain it."

"If that's a recruiting speech, you've taken the wrong line."

"Make up your mind."

I walked toward them and they parted, fell in beside me, trailed me across toward the entrance. Beyond it, crimson twilight stained the rocks.

"We need you, Tarleton," Heavy said. "We need what Danton found! If he were alive today, he'd want us to have it."

"You can't afford to let me stay here," I said, not looking at him. "I might listen in on your war councils, then hot-foot it across the sands to spill the beans to Cymraeg and company. And you can't afford to merely throw me out, for the same reason . . ." As I spoke, I took another casual step or two toward the outer air; Blane kept pace with me. I had no conscious plan of action; it was no more than an instinct, perhaps, to move toward space and freedom.

"Don't talk nonsense, Tarleton," Heavy said sharply from behind me. "We don't intend—"

"Perhaps *you* don't," I cut in. "But I think Blane is prepared to do what has to be done." On the last word I caught his arm as it reached out suddenly toward me, jerked him unexpectedly toward me, ducked past him and was running down across the tallus slope, jumping the scattered rocks. There were yells and feet were pounding close behind me. In seconds, my wind was gone. I ducked aside, caught a glimpse from the corner of my eye of Blane, wild-eyed, closing fast, Heavy a pace or two behind. A dark crevice loomed between upslanted rocks; I sprinted for it, stumbled on loose pebbles, almost caught myself, stumbled again, went down hard and rolled. Blane's hand grazed my foot as he skidded, checking his dash, and dived for me. But a larger body hurtled across his path, slammed against him. Heavy and Blane went down together, and I was back on my feet, limping on a twisted ankle. I reached the open fissure I had seen, squeezed inside, forced my way back between close walls. Another cleft opened to my left; I took it, climbed up to reach a higher transverse crack, kept going. There were shouts behind me, to my left, then to the right. I eased under an overhanging lip of rock and wedged myself as far back under it as possible, and breathed as silently as I could, with my mouth wide open. It was almost cool here. I lay for a while, and heard the shouts gradually recede as they worked past me. I think I dozed. The color was gone from the air. I waited until the chill had begun to seep through my bones; then I crept out, made my way up to the top of the great fractured slab.

A few hundred yards distant cheery light glowed from the cavern mouth. A bulky silhouette paced there, pausing to stare out into the darkness. Heavy—had he intentionally blocked Blane? I tried to believe he had.

It wasn't too late for me to go back, express contrition, and join the Grand Army of the Revolution. The end might be the same, but at least it would be deferred. But the price of membership was a secret I didn't have, that they would never believe I didn't have.

"And if I did . . ." I started to mutter, and checked myself. I wasn't sure any longer. All the simple, clear answers seemed to have gone the way of the clear, simple life.

I tried again: "I'm a refugee from the outcasts of the exiles," I told the empty desert. "But I'm not a traitor."

"Well, good for you," another part of me answered. "Remember to apply for your Eagle Badge for riding the wreckage down in flames."

Above, Roseworld's sister planets winked, shedding pale light on gray rock and sand. I took a bearing on the same constellation that had guided me on my last trek and set off, not very rapidly, favoring my ankle.

Twelve

Night and the desert, large amounts of both. Bitter cold; loose sand that slipped away underfoot; pebbles to stumble over, rocks to trip on, boulders to blunder into. No food, no water, no destination. The twisted ankle hurt, but I ignored that. Pain is just nature's danger signal, and all that seemed quite extraneous now. I could either stop where I was and die, or go a little farther and die. I kept going, wondering why I bothered. Perhaps it was only a petty desire to let Blane and his little band of anti-patriots sweat over the question of whether I had made it back to Hen to bring the avengers down on them. Or it might have been the same instinct that makes a shipwrecked sailor cling to a floating spar as long as there's any strength left in his fingers.

I named the two planets Cherry and Grape, because of their color. Cherry was the bigger of the two. They danced in the air, rushing closer and then retreating. They kept wandering aside, slipping across the sky, but I wasn't fooled. I turned the world under me and pursued them, not swiftly, but persistently.

Somehow Cherry and Grape had gotten directly overhead. Outfoxed at last. How do you march toward zenith? Can't fly. Can't even walk. Crawl, then. Another yard. Another foot. Another inch.

No, not even another inch. All done, Tarleton. All done. Lie down and sleep and never wake up. . . . End of the line.

. . . light shining in my face. Everybody on deck on the double; you too, Tarleton! My eyes were open and there was a red-hot patch on the gray wall opposite me. Not a drill; real thing; ship's on fire. . . . !

The gray wall shimmered and became a gray sky. The glowing metal shrank away into remote distance and was merely a sun.

Sunrise on Roseworld.

And still alive.

It all seemed rather silly. I enjoyed a brief chuckle which began to sound like a woman's sobbing. I cut it off and twitched various bruised muscles and was sitting up. Tall rocks loomed around me like weathered tombstones. The Devil's graveyard. What was one more corpse, more or less? Not worth the effort. I lay back and was dreaming:

Paul Danton climbed up from a hole in the ground, holding something in his hands. I craned my neck to see what it was, but he moved away, concealing it with his body. I tried to call to him to show it to me, but my voice wouldn't work. Suddenly I was burning with thirst. The fire licked up around my face. I inhaled to breathe in the flames and end the farce, but that made me cough. I coughed until the tears ran from my eyes. I wiped them away and squinted against the scarlet glare of the sunlight reflecting from the rocks. A fine system for roasting a fowl evenly on all sides. There was a velvet-soft slab of deep purple shadow not far away. I used the stumps of amputated limbs to crawl there before I collapsed again.

The sun made a jump and sliced away half my pool of shade. I pulled my legs up. Barely room to lie now, huddled against the base of the slab. Very hot now. Difficult to breathe. I was looking down a slope between rocks. Deeper shadows there; they flickered and moved, like rock-sprites, beckoning. I wasn't aware of making a momentous policy decision, but I found myself half crawling, half sliding down the slope. The shadow I had seen was a deep, narrow cut. It wasn't necessary for me to consider what I would do about that. I slid over the edge and fell a yard or two onto a drift of rubble. Coolness washed over me, and I took a deep breath so as to drown quickly, and was surprised to find that I could breathe shadow just as if it were air. It seemed a remarkable discovery, one which I should report as soon as possible to the scientists in charge of the experiment.

"Men can live and breathe in shadow," I announced. Someone nearby made a weak croaking sound. Always a skeptic in the crowd. But it was true. And if I could breathe, perhaps I could also swim; glide like a fish in the deep darkness, effortless, mindless. . . .

It seemed I had had that thought before. I tried a few strokes, but found it painful. I was on the bottom of the bowl, where the colored pebbles are. Dark here, lights up above. Must turn lights off, otherwise fish, lacking a laziness instinct, will swim until they die. . . .

I was awake again, lying on my side at the bottom

of a narrow cut in the rock which trended downward at a slight angle to disappear into an even deeper blackness some five yards away. It occurred to me that all the shadow would drain away through the hole and leave me gasping on the beach, and I felt a momentary panic; but if I could plug the gap, block it with stones. . . .

I swam toward it, having a certain amount of difficulty due to the fact that my ventral side was still dragging bottom. I reached the hole and swam through.

I was in a cave.

Where there were caves there were lichens.

"Where there are caves," I said aloud, speaking carefully so as to get it just right, "there are lichens."

No one answered. At least no one contradicted me. That was a good sign. And somewhere nearby there were lichens; I knew this because someone had just said so. Later I would have to thank whoever it was for the information, but at the moment the steak dinner was more important. In fact, it wasn't even necessary that I have steak. Hot sausage and mustard would do. Oliver Twist had liked hot sausage and mustard. Fat, tender, juicy sausages, spread with sharp, acidulous, aromatic mustard. . . .

Needles jabbed into the sides of my jaws and I started chewing, but discovered I hadn't yet bitten into the sausage. In fact, I hadn't yet reached the sausages. But they were *that* way; I could smell them. I went toward the source of the aroma. . . .

It seemed to take a long time to reach the place where the food waited. But the odor grew stronger, more compelling, urging me on.

"How much farther?" I asked.

"Not far, sir," the waiter said. He was a small man, not over two feet tall, with a smooth head like a turnip, and an odd way of walking. "Just a little farther," he said, backing away before me. I wanted to ask him why a table couldn't be set up right here, but I needed all my breath to keep up. Terrible service. Plenty of empty tables here, but no, this dining room is not open, sir. Just a little farther, sir. This way, sir. . . .

My hands touched something yielding, and I seized it and broke off a wad and put it in my mouth. It was magnificently seasoned, lovingly smoked, juicy and succulent. I had never before had sausage in precisely this form, but that was one of the secrets of the old sausage maker. I wouldn't pry. And the mustard—ah, there it was! Not too sharp, not too bland, just right. Oliver Twist was on to something. And there was lots more. But mustn't eat it all at once, somebody cautioned me. Damned impertinence on the part of the waiter, but couldn't afford to offend. After all, he *had* led me to a table. To a bed. I was lying in a bed, wide, soft, smooth, with silken sheets, a fleecy blanket against the cool. Ingracious not to accept. Could do with a nap. Tired. So tired. . . .

My last thought was of a dream I had had about a fish. Silly dream. Odd I had had it while I was awake. But it was too hard to think about that now. I moved my fins gently in the dark current and let it carry me away into peaceful depths.

2

I woke clear-headed, aching all over, but more especially on my knees and the palms of my hands. Sitting up was an undertaking to rank with the construction of the Gibraltar Dam but I managed it.

Faint light glowed along the cavern wall, showing

me a low, lime-encrusted ceiling, fissured walls, the bare, runnelled floor on which I lay. The palms of my hands were slashed and scraped raw. The knees of my suit were intact, but inside it the knees themselves felt like hamburger. It seemed I had come a considerable distance on all fours. My chin hurt, too, and the end of my nose. I must have walked part of the way on my face. And here I was.

The Zephyrs would be scouting the desert for me now, wondering if the cat was out of the bag and all their world-beating plans brought to naught. I grinned foolishly and then stopped grinning. Perhaps they were right to take up arms against a sea of troubles, and by opposing end them—in the only way they could end.

My thoughts swung in toward my own situation, and veered away again, like the man in the graveyard who won't look back because he knows that close behind a fearful fiend doth tread. I didn't have to think about that, didn't have to think about anything.

Outside, in the big world, men would be killing each other, battling for their various ideas of how things ought to be. But not me. I was retired.

I had battled the best I could, and lost, all along the line. I had tried to cling to my principles, and my principles had turned around and bit me. I was for peace and order, and peace and order had thrown me to the wolves—and the wolves had chased me into the desert—and the desert had tried to kill me. That was enough. I was no fool. I got the idea.

"This just wasn't your round, Tarleton," I told myself. "Try again in your next incarnation. . . ."

And in the meanwhile . . . ?

Well, I had a nice, cool spot to starve to death in. Curious that I wasn't hungry at the moment. I thought about sausage and felt a mild revulsion. I had had enough sausage to last me . . .

"Correction," I said aloud. "There's no sausage within several light years of this spot."

But I had eaten something. My stomach told me that. I had fed full, and not very long ago. I looked around, not really expecting to see scraped plates and licked spoons, or even small waiters with heads like turnips.

What I saw was a mound of lichen.

I looked at it and thought. I looked at the bare floor, the bare walls. No lichen grew here. So how had it gotten here? Simple. I had gathered it somewhere else and brought it here. It was the only logical thought, and I tried hard to believe in it.

"Fine," I said. Talking aloud to myself could easily become a habit, I realized, but I went right on: "You walked in out of the hot sun, explored a cave system on all fours, located a convenient supply of crunchies, and carried them back to this cosy patch of rock to consume them."

"Not likely," the other half of my rapidly splitting personality came back sharply. "In your condition, you couldn't have gone six inches farther than you had to."

"The alternative," I pointed out, "is that you're going off your rocker."

"Either that—or someone brought the lichen to me."

"Precisely my point. Breakfast in bed, eh? I suppose that's where the little man with the smooth head comes in."

"Whose side are you on?"

"Side? What's in a side? Your bittterest enemies love you, and your faithful friends condemned you to death. The right are wrong and the wrong are right. Up to a point. After that, it's the reverse."

"You're talking to yourself."

"It's all right. I'm not listening."

"Let's get out of here. It's spooky."

"For once we agree. On your feet."

Getting up wasn't impossible, or so I kept telling myself. On the third try I made it. I took a tottery step, then another.

"Look, ma, no hands," I said.

Nobody answered. Even my alter-ego had deserted me. How sad. Poor young Banastre Tarleton, once so full of promise and high ideals, all alone with the bats in his belfry.

Then I saw the footprint.

3

It was clearly printed in a patch of smooth dust drifted behind a ridge in the floor. It was three inches long, two inches wide at the toe end, and half an inch wide at the heel. It might have been made by a splay-footed monkey, except that such were not known to inhabit these environs. It might have been my imagination. But it wasn't.

"It's about the right size for the waiter," I told myself, and sneered, and shivered halfway through the sneer.

My desire for a glimpse of the outer air—red-hot sun, pink dust and all—had suddenly become more urgent. It was fifty feet to the curve in the passage from which the dim light came. I made it, with only two falls, rounded the turn. The light came from a fissure in the roof. No way out there.

I went on. The passage twisted and turned, dipped, rose. The light faded. I turned back, found another branch. It ended in darkness. I retraced my steps, but the light was gone now. For another hour I searched for the route, before I fell for the last time. Lying in the total darkness, I could hear my heart thump. I could hear ghosts whispering in the wings. I could hear the patter of little feet. I could hear myself starting to snicker.

"You're lost, Tarleton," I said, and didn't like the sound of my voice. "You got in, but you can't get out. This settles it. This is the end, the last bow after the last act. You're buried, and in a little while you'll be dead, in the wrong order perhaps, but nobody's going to complain about that."

"Take it easy, Ban," Paul Danton's voice said.

4

At this juncture, other, lesser minds might have snapped. But mine didn't. I had fooled them; mine had snapped hours ago. Or was it days? And hearing voices wasn't so bad. Nothing like a little delirium to keep one occupied. Talking with a friendly hallucination was better than no company at all.

"Glad you came, Paul," I said. "I've been wanting to tell you I'm sorry you didn't trust me enough to tell me what it was you were involved in. I think perhaps you wanted to, just after Blane was cashiered; but I suppose I didn't give you much encouragement."

"You need rest, Ban. Lie here awhile, and sleep. You're in bad shape, Ban. Your body is nearly dead."

For a moment it seemed to me that I was lying on my bunk in my suite aboard *Tyrant*, but I made an effort and got back to reality—my slightly edited version of reality. Imaginary voices that seemed to be speaking between my ears were all right under the circumstances, but imaginary bunks were too much.

"A few harmless delusions, for medicinal purposes only." I laid down the law severely. "Otherwise, I'd be imagining myself lying on the beach at Monte Bello Island with a shapely girl named Janet-Anne beside me, quaffing iced champagne and contemplating another dip in the surf. . . ."

White light burned through my eyelids; coarse sand creaked under my hand. Lively music sang from the portable trideo. I could smell the sea-water, hear the boom of the lazy surf. I turned my head and opened one eye and saw the curve of a long, smooth thigh—

"No!" I yelled, and sat up. "Leave my brain alone!"

"We mean you no harm, Ban," someone answered in my head. I clamped my hands over my ears and scuttled backwards, came up sharp against a rough-surfaced wall of cold stone.

"Stay out of my head," I said. It was hard to talk because my teeth wanted to chatter. It wasn't a joke any more. I was afraid—more afraid than I had ever been.

"Don't be afraid, Ban," the voice said.

"I *am* afraid, damn you!" I yelled, and scrubbed my hands harder against my ears, not that that would help, because the voice wasn't coming through my auditory system; it was *there,* inside. . . .

And the sand grains adhering to my cut palms raked my skin. Coarse sand. Sand of a kind that couldn't be here. The cave floor was water-worn stone, with some scattered dust. No sand. Especially no sharp-edged, silicon sand. Sand such as made up the beach at Monte Bello.

I whimpered.

"I'm going to die, I know that," I pleaded with someone, something. "But not insane. Just let me fade out in my right mind. Let me die knowing who I am and where I am, not with a handful of imaginary sand from a beach ten light years away. That isn't too much to ask, is it?"

"Do you want to die, Ban?" Paul asked me. *"But no, I see you don't . . ."*

"Go away," I said. "Leave me alone!"

"Why are you afraid, Ban?"

"I'm afraid of things I can't see that talk inside my head," I yelled. "I'm afraid of going crazy, of not being *me* anymore! I'm afraid of the dark!" I had to stop shouting then, because the mental picture of myself, wild-eyed, screaming to myself in an underground cell paralyzed my vocal organs. It was like coming into a dark room and confronting your reflection in a mirror, and for a moment, before you know it's a mirror, you freeze in nameless terror, staring into those alien eyes.

"Be soothed, Ban," the voice said. And as suddenly as that, the fear was gone.

I sat in a tense crouch, my eyes shut tight, hands clenched around the impossible grit, and waited.

"We're sorry we frightened you, Ban," the voice said. It was different now, no longer Paul Danton; and yet it was the same voice. *"We want to help you."*

I became aware that a faint light was shining; I could sense it through my closed eyelids. I opened them. A pearly light like dawn in a sea-cave shone from nowhere on three small creatures with turnip heads who squatted in a row with their blind faces turned toward me.

5

It took them a long time to convince me that they were real, and harmless, and helpful. They were the Ancil, they said, but seemed unsure whether this was a generic term or the name of a Special Committee for the Rescue of Distressed Spacemen. They had always lived in the caves, they said, tending their lichen crops and listening to the voices of the past while the ages rolled by overhead. They told me all this in familiar, friendly voices that came into being somewhere behind my eyes, as if there were a small radio receiver buried there, tuned to their special wavelength.

There were a thousand questions I should have asked; but I was suddenly very tired. . . .

"*. . . Ban!*" I became aware that one of them was calling me. "*Ban, your lifelight grows dim! You must mend yourself now, quickly, before it flickers out!*"

I'm fine, I said, not in words, but the other way, the easy, mind-to-mind way. *I feel better than I have for a long time. The aches and pains are gone. I'll just rest here awhile and then we'll talk some more . . .*

"*He fades, he fades,*" one of the others said. "*Hold him, each and all!*"

I felt cold fingers of thought slide into my brain, probing, touching, exploring. Many voices were clamoring together:

"*. . . a strange configuration . . . and yet, not without logic . . .*"

"*. . . massive damage to this system . . . and to this. These organs fail; the level falls . . .*"

"*Ban! Listen to me!*" Paul's voice came through loud and clear. "*We can help—but you must join with us! Wake up, Ban! Join with us! Fight!*"

I wanted to answer, to tell them that the time for fighting was long gone; that now I was within reach of a comfortable blackness that I could sink into, that would demand nothing of me, that was reward enough for all my efforts. I wanted to tell them this, but it was too hard; they were too far away, their voices faint cries in a gathering dusk that was deeper and more final than any night I had ever known. . . .

But they wouldn't let me rest. They jabbed and prodded and called.

"Try, Ban! Help us!"

"Why should I?"

"The lifelight is a precious thing, not to be relinquished easily, Ban! Hold it! Cling to it! and help us, Ban!"

"Help you . . . how?"

"Thus, Ban!" A firmer, surer hand touched my brain. Barriers fell. Pseudo-light gleamed in a vast cavern, dimensionless, substanceless. *"This way, Ban!"*

The voice led. I followed, among abstract shapes of thought, bodiless relationships that loomed up, shifting, changing, in a dimming flow of dying life. Energy flowed, weaving intangible patterns, fading and incomplete. I saw the dark places, the broken webs and shattered mosaics. And following the guiding hand and the urging voice I touched, lifted up, restored, rebuilt. At last the glow held steady, then began to rise. I felt the stir of renewed function, the building flow of currents in the immaterial structures of mind-stuff.

"The lifelight steadies, Ban! Now come! We must rebuild!"

Together we swept on, deep, deep into blinding intricacies, incomprehensible complexities. Directed by the small voices, I moved among them, restoring, repairing, reassembling. There was no time, no space, no substance. Only patterns; patterns broken and now renewed. Patterns within patterns, patterns that interlocked and became greater patterns. Patterns of thought, impressed on patterns of energy.

Then it was finished, and I drifted in the center of a structure of light and form and flow that filled infinity, vibrating in symphonic resonance with the beat of eternity.

"It's done, Ban," the voices called; small voices, far away, dwarfed by the immensity around me. *"Come away now, Ban. Come back, rest, sleep, renew. . . ."*

They touched me, guiding me back out, away from the glory I had erected around me, back into comforting narrowness, soothing darkness, easeful emptiness. They dwindled, receded, were gone.

I slept.

6

I woke remembering a strange dream. And I was hungry. And then the Ancils were there, and they were not a dream. They led me back along the dark passages, into a wide cavern where water poured from an opening in the wall, where lichens grew in rectilinear beds. I drank. They watched from shadowy corners, averting their eyeless faces from the light that glowed from the walls.

It wasn't until then that I remembered my aches and pains and weaknesses. Remembered them by their absence. My hands were healed. My knees were whole again. I drew a deep breath, tried my arms and legs, sensed the well-being of a healthy body, a feeling I had almost forgotten.

"How?" I asked them. "How did you do it?"

"*You* did it, Ban," the voices answered. The words

were like those a man enunciates silently in his mind when he thinks to himself in words: clear; precise, unvoiced.

"Any living creature has within himself the ability to mend himself. We merely showed you the way. It was necessary to borrow molecules from where they could best be spared to place them where they were most needed. But now you must eat well, grow strong again."

I rested, ate, explored the cave system. Wherever we went, the walls glowed softly ahead, lighting my way. I saw miles of passages, hundreds of chambers. Some of them were clearly artificially cut from the pink stone.

"Long ago we made them, Ban," the Ancils told me. "Once there were many of us. Now we grow old, Ban. One by one we dim and wink out. The great blackness reclaims us. But you are young, Ban, so young. The history of your race stretches before you into unthinkable dimensions."

I didn't argue the point. I lived in a strange half-dreaming state of mind, drugged with the sense of physical well-being, of total divorcement from the entanglements of a life I had failed at long ago. My strength returned; my arms and body filled out, my appetite was healthy, I slept deep and dreamlessly. My teeth, I discovered, had regenerated completely: no cavities, no fillings. My hair felt thick and vigorous; my eyesight was as keen as it had been when I had fired on the Academy handgun team, an eternity ago.

One day I felt an urge to see the sunlight and smell the outer air. They led me to the surface, and hung back while I walked out into the pink glare of later afternoon. The sunlight hurt my eyes; I opaqued the corneas to a comfortable level and strolled for a while across the desert. I found myself thinking of the Zephyrs, wondering what they were doing now. Had young Blane led his foolish little attack on Llywarch Hen? How many of them had lived through it? Or were they still hiding in their caves, holding insanity at bay by spinning long schemes that would never come to pass? But there was no urgency in it. It was like thinking of the Punic Wars, or the building of the pyramids, musing over the motives and feelings of men long dead, in another world.

My world was pink stone formed from the fossil carapaces of an incredibly abundant sea-life that had swum in the shallow oceans of Pink Hell when it had been an ocean world, millions of years ago. They had lived and died, each depositing his grain of rose-colored mineral on the beds that floored the sea. As a man lived and died, leaving not even that much evidence of his life's worth.

The setting sun shone across the peaks of a fossil reef, casting long, deep-purple shadows across the sand. I remembered the coarse, red sand that I had found between my fingers when I woke from my long nap, after the dream-journey in which I had laid hold of the building blocks of my mind and body and rebuilt them to specifications. I had asked the Ancils about them, but their answers had been vague. I had yearned greatly for the feel of that beach under my hand; and it had come to me, or me to it; or I had thought it had, had believed in it, and in the sandy evidence of it. . . .

I absorbed their attitude of indifference to such questions. What did it matter? I was here, I was alive, I ate, I slept, my senses monitored the cycle of physical phenomena that flowed around me, savoring the myriad tiny evidences of life, measuring them against the Universe-sized backdrop of not-life, the one balanced with the other in the poised equation of existence.

I stood on a shelf of rock and watched the sun slide behind the peaks half a mile away. It was time to go back. The sand was midnight purple below me. Halfway down the giant's staircase I had climbed to reach my perch, a slash of vivid light spilled across the dull stone. I looked back. The sun had found a chink through the multiple barrier of ringwall and earthquake-spilled rockslabs. It bored like a spotlight through the circular opening formed by a notch in a searside spire. It was as perfect a bore as if it had been cut by a half-mile-long-forty-foot-diameter drill.

I turned and looked down along the path of light. The beam fell along a weathered, rubble-filled groove that ended in a ragged, forty foot cave mouth at the base of a rock ridge.

I finished the descent to the desert floor, walked across in deepening darkness to the scored cut, followed along its edge to the cave. The rock around the entry was fused. Erosion had cut at it, crumbled the regular outline; but it was still obvious that the tunnel mouth had once been perfectly round.

But that had been a very long time ago.

"Simple," I told myself. "The Ancils cut it, way back when."

"But their tunnels are smaller, rectangular," I objected. "What would they make a forty-foot tunnel for? And why cut through the reef walls?"

"Ask them."

That seemed to be a reasonable suggestion. I sensitized my retinae to the infra-red emitted by the sun-warmed rocks and by their eerie light made my way back to the Home Cavern.

7

The Ancils seemed not much interested in my questions. No, they knew nothing of the round-mouthed cave. They had seen it, perhaps, long ago, venturing out by night, but it was a dead thing, of no interest.

"It looks as if something hit there, some projectile," I said. "Not a meteorite; the cut's too regular. Something artificial."

"Yes, perhaps, Ban," they said. "Once we knew, perhaps, but we have forgotten."

"From the angle at which it struck, it must have buried itself near the southern end of the cave system," I said. "Have you seen anything underground there?"

"Yes, yes, perhaps, Ban."

"Show me."

They led me through the twisting, time eroded tunnels to a smaller opening cut in the side wall of a dead-end spur, choked with broken rock. It appeared to have been blocked intentionally. They complained when I started in to clear it, but couldn't explain why.

It took many hours of hard labor to remove the rubble and open a route in to the cave at the far end. I pushed the last stone aside and crawled through and was in a high, wide chamber almost filled by a pitted, scarred, and tarnished shape of crystalline mineral. It was nothing that had ever been built by the hand of men, but there was no faintest doubt as to what it was.

A spaceship.

Thirteen

There was just room in the cavern for a man to walk beside the hundred and fifty foot tapered conic shape, to round the blunt prow, to come back along the other side. There were markings on the hull, curious shaped projections, a circular port high on one side, standing half open. The Ancils followed me, stood in a group beside me as I looked up over the curve of age-blackened hull at the entry.

"No, Ban," they said. "We begin to remember, now. This is not a good thing, Ban. It is a thing better lost and forgotten."

"How did it come to be here? How long has it been here?"

"Our memories tell us that this is a cave-that-moved, Ban. Once there were many such. In them we moved from world to world, knowing the light of many suns, drawing the arms of the Galaxy into the nets of our understanding. Then . . . evil befell us. Our great cities, so cunningly carved beneath the crusts of a thousand worlds, were shattered and killed. We died, Ban. Oh, we died. . . .

"They tracked us, where we fled. Great were our powers, but as nothing under the onslaught of the Axorc. By the energies emitted by our vessels they followed, and they slew, and slew. In the end, we last ones, we few, came here to the sea-world; we concealed our vessels, and in the shallow caves beside the pounding surf we hid ourselves.

"Time passed, and the seas are gone, Ban. But still we live, and still we fear. For the Axorc are many, and great is their power for evil."

"I thought of the eons that must have rolled past while the oceans of Roseworld dried up. Ten million years? A hundred million?

"We have seen and remembered, Ban," they said. "Now let us go, and re-seal the chamber, and again forget that which once was, the evil that drove us here."

"These Axorc: what were they like?"

"They are the whirlwinds of destruction, jealous of lifelight, that only theirs should shine across the Galaxies. Now perhaps they have forgotten us, as we had forgotten them."

"I'm going to have a look inside," I said. They complained, but I ignored them. In the end they threatened, and for the first time since the night we had met I felt their ghost-touches in my mind; but I thrust them out, and began to climb.

"Now are you healed indeed, Ban," they called after me, sadly rather than angrily. "And great is the power of your mind-force. But as your young vigor is to our withered vitality, so is the might of the Axorc to your force. Beware, Ban. Touch nothing; disturb nothing, let the ogre sleep in peace."

"I'm not going to summon up any demons," I told them. "I just want to see."

In the end they followed me.

2

The hatch stood ajar, as the last Ancil had left it, at a time when the first great saurians were depositing their gallon-sized eggs on the young beaches of Earth. But the imperishable alloy was still as sound as it had been that long-ago day. The heavy, foot-thick disk swung aside at a touch, and I stepped over the threshold into a low-ceilinged passage. A faint glow sprang up before me, showing me doors, a branching passage, a companionway leading down, all scaled to a ten year old boy; cramped for me, but roomier than needed for the Ancils.

"*Once we were larger, Ban,*" they told me. "*But what need in our close world for great size? And so we dwindled. Now the works of our youth appear as the craftsmanship of giants.*"

I went along the corridor, looked into rooms furnished with chairs and beds not much different from the ones I had been using all my life, except for the slight degree of miniaturization. The dust was half an inch thick—the remains of whatever perishable materials had been aboard. There was no decoration, nothing that wasn't strictly functional. I went down to the lower deck, looked in on equipment rooms, storage spaces, a navigation section with recognizable instruments. I found the command section forward, a maintenance shop aft. In the prow a battery of what looked like weapons were mounted. The Ancils explained that they were the heat-projectors that had been used to vaporize the rock, cutting the bore for the concealment of the ship.

I pictured the vessel, hovering half a mile above the ancient atoll, suspended on pressor beams, pouring the torrents of invisible light into the wet, pink rock, the steam and vapor boiling upward . . .

"There's something missing," I said. "Where's the Power Section? I want to see the engines."

The Ancils started wailing again.

"No, Ban, come away now, we remember danger! Danger, Ban! Come, come away . . . !"

I insisted; they moaned and pleaded, but in the end they led the way to a small door set chest-high in the wall, like an incinerator hatch.

"There, Ban. But you must not—must not! touch this!"

I pulled down the door. A tray slid out. In its center lay a glistening white object some four inches long, an inch and a half in diameter, smoothly rounded. There were perforations at one end; otherwise it was as featureless as an egg. I had never seen anything like it before—but I had heard it described: it was what Blane had seen in *Tyrant*'s Power Room, just before he was clubbed down and thrown out of the Navy.

A Starcore, he had called it. A thing no bigger than a goose egg, he had said, that poured out a Niagara of energy to power a ship of the line. A device that powered the industry and technology of Earth; a device without which the economy would collapse in an hour. The proprietary property of Lord Imbolo and the Starlords, the five men who owned the world.

Five thieves.

3

I was delivering a lecture to myself: "Imbolo's grandfather was one of the early astronauts. He went off course on a one-man Jupiter shot, sometime in the late 20th Century. He was given up for lost. Later—he came back. He had a story of a miraculous three-cushion shot among Saturn's moons that swung him back onto course. There were questions, but the fact that he was home—three months late—seemed to prove his contention. After all, there was no fueling station out there. His reentry craft was never found; he landed via chute in the Canadian Rockies. They didn't find him for two days, wandering in the woods.

"He left the service after that, used his bonus to start up a small research company. In ten years he had taken in four monied partners and parlayed his patents into the biggest industrial empire in the world. All built on cheap, plentiful power . . ."

"*Come away now, Ban,*" the Ancils called. They weren't listening. It didn't matter. I was talking to myself, trying to get the picture straight. The picture of a lost astronaut in a primitive ship, wandering off course, out to Saturn, bringing his craft in to a landing on one of her moons, exploring on foot, finding—what? A ruined city? An abandoned ship, like the one I had ferreted out buried in the rock? Finding the Starcore, bringing his cockleshell back with the fabulous find safely tucked away in a pocket, hiding it, getting away clean with a treasure worth more than all the money spent on space research since Sputnik I.

"It explains so many things; the Company space monopoly with the Navy as a police force, to insure that no one else stumbles on anything."

I picked up the glistening, floss-white Starcore. It was abnormally heavy, with a soapy feel in my hand. My eyes fell on the fitted hollow in which it had been nestled. I had seen a hollow like that before: in the piece of stone Paul had cut from the floating boulder in the Rings; the one I had taken from Hatcher's body. I had held it in my hand a thousand times on the long run back; I had run my fingers over the curved depression, wondering what it was, what it meant.

Now I knew.

No wonder they had killed Paul Danton. He had found the secret that would destroy their world.

And so had I.

I became aware again of the chorus of Ancil voices, "How does it work?" I demanded.

"Ban—hear us! Understand your peril! If you touch the Starcore with your mind—if you tap its heart for energy—the signal leaps out, at the square of the velocity of light—to warn the Axorc! Then nothing can save us, Ban! Then they come again with their world-destroying fires, and Ancil and Man alike go down to eternal death!"

"It's been a long time," I said. "Your old enemy is dead. Tell me—"

"Not so, Ban! What are a few millions of years to a race older than time? They live—and will come again!"

"The Starcore has been in everyday use for a hundred and fifty years," I said. "Imbolo and Company must have found quite a trove of them—or learned to duplicate them. Nothing has happened."

For a long moment there was absolute silence—physical and mental. Then a wave of sick despair struck me like a thirty-foot comber smashing down out of the dark, a chorus of moans and wails like all the lost souls in all the hells.

"Then are we truly doomed, Ban," the message came through like a bell tolling disaster. *"Now nothing can save us. Great Axorc dwells far away, in the*

satellite system you call the Lesser Magellanic Cloud. Yet the message would have reached him mere months after the first of your kind blundered on the Starcore. They knew then that once again a rival mindlight glows here in the Galaxy. They will not have delayed, Ban. Even now they come, they come!"

"The Lesser Magellanic Cloud is three hundred thousand light-years away—"

"Great Axorc can cross space at a multiple of the velocity of propagation of radiation, Ban. It may be long—a thousand years, or ten thousand—but come they will. Nothing can stop them, now."

"But . . . perhaps . . ." another Ancil voice spoke up. *"Man is a young race; their potential is unrealized. Perhaps they can stand against Axorc—with our help."*

"How could they succeed where we failed?"

"They are not like us; their kind can kill smiling—and face the knowledge of mortality with laughter. In them may be the seeds of a greatness that we could never know."

"These rough beasts, a single Great Century from mindlessness—win out where we with a hundred times that span of culture—died?"

"Nothing will be lost if we try."

"Would you unleash the power to ignite suns among these primitives? What then of us?"

"Our time is done. Yet our bequest may give them a chance at life."

"Just show me how it works," I cut into the babble. "That's all I need!"

"This is no easy trick, Ban. Your mind may break under the knowledge."

"I'll take the chance."

There was a moment of silence—or perhaps they communicated at a level inaudible to me then.

"We will try, Ban. Good luck."

For a moment longer, nothing happened. Then a bomb burst inside my head, and drowned me in a torrent of light.

4

An intangible finger of thought traced a pattern in my mind. I saw how the crystalline matrix of the Starcore was arranged, the forces in balance. I saw how, by a slight realignment, a channel was opened, tapping a bottomless well of energy—the power-flow which is the substance of space/time.

I tried a tentative touch, explored the interior of the egg-shape, sensed the fantastic forces held in precarious equilibrium. Molecule by molecule I picked my way, found the nexial point, touched it with infinite delicacy—

Energy fountained up like a shower of fire. Instantaneously, the Ancils clamped down on it, shut it off at the source—

I forced them back, resumed control. They struggled to resist me, but I erected a shaped barrier enclosed their assault, compressed it in on itself, forced it out of my mind as a splinter might be forced by thumb-pressure out of swollen flesh.

And the Starcore pulsed in my hand; alive.

5

Around me the Ancils fluttered, emitting faint, unfocused pulses of distress and confusion. I ignored them. The apathy of many months was gone. I knew now what I had to do. I left the ship, closed off the tunnel, returned to the cavern that had been my unquestioned home for so many weeks, now no more than a gloomy den carved in the cold rock of an alien world. I made my way up to the cave mouth. It was early dusk. The scarlet sky seemed strangely deep and luminous. Cherry and Grape glowed with a lambent fire, low in the west.

"I'm going now, Ancils," I said. "Thank you—for everything."

There was no answer. Without a backward look I walked away across the desert.

6

The Zephyrs failed to recognize me at first; by the time they did, I had told them enough to restrain them from making any abrupt errors in judgment. I showed them the Starcore, let them pass it from hand to hand. Blane confirmed that it was the twin to the thing he had seen in *Tyrant's* Power Room. He weighed it on his palm, looked at me, frowning.

"Good work, Jonah," he said. "I'll keep this. It may be useful in some way—"

"I'll have it back now," I said. "I have a use for it, you may rest assured."

Blane's face darkened. "Jonah, you're here on sufferance. I suggest you conduct yourself with great circumspection—"

"The time for circumspection is past," I cut him off. "I'm going to Llywarch Hen tonight. You may come along if you wish."

Blane made a motion and a man behind me stooped to scoop up a stone of skull-crushing size. I touched his sleep center lightly, he crumpled on his face and snored. Two other men started toward me from opposite sides. They tripped and were unable to get up. The others moved back, looking suddenly frightened. I held Blane where he was, lifted the Starcore from his palm and dropped it in my pocket.

"As you see, I'm in command now," I said. "Does anyone dispute the point?"

No one did. We rested that day, and at nightfall set off for Hen.

7

Cymraeg's men met us two miles out, eight men standing beside their carryall where it had stalled at the crest of a rise. Two of them carried standard prison-guard issue handguns of the type energized by broadcast power from a central transmitter—a safety measure in the event the weapons fell into the wrong hands. I felt out for the transmitter, found the Starcore, shut it down.

"Close enough," one of the men called when we were fifty feet from them.

We halted.

"I don't know what you monkeys had in mind," the spokesman said. "But it just flunked out. Line up in a column of twos, hands behind the heads."

I walked toward him. He barked at me. I kept coming. He raised the gun and aimed between my eyes and sweat popped out on his forehead. He yelled at me to halt, and when I didn't he squeezed the firing stud.

His expression when nothing happened was like a silent scream. The other armed man jumped front and center and made firing motions. His gun failed to function. He drew his arm back to throw it at me and I blacked him out. I felled three more of them before they understood. I ordered the Zephyrs into the vehicle, reactivated the power unit. The former owners watched with numb expressions as we drove down toward Hen.

There was very little trouble in the camp. I found Cymraeg busy shouting a report into a dead comm screen and silenced him. My men gathered in his cadre, locked them in a barracks, recruited forty-three inmates, loaded the carryall with food and water. We headed west.

It was a four day hike to Base Station. I had left a volunteer behind at Hen to man the reactivated comm screen, in case one of the infrequent calls from the Station came through before we arrived. In spite of that, they were waiting for us; I could see the crew around the lone power cannon mounted atop the Admin building as we came up.

"Keep going," I told the driver. When we were half a mile out, a PA voice boomed across the flats, ordering us to halt. We did not comply. There was a flurry of activity around the gun, then a pause, then a more frantic flurry. A man left the gun and dashed away. Other men emerged from the stairhead onto the roof, hurried over to try their hands at the malfunctioning cannon. As we crossed the perimeter line, they were still pounding at it, swearing.

Men came running from the guard barracks as we halted in front of it. Their guns failed to fire. My troops gathered them in—there were nineteen guards in all—and locked them up. The Station commandant sat in his chair with a fury-white face and trembled as I gave him his instructions. He was stubborn; I touched his pain center three times with increasing severity before he broke and transmitted the emergency call to the cutter standing by on picket detail off-planet.

There was a three hour wait then. I found a corner table in the mess hall and sipped a cold drink from Cymraeg's private bar stock. Faintly, at the edge of sensitivity, I could sense the tiny energy-pattern of the distant vessel as it drove toward Pink Hell at full disaster acceleration. As I withdrew, the man called Heavy sat down opposite me. He seemed nervous, but determined.

"You've changed, Tarleton," he said. "What happened to you out there? What did it turn you into?"

I didn't answer; my thoughts were elsewhere.

"You're not well, Tarleton. You move like a zombie. Your eyes are strange. And these—miracles you perform: It's eerie. The men are all afraid of you. I'm afraid of you too."

"Follow instructions and you will not be injured," I reassured him.

"We were friends, once," he said. "Whatever you may believe, I had no ulterior motives. I kept Blane from catching you. Later I searched for you, to bring you back—"

"What is it you want of me?" I asked.

"Tarleton—listen to me: I want you to step down, let the rest of us handle it from this point on."

"That will not be possible."

I sensed movement around me, and scanned, and struck. Men fell, lay breathing hoarsely. Heavy edged back in his chair and watched me warily.

"Don't try it again," I said. "If you should interfere at a critical moment, the results might be serious." I walked out past the men on the floor and the equally silent men at the tables. The mid-morning sun was hot.

There were two hours and forty minutes still to wait.

8

There was no difficulty. The cutter assumed a parking orbit and dropped a launch. I followed it down, waited until it had settled in, half a mile from Base, then deactivated it. There was some slight resistance—fists and impromptu clubs—but in a quarter of an hour we had rounded up the thirty-man riot detail and marched them off to be detained. I took ten men and lifted the launch, less than an hour after it had touched down.

It was strange to be in space again. Old thoughts came crowding, but I pushed them back. The business at hand required all my attention. The cutter hailed us as we took up orbit twenty miles from her, preparatory to assuming a closing course. I answered, told them to stand by to take us aboard.

They ordered us to stand clear or be fired on. I damped down their Starcore and moved in. When we had grappled to the hull, I restored power, used it to cycle the boat-deck hatch, moved the launch inside.

All ten of my men had handguns, tuned to the Starcore I carried with me. The 'stabs who met us were also armed, but their weapons failed to fire. When I demonstrated that we were under no such handicap, they surrendered.

My interview with the cutter's captain was brief and businesslike. He seemed eager to inform me of the terrible punishment awaiting all of us, myself in particular; but I had no time to indulge his fancies. I ordered him to transmit an urgent SOS to the nearest battlewagon: *Belthazar*, on out-system patrol a week's run Sol-ward.

He refused.

I touched his pain center, but his conditioning held. He blacked out. I transmitted the call myself. Aboard *Belthazar,* the commodore might wonder; but he would come. For what could resist the armed might of a ship of the line?

9

For seven days, while my men stood guard over the ninety-man complement of the cutter, I waited, sleeping, eating, monitoring the actions of all one hundred men, feeling outward for the battleship's telltale energy pattern. It appeared, grew stronger; at a distance of ten thousand miles, I sensed the readying of warheads. Company policy, I saw, allowed no room for half-measures. Before she could launch, I cut her power. Now fifty million tons of dead metal rushed toward me out of the immense blackness of interstellar space.

It was the work of nine hours to match course and velocity with her, draw alongside at a distance of ten miles. Then I reopened communications:

"Your armament is dead. I suspect conditions inside are rapidly becoming untenable, in the absence of heat, light, air circulation, and so on. I have only one battery, but it functions effectively. I call on you to surrender."

I restored power to enable her to answer, and at once six torpedoes leaped toward us. I was forced to detonate them instantly. The resultant blasts did heavy damage to *Belthazar*'s port quarter. I renewed my demand for her surrender.

There was no response for another hour. Then she

fired a signal flare, indicating acceptance of the inevitable.

I boarded her alone, and was conducted to the suite of the Commodore Commanding.

10

His name was Thatch; he was a man I had once known. I silenced his questions and expostulations, told him what he was to do. He was aware that he and all his crew of over twenty thousand were at my mercy; he transmitted a message to the Chief of Naval Operations requesting an immediate rendezvous of the entire out-system flotilla at a point designated by me. His arguments were convincing. If indeed battleships were helpless against me, they had no choice but cooperation; and if not, it would be as well to bring all available force against me in a conclusive counter-attack.

Again I waited, keeping to the closely-guarded environs of the Commodore's suite. I had restored power to the ship, after seeing to the disarming of her batteries.

The cutter's ninety man crew had been transferred to the battleship. Manned now by my ten men, she trailed us, ready to open fire on command. There was no trouble. Nine great vessels of war approached, found themselves suddenly without power, disarmed, helpless. My crew went aboard each in turn, as I held *Belthazar*'s battery on them, destroyed the fire-control center, after which their captains were amenable to instruction. I called the latter to a conference aboard the flagship. For the occasion, I dressed myself in a regulation Naval uniform, but without insignia of rank or organization.

Two captains, five commodores, two rear admirals, and a vice admiral awaited me; be-ribboned gray veterans of a long campaign more grim than battle. These were the men who implemented the Starlords' policies. I wasted no time on amenities.

"You are here to surrender the Fleet," I told them. "Your ships will return to Earth orbit and disembark your crews."

There was a great deal of talk, and one effort to rush me. The four man Marine guard detail and three of the elderly officers lay on the deep-pile rug before they recognized the futility of it.

Admiral Constant made one last effort:

"Tarleton, you'll be reinstated—with an immediate jump in grade to captain. I personally guarantee your star in the statutory minimum time! I'm sure that there'll be a decoration in it for you—a very high decoration—and unofficially, other rewards—"

"I'm not susceptible to bribes," I told him.

In the end they accepted the *fait accompli.* They had no choice, no possibility of resistance. The Navy was the planet's sole armed force, the Starcore its sole power source. And I controlled the Starcore.

The flotilla returned to Earth. One by one the great ships discharged their complements. I did not permit even skeleton crews to remain aboard. For the first time since their launching in the previous century, the dreadnaughts drifted, lightless and unmanned.

The man known to me as Heavy came to the bridge of the flagship, from which I had observed the disembarkation.

"All right," he said. "You've captured the Fleet without a shot. Now what?"

"We're going down," I said.

"Have you lost your mind, man? You're holding the situation in the palm of your hand—as long as you're here, sitting behind the big guns. Go down, and you've thrown it all away!"

"I have unfinished business on-planet."

"Do you have any idea what conditions will be like down there when word gets around that the Navy's disbanded—"

"That's not my concern. My business is with Lord Imbolo."

"Stop and think for a minute, Tarleton. You've spiked his guns; you can dictate policy. Isn't that enough?"

"I intend to destroy the disease at its source."

"Tarleton—even a bad system is better than no system at all. Killing Imbolo is nothing—but the anarchy that will come afterwards will throw the whole world back to the Neolithic!"

"Perhaps."

"Poor, bitter, disillusioned young Tarleton," Heavy said sardonically. "He got a bad deal; his idols turned out to be clay from the neck down; all his cherished ideals turned out to be solid brass. So he makes his grand gesture and then breaks his toys! Sure, what are a few billion people, so long as you have your big moment, eyeball to eyeball with the villain of the piece! To hell with you, Lieutenant!"

"Prepare a G-boat," I said. "Get the men aboard. We leave in half an hour."

FOURTEEN

The fifty acre fortress-palace known as Imbolo Tower had been built on an island off the Carolina coast. We landed at the port outside the town. No ground crew met us. The terminal was deserted. Already, scraps of paper were blowing across the formerly immaculate ramp. We selected a pair of limousines from among the vehicles abandoned outside the terminal building and drove out through the open gates, past empty guard posts.

There were a few people abroad in the village. They stared as we went past. I saw a few broken windows; a wrecked car sat unattended across a sidewalk. There were no other signs of disorder.

The palace gates stood open. We drove in along the wide, curved drive, into the shadow of the tower that reared up half a mile above us. I reached out cautiously, but could detect no mind within my range of sensitivity.

Suddenly the car veered to the left, leaving the pavement. The drive unit died. I caught the wheel, steered it to a halt. The driver was slumped sideways, his face slack. The other four men sprawled unconscious in their seats. There was a rending crash behind me. I turned to see the second car on its side against a tree from which a great section of bark had been gouged. No one moved inside it.

I got out of the car, stood on the flat green lawn under the spreading trees. Vivid flowers grew in beds beside the drive. In the silence, I heard the hum of insects, the twittering of a bird. The sun shone down brightly from the blue sky. Across the park, the white facade of the palace stood unguarded. I walked toward it, alert for attack; but no attack came.

Inside the palace, all was silent, the offices empty, the corridors dark. I knew that Lord Imbolo's apartments were situated in the Upper Tower. In the grand foyer a bank of elevators stood with open doors. I rode one to the highest level to which it gave access, continued my climb on foot.

Twice, I encountered doors secured by powerlocks which I opened with a touch of my mind. A more elaborate device protected the ornate doors controlling access to the one hundred and eighty-fifth level, but it, too, opened to my touch.

I found myself in a wide, gray-carpeted room, softly-lit, furnished with low chairs and tables, a desk at one side, a pair of wide, carved doors beyond it. They opened without resistance into an unadorned passage leading to still another pair of doors. As I approached, they swung open before me. I passed through them and was in the presence of a man.

2

He was a figure carved from basalt, weathered by time and hard usage. His skull was small, round, hairless, set close against wide, still powerful shoulders. His eyes were large, with yellowish white, steady on me as I looked across at him. His hands, large, dusty-black, coarse-knuckled, were folded on the desk before him.

"Come in, Mr. Tarleton," he said in a deep voice as soft as crumpled velvet. "Sit down. You and I have matters which require discussion." He spoke with great assurance, as if I were a routine caller, dropping in on invitation. I reached out to touch his mind—

And encountered a surface as smooth and impermeable as polished steel.

"I knew this day would come, in time," he said, speaking easily, as if he had noticed nothing. "Space is too wide, men are too curious. And Roseworld was a mistake, of course. We had found traces there, and it seemed a clever solution to use the exiles to carry out the search. Perhaps I'd grown over-confident in my old age. Perhaps it was mere luck." He smiled, but it seemed to me that I detected a trace of tension under the blandness.

"I congratulate you on your abilities," he went on when I made no answer. "In some ways you've learned more in a few months than I in all my years of experimentation." He leaned back in his chair, still smiling a little. "But for all your cleverness, you've walked into my trap as neatly as though I'd led you on a rope." His smile grew a little wider, a remarkably youthful, white-toothed smile in his dark face.

"I point this out, not in a spirit of boastfulness, but only to make it clear to you that you're overmatched. And even if you'd kept your distance, attacked me indirectly, in the end the result would have been the same. I could have stopped you sooner, of course, but this way we save time, eh?"

As he spoke, I had again extended my awareness, with the greatest delicacy had scanned the surface of that incredible shield that protected his mind. What I found was not precisely a weakness, but a point of focus, where the lines of force came together. Retaining only the most tenuous contact, I again withdrew.

"I've followed your career with great interest, you know," he said, almost dreamily. "I knew your father, of course. A vigorous young man—and an even more vigorous old one." His expression became grim.

"Over the years I've been forced to do many things that caused me pain, Tarleton. But they were necessary." He turned to stare out the wide, curved window, waved a hand. "A pleasant view, is it not? A garden city, busy, prosperous, happy. A garden world. Man's old dream of peace and order realized." He swung back to stare into my face. "A dream worth protecting, Mr. Tarleton. A dream worth elaborate measures of security. A dream worth whatever it may have cost."

"Curious that other men have always paid the cost, Imbolo," I said. "Your bill is long overdue."

He laughed, a quiet, patient chuckle.

"I didn't entice you here to destroy you," he said. "Far from it. I need you Mr. Tarleton, I'm free to admit it. The burdens grow greater, and I grow weary. I need help; understanding help, someone to share the burden of superiority."

"You misunderstand," I said. "I'm in no danger of destruction."

A frown flicked across his face like a shadow. "Don't be a fool, young man. There's nothing to be gained by conflict between us. We two hold the power. The others—Catrice, Banshire and the rest: they're puppets, nothing more. They were wise enough to back me with their fortunes in the beginning; in gratitude I've kept my promises to them. But you and I—we're a different matter, boy! We hold the key, we two alone of all the billions— "

He struck without warning, a hammer-blow aimed at my mind. My vision blacked out; for a time outside of time the pressure crushed at me, while I strained against it with every erg of power I could summon. . . .

Suddenly the pressure was gone. I blinked away dimness. Sweat was running down across the fine wrinkles of Imbolo's face. He looked at me, his mouth curved in a smile without meaning.

"So—you surprise me, boy. I meant only to give you a touch of the quirt, as it were. But I see you're not yet broken to the whip." He shook his head like a man dazed by a blow. "All the better. I need a partner, not another underling. Things are falling apart, Tarleton. I confess this to you. It's gotten too big, too complex; too many pressures have built, too many repercussions of repercussions. What they don't understand, they fear—and when they fear, they hate. You'll learn that, Tarleton. Perhaps you already have. The price of your supremacy is the love of your fellow man."

"Things are worse than you realize, Imbolo," I said—and this time I struck first. The featureless shield held firm for an instant; then split, and I lanced in past the motor control centers, past the volitional node, toward the brilliant point of pseudo-light that was the essential ego of the man—

And merged.

3

His mind lay bare to me, as mine to him. I saw his memories: the long-ago days of his youth, the early aspirations, the years of dedication, the fears, mastered at last, the beginning of the long journey outward into the unknown. I saw disaster strike as a gyro malfunction aborted his Jupiter approach, felt with him the panic, and then the acceptance, and the terrible loneliness as his primitive vessel fell outward toward the emptiness of interstellar space.

I watched as he gathered his forces, cleared away the paralysis; I saw the focusing of a brilliant intellect, the analysis of the situation, the rebirth of hope. I followed as he calculated, planned, waited—and at the proper moment, used the last of his fuel in a forlorn effort to throw the vessel into orbit around Saturn's outermost moon. Not in hope of saving his own life—he knew there was no chance of that—but to preserve the ship intact for the study of those who followed, a lonely act of heroism and desperation.

Then the waiting, the growing awareness that he had failed again, that the ship was falling in past Europa; and then again hope, as it took up an eccentric orbit that brought it close to Ganymede. Close enough for a final desperate attempt, using the atmospheric braking jets, to maneuver for a landing—and to succeed.

And the dawning wonder as he realized that the

time-eroded shapes around him were those of a city fallen into ruin.

In his space suit, he had emerged from the tiny vessel, tramped through the dust- and ice-covered avenues, silvery in the light of the ringed impossible world that hung swollen in the black sky. I saw him, light-headed with starvation, stumble on the chamber where the white egg-shapes lay racked, saw how his mind, half-freed from his body, groped out instinctively, touched the triggering impulse—and awoke the power of the Starcore.

Alone, without instruction, in a state bordering delirium, he had learned to tap the energy source, direct its flow into his ship's power system, had re-energized the synthesizer system which converted inert mineral matter into edible organics, had regained his strength, lifted from the barren world, and begun his return voyage to Earth.

And on the way, he had considered the results of his discovery. He had visualized the impact of a perpetual, inexhaustible power source on the tortured world, assessed his culture's ability to use it wisely—and found it wanting.

I agonized with him as he recognized—and accepted—the burden that devolved on him.

The years of struggle, planning, of the gradual shaping of order, the lessons learned, the controls imposed, the growing weariness. . . .

The rise of the Hateniks, an expression of the formless urge of humanity for change. The threat, ever-present that the secret of the Starcore would fall into the hands of one who would misuse it.

Culminating in the arrival of the brash young man with the strange eyes . . .

Myself.

I saw the welcome in his heart, the overwhelming desire to relinquish the terrible power he had held so long to another, younger man, to rest at last. But first, the need to be sure of his successor's abilities, his intentions. The need to teach him, to pass along the bitterly-won lessons of his long life. . . .

"Now you see, Tarleton," his voice came from far away. "Now you understand."

"You made mistakes, Imbolo," I said. "There were things you didn't know. The Ancils still live, they can teach us. . . ."

"Now I understand. Too late, Tarleton. Too late for me. I underestimated you. You struck too hard. . . ."

The light of his mind was fading. I tried to grapple to it, to breathe new life into it, but I was too slow, too clumsy.

Then I was alone in darkness.

4

Lord Imbolo sat in the chair behind the gleaming desk, his eyes half open, the faint smile still on his dead mouth.

I made my way out of the suite, down the stairs, out of the building. On the wide terrace they waited for me, warily.

"You went in—and you came back alive," Heavy said. "I suppose that means you've done what you came for. Now you hold all the cards. What game are you calling?"

"I'm throwing in my hand," I said. "You take over."

He stepped forward and caught my arm. "You're yourself again," he said. "What happened?"

"I discovered what playing God means. I'm not up

to the job." I shook his hand off. I had taken two steps when a familiar touch brushed my mind:

"Ban . . . we have followed with you, directed you, through your eyes seen the nature of your young kind. Brutal you are, and primitive; but the seeds of greatness are in you. Our long era ends, yours begins. You must play your role, as have we."

"I'm finished," I said. "I'm tired. I want to rest."

"Alas, Ban," the Ancils mourned; their voices were faint with distance. *"For you there is no rest. And in a thousand years, perhaps, you will know the true meaning of weariness. You have assumed a burden you cannot discard: embarked on a path from which you cannot depart.*

"And yet—you are young, and life is sweet. Go forth, breathe the clear air, look on your green world. When your mind is healed—come back."

"Tarleton," Heavy was saying. "I've already talked with Admiral Grayson. He wants permission to hold the Navy together as a peace-keeping force until you've . . . made other arrangements. I think we ought to cooperate. We have to begin somewhere. Rebuilding a world from scratch is a bigger job than any of us ever considered."

"Yes," I said, "hold it together. Make it work. Imbolo is dead, but the world lives on."

"Where are you going, Tarleton? What are your plans?"

"Plans?" I looked up at the toy clouds drifting across the sky. "I have no plans. I'm going out there . . ." I waved a hand that encompassed the world ". . . and see if there's anything worth preserving. If so . . . one day perhaps I'll be back."

I walked away under the green trees. A soft breeze

carried the perfume of flowers. A fountain tinkled. A bird sang.

Perhaps in a thousand years—or ten thousand—a destroying horde known as the Axorc would burst from the deeps of intergalactic space to sweep us away. Perhaps they would succeed—and perhaps we would surprise them. Or perhaps they had died a thousand centuries ago, and their threat was an empty bugaboo.

But if the Axorc did not exist, there would be other, even greater threats to Man. And of these, the greatest would be Man himself.

"*And if you master yourselves, who then can you fear?*" a voice whispered from far away.

"Who indeed?" I said aloud, and laughed, and passed through the gate into the wide world.

THE END

A Relic of War

I

The old war machine sat in the village square, its impotent guns pointing aimlessly along the dusty street. Shoulder-high weeds grew rankly about it, poking up through the gaps in the two-yard-wide treads; vines crawled over the high, rust-and guano-streaked flanks. A row of tarnished enamel battle honors gleamed dully across the prow, reflecting the late sun.

A group of men lounged near the machine; they were dressed in heavy work-clothes and boots; their hands were large and calloused, their faces weather-burned. They passed a jug from hand to hand, drinking deep. It was the end of a long workday and they were relaxed, good-humored.

"Hey, we're forgetting old Bobby," one said. He strolled over and sloshed a little of the raw whiskey over the soot-blackened muzzle of the blast cannon slanting sharply down from the forward turret. The other men laughed.

"How's it going, Bobby?" the man called.

Deep inside the machine, there was a soft chirring sound.

"Very well, thank you," a faint, whispery voice scraped from a grill below the turret.

"You keeping an eye on things, Bobby?" another man called.

"All clear," the answer came: a bird-chirp from a dinosaur.

"Bobby, you ever get tired just setting here?"

"Hell, Bobby don't get tired," the man with the jug said. "He's got a job to do, old Bobby has."

"Hey, Bobby, what kind o' boy are you?" a plump, lazy-eyed man called.

"I am a good boy," Bobby replied obediently.

"Sure Bobby's a good boy." The man with the jug reached up to pat the age-darkened curve of chro-malloy above him. "Bobby's looked out for us."

Heads turned at a sound from across the square: the distant whine of a turbocar, approaching along the forest road.

"Huh! Ain't the day for the mail," a man said. They stood in silence, watched as a small, dusty cushion-car emerged from deep shadow into the yellow light of the street. It came slowly along to the plaza, swung left, pulled to a stop beside the board-walk before a corrugated metal storefront lettered *Blauvelt Provision Company.* The canopy popped open and a man stepped down. He was of medium height, dressed in a plain city-type black coverall. He studied the storefront, the street, then turned to look across at the men. He stepped down into the street and came across toward them.

"Which of you men is Blauvelt?" he asked as he came up. His voice was unhurried, cool. His eyes flickered over the men.

A big, youngish man with a square face and sun-bleached hair lifted his chin.

"Right here," he said. "Who're you, Mister?"

"Crewe is the name. Disposal Officer, War Materiel Commission." The newcomer looked up at the great machine looming over them. "Bolo *Stupendous*, Mark XXV," he said. He glanced at the men's faces, fixed on Blauvelt. "We had a report that there was a live Bolo out here. I wonder if you realize what you're playing with?"

"Hell, that's just Bobby," a man said.

"He's town mascot," someone else said.

"This machine could blow your town off the map," Crewe said. "And a good-sized piece of jungle along with it."

Blauvelt grinned; the squint lines around his eyes gave him a quizzical look.

"Don't do getting upset, Mr. Crewe," he said. Bobby's harmless—"

"A Bolo's never harmless, Mr. Blauvelt. They're fighting machines, nothing else."

Blauvelt sauntered over and kicked at a corroded tread-plate. "Eighty-five years out in this jungle is kind of tough on machinery, Crewe. The sap and stuff from the trees eats chromalloy like it was sugar candy. The rains are acid, eat up equipment damn near as fast as we can ship it in here. Bobby can still talk a little, but that's about all."

"Certainly it's deteriorated; that's what makes it dangerous. Anything could trigger its battle reflex circuitry. Now, if you'll clear everyone out of the area, I'll take care of it."

"You move kind of fast for a man that just hit town," Blauvelt said, frowning. "Just what you got in mind doing?"

"I'm going to fire a pulse at it that will neutralize what's left of its computing center. Don't worry; there's no danger—"

"Hey," a man in the rear rank blurted. "That mean he can't talk anymore?"

"That's right," Crewe said. "Also, he can't open fire on you."

"Not so fast, Crewe," Blauvelt said. "You're not messing with Bobby. We like him like he is." The other men were moving forward, forming up in a threatening circle around Crewe.

"Don't talk like a fool," Crewe said. "What do you think a salvo from a Continental Siege Unit would do to your town?"

Blauvelt chuckled and took a long cigar from his vest pocket. He sniffed it, called out: "All right, Bobby—fire one!"

There was a muted clatter, a sharp *click!* from deep inside the vast bulk of the machine. A tongue of pale flame licked from the cannon's soot-rimmed bore. The big man leaned quickly forward, puffed the cigar alight. The audience whooped with laughter.

"Bobby does what he's told, that's all," Blauvelt said. "And not much of that." He showed white teeth in a humorless smile.

Crewe flipped over the lapel of his jacket; a small, highly polished badge glinted there. "You know better than to interfere with a Concordiat officer," he said.

"Not so fast, Crewe." A dark-haired, narrow-faced fellow spoke up. "You're out of line. I heard about you Disposal men. Your job is locating old ammo dumps, abandoned equipment, stuff like that. Bobby's not abandoned. He's town property. Has been for near thirty years."

"Nonsense. This is battle equipment, the property of the Space Arm—"

Blauvelt was smiling lopsidedly. "Uh-uh. We've got salvage rights. No title, but we can make one up in a hurry. Official. I'm mayor here, and District Governor."

"This thing is a menace to every man, woman, and child in the settlement," Crewe snapped. "My job is to prevent tragedy—"

"Forget Bobby," Blauvelt cut in. He waved a hand at the jugle wall beyond the tilled fields. "There's a hundred million square miles of virgin territory out there," he said. "You can do what you like out there. I'll even sell you provisions. But just leave our mascot be, understand?"

Crewe looked at him, looked around at the other men.

"You're a fool," he said. "You're all fools." He turned and walked away, stiff-backed.

II

In the room he had rented in the town's lone boarding house, Crewe opened his baggage and took out a small, gray plastic-cased instrument. The three children of the landlord who were watching from the latchless door edged closer.

"Gee, is that a real star radio?" the eldest, a skinny, long-necked lad of twelve asked.

"No," Crewe said shortly. The boy blushed and hung his head.

"It's a command transmitter," Crewe said, relenting. "It's designed for talking to fighting machines, giving them orders. They'll only respond to the special shaped-wave signal this puts out." He flicked a switch, and an indicator light glowed on the side of the case.

"You mean like Bobby?" the boy asked.

"Like Bobby used to be." Crewe switched off the transmitter and put it aside.

"Bobby's swell," another child said. "He tells us stories about when he was in the war."

"He's got medals," the first boy said. "Were you in the war, Mister?"

"I'm not quite that old," Crewe said.

"Bobby's old, he's older'n Granddad."

"You boys had better run along," Crewe said. "I have to . . ." He broke off, cocked his head, listening. There were shouts outside; someone was calling his name.

Crewe pushed through the boys and went quickly along the hall, stepped through the door onto the boardwalk. He felt rather than heard a slow, heavy thudding, a chorus of shrill squeaks, a metallic groaning— A red-faced man was running toward him from the square.

"It's Bobby!" he shouted. "He's moving! What'd you do to him, damn you, Crewe!"

Crewe brushed past the man, ran toward the plaza. The Bolo appeared at the end of the street, moving ponderously forward, trailing uprooted weeds and vines.

"He's headed straight for Spivac's warehouse!" someone yelled.

"Bobby! Stop there!" Blauvelt came into view, running in the machine's wake. The big machine rumbled onward, executed a half-left as Crewe reached the plaza, clearing the corner of a building by inches. It crushed a section of boardwalk to splinters, advanced across a storage yard. A stack of rough-cut lumber toppled, spilled across the dusty ground. The Bolo trampled a board fence, headed out across a tilled field. Blauvelt whirled on Crewe.

"This is your doing, damn you! We never had trouble before— "

"Never mind that! Have you got a field-car?"

"We—" Blauvelt checked himself. "What if we have?"

"I can stop it—but I have to be close. It will be into the jungle in another minute. My car can't navigate there."

"Let him go," a man said, breathing hard from his run. "He can't do no harm out there."

"Who'd of thought it?" another man said. "Setting there all them years—who'd of thought he could travel like that?"

"Your so-called mascot might have more surprises in store for you," Crewe snapped. "Get me a car, fast! This is an official requisition, Blauvelt!"

There was a silence, broken only by the distant crashing of timber as the Bolo moved into the edge of the forest. Hundred foot trees leaned and went down before its advance.

"Let him go," Blauvelt said. "Like Stinzi says, he can't hurt anything."

"What if he turns back?"

"Hell," a man muttered. "Old Bobby wouldn't hurt *us*. . . ."

"The car," Crewe snarled. "You're wasting valuable time."

Blauvelt frowned. "All right—but you don't make a move unless it looks like he's going to come back and hit the town, clear?"

"Let's go."

Blauvelt led the way at a trot toward the town garage.

III

The Bolo's trail was a twenty-five feet wide swathe cut through the virgin jungle; the tread-prints were pressed eighteen inches into the black loam, where it showed among the jumble of fallen branches.

"It's moving at about twenty miles per hour, faster than we can go," Crewe said. "If it holds its present track, the curve will bring it back to your town in about five hours."

"He'll sheer off," Blauvelt muttered.

"Maybe. But we won't risk it. Pick up a heading of two hundred and seventy degrees, Blauvelt. We'll try an intercept by cutting across the circle."

Blauvelt complied wordlessly. The car moved ahead in the deep green gloom under the huge shaggy-barked trees. Oversized insects buzzed and thumped against the canopy. Small and medium lizards hopped, darted, flapped. Fern leaves as big as awnings scraped along the car as it clambered over loops and coils of tough root, leaving streaks of plant juice. Once they grated against an exposed ridge of crumbling brown rock; flakes as big as saucers scaled off, exposing dull metal.

"Dorsal fin of a scout-boat," Crewe said. "That's what's left of what was supposed to be a corrosion resistant alloy."

They passed more evidence of a long-ago battle: the massive shattered breech mechanism of a platform-mounted Hellbore, the gutted chassis of what might have been a bomb car, portions of a downed aircraft, fragments of shattered armor. Many of the relics were of Terran design, but often it was the curiously curved, spidery lines of a rusted Axorc microgun or implosion projector that poked through the greenery.

"It must have been a heavy action," Crewe said. "One of the ones toward the end that didn't get much notice at the time. There's stuff here I've never seen before, experimental types, I imagine, rushed in for a last-ditch stand."

Blauvelt grunted.

"Contact in another minute or so," Crewe said. As Blauvelt opened his mouth to reply, there was a blinding flash, a violent impact, and the jungle erupted in their faces.

IV

The seat webbing was cutting into Crewe's ribs. His ears were filled with a high, steady ringing; there was a taste of tarnished brass in his mouth. His head throbbed in time with the heavy thudding of his heart.

The car was on its side, the interior a jumble of loose objects, torn wiring, broken plastic. Blauvelt was half under him, groaning. He slid off him, saw that he was groggy but conscious.

"Changed your mind yet about your harmless pet?" he asked, wiping a trickle of blood from his right eye. "Let's get clear before he fires those empty guns again. Can you walk?"

Blauvelt mumbled, crawled out through the broken canopy. Crewe gropped through debris for the command transmitter—

"Mother of God," Blauvelt croaked. Crewe twisted, saw the high, narrow, iodine-dark shape of the alien machine perched on jointed crawler-legs fifty feet away framed by blast-scorched foliage. Its multiple-barreled microgun battery aimed dead at the overturned car.

"Don't move a muscle," Crewe whispered. Sweat trickled down Crewe's face. An insect, like a stub-winged four inch dragonfly, came and buzzed about them, moved on. Hot metal pinged, contracting. Instantly, the alien hunter-killer moved forward another six feet, depressed its gun muzzles.

"Run for it!" Blauvelt cried. He came to his feet in a scrabbling lunge; the enemy machine swung to track him—

A giant tree leaned, snapped, was tossed aside. The great green-streaked prow of the Bolo forged into view, interposing itself between the smaller machine and the men. It turned to face the enemy; fire flashed, reflecting against the surrounding trees; the ground jumped once, twice, to hard, racking shocks. Sound boomed dully in Crewe's blast-numbed ears. Bright sparks fountained above the Bolo as it advanced. Crewe felt the shock as the two fighting machines came together; he saw the Bolo hesitate, then forge ahead, rearing up, dozing the lighter machine aside, grinding over it, passing on, to leave a crumpled mass of wreckage in its wake.

"My God, did you see that, Crewe?" Blauvelt shouted in Crewe's ear. "Did you see what Bobby did? He walked right into its guns and smashed it flatter'n crock-brewed beer!"

The Bolo halted, turned ponderously, sat facing the men. Bright streaks of molten metal ran down its armored flanks, fell spattering and smoking into crushed greenery.

"He saved our necks," Blauvelt said. He staggered to his feet, picked his way past the Bolo to stare at the smoking ruins of the smashed adversary.

"That thing was headed straight for town," he said. "My God, can you picture what it would have done?"

"Unit nine-five-four of the line, reporting contact with hostile force." The mechanical voice of the Bolo spoke suddenly. "Enemy unit destroyed. I have sustained extensive damage, but am still operational at nine point six percent base capability, awaiting further orders."

"Hey," Blauvelt said. "That doesn't sound like . . ."

"Now maybe you understand that this is a Bolo combat unit, not the village idiot," Crewe snapped. He picked his way across the churned-up ground, stood before the great machine.

"Mission accomplished, Unit nine-five-four," he said. "Enemy forces neutralized. Close out Battle Reflex and revert to low alert status." He turned to Blauvelt.

"Let's go back to town," he said, "and tell them what their mascot just did."

Blauvelt stared up at the grim and ancient machine; his square, tanned face looked yellowish and drawn. "Yeah," he said. "Let's do that."

V

The ten-piece town band was drawn up in a double rank before the newly-mown village square. The entire population of the settlement—some three hundred and forty-two men, women, and children—were present, dressed in their best. Pennants fluttered from strung wires. The sun glistened from the armored sides of the newly-cleaned and polished Bolo. A vast bouquet of wild flowers poked from the no longer sooty muzzle of the Hellbore.

Crewe stepped forward.

"As a representative of the Concordiat government I've been asked to make this presentation," he said. "You people have seen fit to design a medal and award it to Unit nine-five-four in appreciation for services rendered in defense of the community above and beyond the call of duty." He paused, looked across the faces of his audience.

"Many more elaborate honors have been awarded for a great deal less," he said. He turned to the machine; two men came forward, one with a stepladder, the other with a portable welding rig. Crewe climbed up, held the newly-struck decoration in place beside the row of century-old battle honors. The technician quickly spotted it in position. The crowd cheered, then dispersed, chattering, to the picnic tables set up in the village street.

VI

It was late twilight. The last of the sandwiches and stuffed eggs had been eaten, the last speeches declaimed, the last keg broached. Crewe sat with a few of the men in the town's lone public house.

"To Bobby." A man raised his glass.

"Correction," Crewe said. "To Unit nine-five-four of the line." The men laughed and drank.

"Well, time to go, I guess," a man said. The others chimed in, rose, clattering chairs. As the last of them left, Blauvelt came in. He sat down across from Crewe.

"You, ah, staying the night?" he asked.

"I thought I'd drive back," Crewe said. "My business here is finished."

"Is it?" Blauvelt said tensely.

Crewe looked at him, waiting.

"You know what you've got to do, Crewe."

"Do I?" Crewe took a sip from his glass.

"Damn it, have I got to spell it out? As long as that damned machine was just an oversized half-wit, it was all right. Kind of a monument to the war, and all. But now I've seen what it can do—my God, Crewe—we can't have a live killer in the middle of our town, us never knowing when it might take a notion to start shooting again!"

"Finished?" Crewe asked.

"It's not that we're not grateful—"

"Get out," Crewe said.

"Now, look here, Crewe—"

"Get out. And keep everyone away from Bobby, understand?"

"Does that mean—?"

"I'll take care of it."

Blauvelt got to his feet. "Yeah," he said. "Sure."

After he was gone, Crewe rose and dropped a bill on the table; he picked the command transmitter from the floor, went out into the street. Faint cries came from the far end of the town, where the crowd had gathered for fireworks. A yellow rocket arced up, burst in a spray of golden light, falling, fading. . . .

Crewe walked toward the plaza. The Bolo loomed up, a vast, black shadow against the star-thick sky. Crewe stood before it, looking up at the already draggled pennants, the wilted nosegay drooping from the gun muzzle.

"Unit nine-five-four, you know why I'm here?" he said softly.

"I compute that my usefulness as an engine of war is ended," the soft, rasping voice said.

"That's right," Crewe said, "I checked the area in a thousand mile radius with sensitive instruments.

There's no enemy machine left alive. The one you killed was the last."

"It was true to its duty," the machine said.

"It was my fault," Crewe said. "It was designed to detect our command carrier and home on it. When I switched on my transmitter, it went into action. Naturally, you sensed that, and went to meet it."

The machine sat silent.

"You could still save yourself," Crewe said. "If you trampled us under and made for the jungle it might be centuries before . . ."

"Before another man comes to do what must be done? Better that I die now, at the hands of a friend."

"Good-bye, Bobby."

"Correction: Unit nine-five-four of the line."

Crewe pressed the key. A sense of darkness fell across the machine.

At the edge of the square, Crewe looked back. He raised a hand in a ghostly salute; then he walked away along the dusty street, white in the light of the rising moon.

Test to Destruction

The late October wind drove icy rain against Mallory's face above his turned-up collar where he stood concealed in the shadows at the mouth of the narrow alley.

"It's ironic, Johnny," the small, grim-faced man beside him muttered. "You—the man who should have been World Premier tonight—skulking in the back streets while Koslo and his bully boys drink champagne in the Executive Palace."

"That's all right, Paul," Mallory said. "Maybe he'll be too busy with his victory celebration to concern himself with me."

"And maybe he won't," the small man said. "He won't rest easy as long s he knows you're alive to oppose him."

"It will only be a few more hours, Paul. By breakfast time, Koslo will know his rigged election didn't take."

"But if he takes you first, that's the end, Johnny. Without you the *coup* will collapse like a soap bubble."

"I'm not leaving the city," Mallory said flatly. "Yes,

there's a certain risk involved; but you don't bring down a dictator without taking a few chances."

"You didn't have to take this one, meeting Crandall yourself."

"It will help if he sees me, knows I'm in this all the way."

In silence, the two men waited the arrival of their fellow conspirator.

Aboard the interstellar dreadnought cruising half a parsec from Earth, the compound Ree mind surveyed the distant solar system.

Radiation on many wavelengths from the third body, the Perceptor cells directed the impulse to the sixty-nine hundred and thirty-four units comprising the segmented brain which guided the ship. *Modulations over the forty-ninth through the ninety-first spectra of mentation.*

A portion of the pattern is characteristic of exocosmic manipulatory intelligence, the Analyzers extrapolated from the data. *Other indications range in complexity from levels one through twenty-six.*

This is an anomalous situation, the Recollectors mused. *It is the essential nature of a Prime Intelligence to destroy all lesser competing mind-forms, just as I/we have systematically annihilated those I/we have encountered on my/our exploration of the Galactic Arm.*

Before action is taken, clarification of the phenomenon is essential, the Interpretors pointed out. *Closure to a range not exceeding one radiation/second will be required for extraction and analysis of a representative mind-unit.*

In this event, the risk level rises to Category Ultimate, the Analyzers announced dispassionately.

RISK LEVELS NO LONGER APPLY, the powerful thought-impulse of the Egon put an end to the discussion. NOW OUR SHIPS RANGE INTO NEW SPACE, SEEKING EXPANSION ROOM FOR THE GREAT RACE. THE UNALTERABLE COMMAND OF THAT WHICH IS GREAT REQUIRES THAT MY/OUR PROBE BE PROSECUTED TO THE LIMIT OF REE CAPABILITY, TESTING MY/OUR ABILITY FOR SURVIVAL AND DOMINANCE. THERE CAN BE NO TIMIDITY, NO EXCUSE FOR FAILURE. LET ME/US NOW ASSUME A CLOSE SURVEILLANCE ORBIT!

In utter silence, and at a velocity a fraction of a kilometer/sec below that of light, the Ree dreadnought flashed toward Earth.

Mallory tensed as a dark figure appeared a block away under the harsh radiance of a polyarc.

"There's Crandall now," the small man hissed. "I'm glad—" He broke off as the roar of a powerful turbine engine sounded suddenly along the empty avenue. A police car exploded from a side street, rounded the corner amid a shriek of overstressed gyros. The man under the light turned to run—and the vivad blue glare of a SURF-gun winked and stuttered from the car. The burst of slugs caught the runner, slammed him against the brick wall, kicked him from his feet, rolled him, before the crash of the guns reached Mallory's ears.

"My God! They've killed Tony!" The small man blurted. "We've got to get out . . . !"

Mallory took half a dozen steps back into the alley, froze as lights sprang up at the far end. He heard booted feet hit pavement, a hoarse voice that barked a command.

"We're cut off," he snapped. There was a rough wooden door six feet away. He jumped to it, threw his weight against it. It held. He stepped back, kicked it in, shoved his companion ahead of him into a dark room smelling of moldy burlap and rat droppings. Stumbling, groping in the dark, Mallory led the way across a stretch of littered floor, felt along the wall, found a door that hung by one hinge. He pushed past it, was in a passage floored with curled linoleum, visible in the feeble gleam filtered through a fanlight above a massive, barred door. He turned the other way, ran for the smaller door at the far end of the passage. He was ten feet from it when the center panel burst inward in a hail of wood splinters that grazed him, ripped at his coat like raking talons. Behind him, the small man made a choking noise; Mallory whirled in time to see him fall back against the wall and go down, his chest and stomach torn away by the full impact of a thousand rounds from the police SURF-gun.

An arm came through the broached door, groping for the latch. Mallory took a step, seized the wrist, wrenched backward with all his weight, felt the elbow joint shatter. The scream of the injured policeman was drowned in a second burst from the rapid-fire weapon—but Mallory had already leaped, caught the railing of the stair, pulled himself up and over. He took the steps five at a time, passed a landing littered with broken glass and empty bottles, kept going, emerged in a corridor of sagging doors and cobwebs. Feet crashed below, furious voices yelled. Mallory stepped inside the nearest door, stood with his back to the wall beside it. Heavy feet banged on the stairs, paused, came his way. . . .

Mallory tensed and as the policeman passed the

door, he stepped out, brought his hand over and down in a side-handed blow to the base of the neck that had every ounce of power in his shoulders behind it. The man seemed to dive forward, and Mallory caught the gun before it struck the floor. He took three steps, poured a full magazine into the stairwell. As he turned to sprint for the far end of the passage, return fire boomed from below.

A club, swung by a giant, struck him in the side, knocked the breath from his lungs, sent him spinning against the wall. He recovered, ran on; his hand, exploring, found a deep gouge that bled freely. The bullet had barely grazed him.

He reached the door to the service stair, recoiled violently as a dirty-gray shape sprang at him with a yowl from the darkness—in the instant before a gun flashed and racketed in the narrow space, scattering plaster dust from the wall above his head. A thick-set man in the dark uniform of the Security Police, advancing up the stair at a run, checked momentarily as he saw the gun in Mallory's hands—and before he recovered himself, Mallory had swung the empty weapon, knocked him spinning back down onto the landing. The cat that had saved his life—an immense, battle-scarred Tom—lay on the floor, half its head blown away by the blast it had intercepted. Its lone yellow eye was fixed on him; its claws raked the floor, as, even in death, it advanced to the attack. Mallory jumped over the stricken beast, went up the stairs.

Three flights higher, the stair ended in a loft stacked with bundled newspapers and rotting cartons from which mice scuttled as he approached. There was a single window, opaque with grime. Mallory tossed aside the useless gun, scanned the ceiling for evidence of an escape hatch, saw nothing. His side ached abominably.

Relentless feet sounded beyond the door. Mallory backed to a corner of the room—and again, the deafening shriek of the SURF-gun sounded, and the flimsy door bucked, disintegrated. For a moment, there was total silence. Then:

"Walk out with your hands up, Mallory!" a brassy voice snarled. In the gloom, pale flames were licking over the bundled papers, set afire by the torrent of steel-jacketed slugs. Smoke rose, thickened.

"Come out before you fry," the voice called.

"Let's get out of here," another man bawled. "This dump will go up like tinder!"

"Last chance, Mallory!" the first man shouted, and now the flames, feeding on the dry paper, were reaching for the ceiling, roaring as they grew. Mallory went along the wall to the window, ripped aside the torn roller shade, tugged at the sash. It didn't move. He kicked out the glass, threw a leg over the sill, and stepped out onto a rusted fire escape. Five stories down, light puddled on grimy concrete, the white dots of upturned faces—and half a dozen police cars blocking the rain-wet street. He put his back to the railing, looked up. The fire escape extended three, perhaps four stories higher. He threw his arm across his face to shield it from the billowing flames, forced his legs to carry him up the iron treads three at a time.

The topmost landing was six feet below an overhanging cornice. Mallory stepped up on the rail, caught the edge of the carved stone trim with both hands, swung himself out. For a moment, he dangled, ninety feet above the street; then he pulled himself up, got a knee over the coping, and rolled onto the roof.

Lying flat, he scanned the darkness around him. The level was broken only by a ventilator stack and a shack housing a stair or elevator head.

He reconnoitered, found that the hotel occupied a corner, with a parking lot behind it. On the alley side, the adjoining roof was at a level ten feet lower, separated by a sixteen foot gap. As Mallory stared across at it, a heavy rumbling shook the deck under his feet: one of the floors of the ancient building, collapsing as the fire ate through its supports.

Smoke was rising all around him now. On the parking lot side, dusky flames soared up thirty feet above him, trailing an inverted cascade of sparks into the wet night sky. He went to the stairhead, found the metal door locked. A rusty ladder was clamped to the side of the structure. He wrenched it free, carried it to the alley side. It took all his strength to force the corroded catches free, pull the ladder out to its full extension. Twenty feet, he estimated. Enough—maybe.

He shoved the end of the ladder out, wrestled it across to rest on the roof below. The flimsy bridge sagged under his weight as he crawled up on it. He moved carefully out, ignoring the swaying of the fragile support. He was six feet from the far roof when he felt the rotten metal crumple under him; with a frantic lunge, he threw himself forward. Only the fact that the roof was at a lower level saved him. He clawed his way over the sheet-metal gutter, hearing shouts ring out below as the ladder crashed to the bricks of the alley.

A bad break, he thought. *Now they know where I am* . . . .

There was a heavy trap-door set in the roof. He lifted it, descended an iron ladder into darkness, found his way to a corridor, along it to a stair. Faint sounds rose from below. He went down.

At the fourth floor, lights showed below, voices sounded, the clump of feet. He left the stair at the third floor, prowled along a hall, entered an abandoned office. Searchlights in the street below threw oblique shadows across the discolored walls.

He went on, turned a corner, went into a room on the alley side. A cold draft, recking of smoke, blew in through a glassless window. Below, the narrow way appeared to be deserted. Paul's body was gone. The broken ladder lay where it had fallen. It was, he estimated, a twenty foot drop to the bricks; even if he let himself down to arm's length and dropped, a leg-breaker. . . .

Something moved below him. A uniformed policeman was standing at a spot directly beneath the window, his back against the wall. A wolf smile drew Mallory's face tight. In a single motion, he slid his body out over the sill, chest down, held on for an instant, seeing the startled face below turn upward, the mouth open for a yell—

He dropped; his feet struck the man's back, breaking his fall. He rolled clear, sat up, half-dazed. The policeman sprawled on his face, his spine twisted at an awkward angle.

Mallory got to his feet—and almost fell at the stab of pain from his right ankle. Sprained, or broken. His teeth set against the pain, he moved along the wall. Icy rainwater, sluicing from the downspout ahead, swirled about his ankles. He slipped, almost went down on the slimy bricks. The lesser darkness of the parking lot behind the building showed ahead.

If he could reach it, cross it—then he might still have a chance. He had to succeed—for Monica, for the child, for the future of a world.

Another step, and another. It was as though there were a vast ache that caught at him with every breath. His blood-soaked shirt and pantsleg hung against him, icy cold. Then feet more, and he would make his run for it—

Two men in the black uniforms of the State Security Police stepped out into his path, stood with blast-guns leveled at his chest. Mallory pushed away from the wall, braced himself for the burst of slugs that would end his life. Instead, a beam of light speared out through the misty rain, dazzling his eyes.

"You'll come with us, Mr. Mallory."

Still no contact, the Perceptors reported.

The prime-level minds below lack cohesion; they flicker and dart away even as I/we touch them.

The initiators made a proposal: *By the use of appropriate harmonics a resonance field can be set up which will reinforce any native mind functioning in an analogous rhythm.*

I/we find that a pattern of the following character will be most suitable. . . . A complex symbolism was displayed.

PERSEVERE IN THE FASHION DESCRIBED, the Egon commanded. ALL EXTRANEOUS FUNCTIONS WILL BE DISCONTINUED UNTIL SUCCESS IS ACHIEVED.

With total singleness of purpose, the Ree sensors probed across space from the dark and silent ship, searching for a receptive human mind.

* * *

The Interrogation Room was a totally bare cube of white enamel. At its geometric center, under a blinding white glare panel, sat a massive chair constructed of polished steel, casting an ink-black shadow.

A silent minute ticked past; then heels clicked in the corridor. A tall man in a plain, dark military tunic came through the open door, halted, studying his prisoner. His wide, sagging face was as gray and bleak as a tombstone.

"I warned you, Mallory," he said in a deep growling tone.

"You're making a mistake, Koslo," Mallory said.

"Openly arresting the people's hero, eh?" Koslo curved his wide, gray lips in a death's head smile. "Don't delude yourself. The malcontents will do nothing without their leader."

"Are you sure you're ready to put your regime to the test so soon?"

"It's that or wait, while your party gains strength. I chose the quicker course. I was never as good at waiting as you, Mallory."

"Well—you'll know by morning."

"That close, eh?" Koslo's heavy-lidded eyes pinched down on glints of light. He grunted. "I'll know many things by morning. You realize that your personal position is hopeless?" His eyes went to the chair.

"In other words, I should sell out to you now in return for—what? Another of your promises?"

"The alternative is the chair," Koslo said flatly.

"You have great confidence in machinery, Koslo—more than in men. That's your great weakness."

Koslo's hand went out, caressing the rectilinear metal of the chair. "This is a scientific apparatus designed to accomplish a specific task with the least possible difficulty to me. It creates conditions within the subject's neural system conducive to total recall, and at the same time amplifies the subvocalizations that accompany all highly cerebral activity. The subject is also rendered amenable to verbal cuing." He paused. "If you resist, it will destroy your mind—but not before you've told me everything: names, locations, dates, organization, operational plans—everything. It will be simpler for us both if you acknowledge the inevitable and tell me freely what I require to know."

"And after you've got the information?"

"You know my regime can't tolerate opposition. The more complete my information, the less bloodshed will be necessary."

Mallory shook his head. "No," he said bluntly.

"Don't be a fool, Mallory! This isn't a test of your manhood!"

"Perhaps it is, Koslo: man against machine."

Koslo's eyes probed at him. He made a quick gesture with one hand.

"Strap him in."

Seated in the chair, Mallory felt the cold metal suck the heat from his body. Bands restrained his arms, legs, torso. A wide ring of woven wire and plastic clamped his skull firmly to the formed headrest. Across the room, Fey Koslo watched.

"Ready, Excellency," a technician said.

"Proceed."

Mallory tensed. An unwholesome excitement churned his stomach. He'd heard of the chair, of its power to scour a man's mind clean and leave him a glibbering hulk.

Only a free society, he thought, *can produce the technology that makes tyranny possible. . . .*

He watched as a white-smocked technician approached, reached for the control panel. There was only one hope left: if he could fight the power of the machine, drag out the interrogation, delay Koslo until dawn . . .

A needle-studded vise clamped down against Mallory's temples. Instantly his mind ws filled with whirling fever images. He felt his throat tighten in an aborted scream. Fingers of pure force struck into his brain, dislodging old memories, ripping open the healed wounds of time. From somewhere, he was aware of a voice, questioning. Words trembled in his throat, yearning to be shouted aloud.

I've got to resist! The thought flashed through his mind and was gone, borne away on a tide of probing impulses that swept through his brain like a millrace. *I've got to hold out . . . long enough . . . to give the others a chance. . . .*

Aboard the Ree ship, dim lights glowed and winked on the panel that encircled the control center.

I/we sense a new mind—a transmitter of great power, the Perceptors announced suddenly. *But the images are confused. I/we sense struggle, resistance. . . .*

IMPOSE CLOSE CONTROL, the Egon ordered. NARROW FOCUS AND EXTRACT A REPRESENTATIVE PERSONALITY FRACTION!

It is difficult; I/we sense powerful neural currents, at odds with the basic brain rhythms.

COMBAT THEM!

Again the Ree mind reached out, insinuated itself into the complex field-matrix that was Mallory's mind, and began, painstakingly, to trace out and reinforce its native symmetries, permitting the natural ego-mosaic to emerge, free from distracting counter-impulses.

The technician's face went chalk-white as Mallory's body went rigid against the restraining bands.

"You fool!" Koslo's voice cut at him like a whipping rod. "If he dies before he talks—"

"He . . . he fights strongly, Excellency." The man's eyes scanned instrument faces. "Alpha through delta rhythms normal, though exaggerated," he muttered. "Metabolic index .99 . . ."

Mallory's body jerked. His eyes opened, shut. His mouth worked.

"Why doesn't he speak?" Koslo barked.

"It may require a few moments, Excellency, to adjust the power flows to ten-point resonance—"

"Then get on with it, man! I risked too much in arresting this man to lose him now!"

White-hot fingers of pure force landed from the chair along the neural pathways within Mallory's brain—and met the adamantine resistance of the Ree probe. In the resultant confrontation, Mallory's battered self-awareness was tossed like a leaf in a gale.

Fight! The remaining wisp of his conscious intellect gathered itself—

—and was grapsed, encapsulated, swept up and away. He was aware of spinning through a whirling fog of white light shot through with flashes and streamers of red, blue, violet. There was a sensation of great forces that pressed at him, flung him to and fro, drew his mind out like a ductile wire until it spanned the Galaxy. The filament grew broad, expanded into a diaphragm that bisected the universe. The plane assumed thickness, swelled out to encompass all space/time. Faint and far away, he sensed the tumultuous coursing of the energies that ravened just beyond the impenetrable membrane of force—

The imprisoning sphere shrank, pressed in, forcing his awareness into needle-sharp focus. He knew, without knowing how he knew, that he was locked in a sealed and airless chamber, constricting, claustrophobic, all sound and sensation cut off. He drew breath to scream—

No breath came. Only a weak pulse of terror, quickly fading, as if damped by an inhibiting hand. Alone in the dark, Mallory waited, every sense tuned, monitoring the surrounding blankness. . . .

I/we have him! The Perceptors pulsed, and fell away. At the center of the chamber, the mind trap pulsed with the flowing energies that confined and controlled the captive brain pattern.

TESTING WILL COMMENCE AT ONCE. The Egon brushed aside the interrogatory impulses from the mind-segmentsa concerned with speculation. INITIAL STIMULI WILL BE APPLIED AND RESULTS NOTED. NOW!

. . . and was aware of a faint glimmer of light across the room: the outline of a window. He blinked, raised himself on one elbow. Bedsprings creaked under him. He sniffed. An acid odor of smoke hung in the stifling air. He seemed to be in a cheap hotel room. He had no memory of how he came to be there. He threw back the coarse blanket and felt warped floor boards under his bare feet—

The boards were hot.

He jumped up, went to the door, grasped the

knob—and jerked his hand back. The metal had blistered his palm.

He ran to the window, ripped aside the dirt-stiff gauze curtains, snapped open the latch, tugged at the sash. It didn't budge. He stepped back, kicked out the glass. Instantly a coil of smoke whipped in through the broken pane. Using the curtain to protect his hand, he knocked out the shards, swung a leg over the sill, stumbled onto the fire escape. The rusted metal cut at his bare feet. Groping, he made his way down half a dozen steps—and fell back as a sheet of red flame billowed from below.

Over the rail he saw the street, lights puddled on grimy concrete ten stories down, white faces, like pale dots, upturned. A hundred feet away, an extension ladder swayed, approaching another wing of the flaming building, not concerned with him. He was lost, abandoned. Nothing could save him. For forty feet below, the iron ladder was an inferno.

It would be easier, quicker, to go over the rail, escape the pain, die cleanly, the thought came into his mind with dreadful clarity.

There was a tinkling crash and a window above blew out. Scalding embers rained down on his back. The iron was hot underfoot. He drew a breath, shielded his face with one arm, and plunged downward through the whipping flames. . . .

He was crawling, falling down the cruel metal treads and risers. The pain across his face, his back, his shoulder, his arm, was like a red-hot iron, applied and forgotten. He caught a glimpse of his arm, flayed, oozing, black-edged. . . .

His hands and feet were no longer his own. He used his knees and elbows, tumbled himself over yet another edge, sliding down to the next landing. The faces were closer now; hands were reaching up. He groped, got to his feet, felt the last section swing down as his weight went on it. His vision was a blur of red. He sensed the blistered skin sloughing from his thighs. A woman screamed.

". . . my God, burned alive and still walking!" a thin voice cawed.

". . . his hands . . . no fingers . . ."

Something rose, smashed at him, a ghostly blow as blackness closed in . . .

The response of the entity was anomalous, the Analyzers reported. *Its life tenacity is enormous! Confronted with apparent imminent physical destruction, it chose agony and mutilation merely to extend survival for a brief period.*

The possibility exists that such a response represents a mere instinctive mechanism of unusual form, the Analyzers pointed out.

If so, it might prove dangerous. More data on the point is required.

I/WE WILL RESTIMULATE THE SUBJECT, the Egon ordered. THE PARAMETERS OF THE SURVIVAL DRIVE MUST BE ESTABLISHED WITH PRECISION. RESUME TESTING!

In the chair, Mallory writhed, went limp.

"Is he . . . ?"

"He's alive, Excellency! But something's wrong! I can't get through to a vocalization level! He's fighting me with some sort of fantasy-complex of his own!"

"Bring him out of it!"

"Excellency, I tried. I can't reach him! It's as though he'd tapped the chair's energy sources, and were using them to reinforce his own defense mechanism!"

"Override him!"

"I'll try—but his power is fantastic!"

"Then we'll use more power!"

"It's . . . dangerous, Excellency."

"Not more dangerous than failure!"

Grim-faced, the technician reset the panel to step up the energy flow through Mallory's brain.

The subject stirs! the Perceptors burst out. *Massive new energies flow in the mind-field! My/our grip loosens . . .*

HOLD THE SUBJECT! RESTIMULATE AT ONCE, WITH MAXIMUM EMERGENCY FORCE!

While the captive surged and fought against the restraint, the segmented mind of the alien concentrated its forces, hurled a new stimulus into the rolling captive mind-field.

. . . Hot sun beat down on his back. A light wind ruffled the tall grass growing up the slope where the wounded lion had taken cover. Telltale drops of dark purple blood clinging to the tall stems marked the big cat's route. It would be up there, flattened to the earth under the clump of thorn trees, its yellow eyes narrowed against the agony of the .375 bullet wound in his chest, waiting, hoping for its tormentor to come to it. . . .

His heart was thudding; under the damp khaki shirt. The heavy rifle felt like a toy in his hands—a useless plaything against the primitive fury of the beast. He took a step; his mouth twisted in an ironic grimace. What was he proving? There was no one here to know if he chose to walk back and sit under a tree and take a leisurely swig from his flask, let an hour or two crawl by—while the cat bled to death—and then go in to find the body. He took another step. And now he was walking steadily forward. The breeze was cool on his forehead. His legs felt light, strong. He drew a deep breath, smelled the sweetness of the spring air. Life had never seemed more precious—

There was a deep, asthmatic cough, and the great beast broke from the shadows, yellow fangs bared, muscles pumping under the dun hide, dark blood shining black along the flank—

He planted his feet, brought the gun up, socketed it against his shoulder as the lion charged down the slope. *By the book,* he thought sardonically. *Take him just above the sternum, hold on him until you're sure. . . .* At a hundred feet he fired—just as the animal veered left. The bullet smacked home far back along the ribs. The cat broke stride, recovered. The gun bucked and roared again, and the snarling face exploded in a mask of red— And still the dying carnivore came on. He blinked sweat from his eyes, centered the sights on the point of the shoulder—

The trigger jammed hard. A glance showed him the spent cartridge lodged in the action. He raked at it vainly, standing his ground. At the last instant, he stepped aside, and the hurtling monster skidded past him, dead in the dust. And the thought that struck him then was that if Monica had been watching from the car at the foot of the hill she would not have laughed at him this time. . . .

Again the reaction syndrome is inharmonious with any concept of rationality in my/our experience, the Recollector cells expressed the paradox with which the captive mind had presented the Ree intelligence.

Here is an entity which clings to personality survival with a ferocity unparalleled—yet faces Category Ultimate risks needlessly, in response to an abstract code of behavioral symmetry.

I/we postulate that the personality segment selected does not represent the true Egon-analogue of the subject, the Speculators offered. *It is obviously incomplete, nonviable.*

Let me/us attempt a selective withdrawal of control over peripheral regions of the mind-field, the Perceptors proposed. *Thus permitting greater concentration of stimulus to the central matrix.*

By matching energies with the captive mind, it will be possible to monitor its rhythms and deduce the key to its total control, the Calculators determined quickly.

This course offers the risk of rupturing the matrix and the destruction of the specimen.

THE RISK MUST BE TAKEN.

With infinite precision, the Ree mind narrowed the scope of its probe, fitting its shape to the contours of Mallory's embattled brain, matching itself in a one-to-one correspondence to the massive energy flows from the Interrogation chair.

Equilibrium, the Perceptors reported at last. *However, the balance is precarious.*

The next test must be designed to expose new aspects of the subject's survival syndrome, the Analyzers pointed out. A stimulus pattern was proposed and accepted. Aboard the ship in its sub-lunar orbit, the Ree mindbeam again lanced out to touch Mallory's receptive brain. . . .

Blackness gave way to misty light. A deep rumbling shook the rocks under his feet. Through the whirling spray, he saw the raft, the small figure that clung to it: a child, a little girl perhaps nine years old, crouched on hands and knees, looking toward him.

"Daddy!" A high, thin cry of pure terror. The raft bucked and tossed in the wild current. He took a step, slipped, almost went down on the slimy rocks. The icy water swirled about his knees. A hundred feet downstream, the river curved in a gray-metal sheen, over and down, veiled by the mists of its own thunderous descent. He turned, scrambled back up, ran along the bank. There, ahead, a point of rock jutted. Perhaps . . .

The raft bobbed, whirled, fifty feet away. Too far. He saw the pale, small face, the pleading eyes. Fear welled in him, greasy and sickening.

Visions of death rose up, of his broken body bobbing below the falls, lying wax-white on a slab, sleeping, powdered and false in a satin-lined box, corrupting in the close darkness under the indifferent sod. . . .

He took a trembling step back.

For an instant, a curious sensation of unreality swept over him. He remembered darkness, a sense of utter claustrophobia—and a white room, a face that leaned close. . . .

He blinked—and through the spray of the rapids, his eyes met those of the doomed child. Compassion struck him like a club. He grunted, felt the clean white flame of anger at himself, of disgust at his fear. He closed his eyes and leaped far out, struck the water and went under, came up gasping. His strokes took him toward the raft. He felt a heavy blow as the current tossed him against a rock, choked as chopping spray whipped in his face. The thought came that broken ribs didn't matter now, nor air for breathing. Only to reach the raft before it reached the edge, that the small, frightened soul might not go down alone—into the great darkness. . . .

His hands clawed the rough wood. He pulled himself up, caught the small body to him as the world dropped away and the thunder rose deafeningly to meet him. . . .

"Excellency! I need help!" The technician appealed to the grim-faced dictator. "I'm pouring enough power through his brain to kill two ordinary men—and he still fights back! For a second there, a moment ago, I'd swear he opened his eyes and looked right through me! I can't take the responsibility—"

"Then cut the power, you blundering idiot!"

"I don't dare, the backlash will kill him!"

"He . . . must . . . talk!" Koslo grated. Hold him! Break him! Or I promise you a slow and terrible death!"

Trembling, the technician adjusted his controls. In the chair, Mallory sat tense, no longer fighting the straps. He looked like a man lost in thought. Perspiration broke from his hairline, trickled down his face.

Again new currents stir in the captive; the Perceptors announced in alarm. *The resources of this mind are staggering!*

MATCH IT! the Egon directed.

My/our power resources are already overextended! the Calculators interjected.

WITHDRAW ENERGIES FROM ALL PERIPHERAL FUNCTIONS! LOWER SHIELDING! THE MOMENT OF THE ULTIMATE TEST IS UPON ME/US!

Swiftly the Ree mind complied.

The captive is held, the Calculator announced. *But*

I/we point out that this linkage now presents a channel of vulnerability to assault.

THE RISK MUST BE TAKEN.

Even now the mind stirs against my/our countrol.

HOLD IT FAST!

Grimly, the Ree mind fought to retain its control of Mallory's brain.

In one instant, he was not. Then, abruptly, he existed. *Mallory,* he thought. *That symbol represents I/we. . . .*

The alien thought faded. He caught at it, held the symbol. Mallory. He remembered the shape of his body, the feel of his skull enclosing his brain, the sensations of light, sound, heat—but here there ws no sound, no light. Only the enclosing blackness, impenetrable, eternal, changeless. . . .

But where was here?

He remembered the white room, the harsh voice of Koslo, the steel chair—

And the mighty roar of the waters rushing up at him—

And the reaching talons of a giant cat—

And the searing agony of flames that licked around his body. . . .

But there was no pain, now, no discomfort—no sensation of any kind. Was this death, then? At once, he rejected the idea as nonsense.

Cogito ergo sum. I am a prisoner—where?

His senses stirred, questing against emptiness, sensationlessness. He strained outward—and heard sound; voices, pleading, demanding. They grew louder, echoing in the vastness:

". . . talk, damn you! Who are your chief accomplices? What support do you expect from the Armed Forces? Which of the generals are with you? Armaments . . . ? Organization . . . ? Initial attack points . . . ?"

Blinding static sleeted across the words, filled the universe, grew dim. For an instant, Mallory was aware of straps cutting into the tensed muscles of his forearms, the pain of the band clamped around his head, the ache of cramping muscles. . . .

. . . was aware of floating, gravityless, in a sea of winking, flashing energies. Vertigo rose up; frantically he fought for stability in a world of chaos. Through spinning darkness he reached, found a matrix of pure direction, intangible, but, against the background of shifting energy flows, providing an orienting grid. He seized on it, hold. . . .

Full emergency discharge! the Receptors blasted the command through all the sixty-nine hundred and thirty-four units of the Ree mind—and recoiled in shock. *The captive mind clings to the contact! We cannot break free!*

Pulsating with the enormous shock of the prisoner's sudden out-lashing, the alien rested for the fractional nanosecond required to restablish inter-segmental balance.

The power of the enemy, though unprecedently great, is not sufficient to broach the integrity of my/our entityfield, the Analyzers stated, tensely. *But I/we must retreat at once!*

NO! I/WE LACK SUFFICIENT DATA TO JUSTIFY WITHDRAWAL OF PHASE ONE, the Egon countermanded. HERE IS A MIND RULED BY CONFLICTING DRIVES OF GREAT POWER. WHICH IS PARAMOUNT? THEREIN LIES THE KEY TO ITS DEFEAT.

I/WE MUST DEVISE A STIMULATION COM-

PLEX WHICH WILL EVOKE BOTH DRIVES IN LETHAL OPPOSITION.

Precious microseconds passed while the compound mind hastily scanned Mallory's mind for symbols from which to assemble the necessary gestalt-form.

Ready, the Perceptors announced. *But it must be pointed out that no mind can long survive intact the direct confrontation of these antagonistic imperatives. Is the stimulus to be carried to the point of nonretrieval?*

AFFIRMATIVE. The Egon's tone was one of utter finality. TEST TO DESTRUCTION.

Illusion, Mallory told himself. *I'm being bombarded by illusions. . . .* He sensed the approach of a massive new wave front, descending on him like a breaking Pacific comber. Grimly, he clung to his tenuous orientation—But the smashing impact whirled him into darkness. Far away, a masked inquisitor faced him.

"Pain has availed nothing against you," the muffled voice said. "The threat of death does not move you. And yet there is a way. . . ." A curtain fell aside, and Monica stood there, tall, slim, vibrantly alive, as beautiful as a roe-deer. And beside her, the child.

He said "No!" and started forward, but the chains held him. He watched, helpless, while brutal hands seized the woman, moved casually, intimately, over her body. Other hands gripped the child. He saw the terror on the small face, the fear in her eyes—

Fear that he had seen before. . . .

But of course he had seen her before. The child was his daughter, the precious offspring of himself and the slender female—

Monica, he corrected himself.

—had seen those eyes, through swirling mist, poised above a cataract—

No. That was a dream. A dream in which he had died, violently. And there had been another dream of facing a wounded lion as it charged down on him—

"You will not be harmed," the Inquisitor's voice seemed to come from a remote distance. "But you will carry with you forever the memory of their living dismemberment. . . ."

With a jerk, his attention returned to the woman and the child. He saw them strip Monica's slender, tawny body. Naked, she stood before them, refusing to cower. But of what use was courage now? The manacles at her wrists were linked to a hook set in the damp stone wall. The glowing iron moved closer to her white flesh. He saw the skin darken and blister. The iron plunged home. She stiffened, screamed . . . .

A woman screamed.

"My God, burned alive," a thin voice cawed. "And still walking!"

He looked down. There was no wound, no scar. The skin was unbroken. But a fleeting almost-recollection came of cracking flames that seared with a white agony as he drew them into his lungs. . . .

"A dream," he said aloud. "I'm dreaming. I have to wake up!" He closed his eyes and shook his head. . . .

"He shook his head!" the technician choked. "Excellency, it's impossible—but I swear the man is throwing off the machine's control!"

Koslo brushed the other roughly aside. He seized the control lever, pushed it forward. In the chair,

Mallory stiffened. His breathing became hoarse, ragged.

"Excellency, the man will die . . . !"

"Let him die! No one defies me with impunity!"

Narrow focus! the Perceptors flashed the command to the sixty-nine hundred and thirty four energy-producing segments of the Ree mind. *The contest cannot continue long! Almost we lost the captive then . . . !*

The probe beam narrowed, knifing into the living heart of Mallory's brain, imposing its chosen patterns. . . .

. . . the child whimpered as the foot-long blade approached her fragile breast. The gnarled fist holding the knife stroked it almost lovingly across the blue-veined skin. Crimson blood washed down from the shallow wound.

"If you reveal the secrets of the Brotherhood to me, truly your comrades in arms will die," the Inquisitor's faceless voice droned. "But if you stubbornly refuse, your woman and your infant will suffer all that my ingenuity can devise."

He strained against his chains. "I can't tell you," he croaked. "Don't you understand, nothing is worth this horror! Nothing. . . ."

Nothing he could have done would have saved her. She crouched on the raft, doomed. But he could join her—

But not this time. This time chains of steel kept him from her. He hurled himself against them, and tears blinded his eyes. . . .

Smoke blinded his eyes. He looked down, saw the faces upturned below. Surely, easy death was preferable to living immolation. But he covered his face with his arms and started down. . . .

Never betray your trust! The woman's voice rang clear as a trumpet across the narrow dungeon.

Daddy! the child screamed.

We can die only once! the woman called.

The raft plunged downward into boiling chaos. . . .

"Speak, damn you!" the Inquisitor's voice had taken on a new note. "I want the names, the places! Who are your accomplices? What are your plans? When will the rising begin? What signal are they waiting for? Where . . . ? When . . . ?"

Mallory opened his eyes. Blinding white light, a twisted face that loomed before him goggling.

"Excellency! He's awake! He's broken through. . . ."

"Pour full power into him! Force, man! Force him to speak!"

"I—I'm afraid, Excellency! We're tampering with the mightiest instrument in the universe: a human brain! Who knows what we may be creating—"

Koslo struck the man aside, threw the control lever full against the stop.

. . . The darkness burst into a coruscating brilliance that became the outlines of a room. A transparent man whom he recognized as Koslo stood before him. He watched as the dictator turned to him, his face contorted.

"Now talk, damn you!"

His voice had a curious, ghostly quality, as though it represented only one level of reality.

"Yes," Mallory said distinctly. "I'll talk."

"And if you lie—" Koslo jerked an ugly automatic pistol from the pocket of his plain tunic. "I'll put a bullet in your brain myself!"

"My chief associates in the plot," Mallory began, "are . . ." As he spoke, he gently disengaged himself—that was the word that came to his mind—from the scene around him. He was aware at one level of his voice speaking on, reeling off the facts for which the other man hungered so nakedly. And he reached out, channeling the power pouring into him from the chair . . . spanning across vast distances compressed now to a dimensionless plane. Delicately, he quested farther, entered a curious, flickering net of living energies. He pressed, found points of weakness, poured in more power—

A circular room leaped into eerie visibility. Ranged around it were lights that winked and glowed. From ranked thousands of cells, white wormforms poked blunt, eyeless heads. . . .

HE IS HERE! The Egon shrieked the warning, and hurled a bolt of pure mind-force along the channel of contact and met a counter-bolt of energy that seared through him, blackened and charred the intricate organic circuitry of his cerebrum, left a smoking pocket in the rank of cells. For a moment, Mallory rested, sensing the shock and bewilderment sweeping through the leaderless Ree mind-segments. He felt the automatic death-urge that gripped them as the realization reached them that the guiding overpower of the Egon was gone. As he watched, a unit crumpled inward and expired. And another—

"Stop!" Mallory commanded. "I assume control of the mind-complex! Let the segments link in with me!"

Obediently, the will-less fragments of the Ree mind obeyed.

"Change course," Mallory ordered. He gave the

necessary instructions, then withdrew along the channel of contact.

"So . . . the great Mallory broke." Koslo rocked on his heels before the captive body of his enemy. He laughed. "You were slow to start, but once begun you sang like a turtledove. I'll give my orders now, and by dawn your futile revolt will be a heap of charred corpses stacked in the plaza as an example to others!" He raised the gun.

"I'm not through yet," Mallory said. "The plot runs deeper than you think, Koslo."

The dictator ran a hand over his gray face. His eyes showed the terrible strain of the last hours.

"Talk, then," he growled. "Talk fast!"

As he spoke on, Mallory again shifted his primary awareness, settled into resonance with the subjugated Ree intelligence. Through the ship's sensors, he saw the white planet swelling ahead. He slowed the vessel, brought it in on a long parabolic course which skimmed the stratosphere. Seventy miles above the Atlantic, he entered a high haze layer, slowed again as he sensed the heating of the hull.

Below the clouds, he sent the ship hurtling across the coast. He dropped to treetop level, scanned the scene through sensitive hull-plates—

For a long moment he studied the landscape below. Then suddenly he understood. . . .

"Why do you smile, Mallory?" Koslo's voice was harsh; the gun pointed at the other's head. "Tell me the joke that makes a man laugh in the condemned seat reserved for traitors."

"You'll know in just a moment. . . ." He broke off as a crashing sound came from beyond the room. The floor shook and trembled, rocking Koslo on his feet. A dull boom echoed. The door burst wide.

"Excellency! The capital is under attack!" The man fell forward, exposing a great wound on his back. Koslo whirled on Mallory—

With a thunderous crash, one side of the room bulged and fell inward. Through the broached wall, a glittering torpedo-shape appeared, a polished intricacy of burnished metal floating lightly on pencils of blue-white light. The gun in the hand of the dictator came up, crashed deafeningly in the enclosed space. From the prow of the invader, pink light winked. Koslo spun, fell heavily on his face.

The twenty-eight inch Ree dreadnought came to rest before Mallory. A beam speared out, burned through the chair control panel. The shackles fell away.

I/we await your/our next command. The Ree mind spoke soundlessly in the awesome silence.

Three months had passed since the referendum which had swept John Mallory into office as Premier of the First Planetary Republic. He stood in a room of his spacious apartment in the Executive Palace, frowning at the slender black-haired woman as she spoke earnestly to him:

"John—I'm afraid of that—that infernal machine, eternally hovering, waiting for your orders."

"But why, Monica? That infernal machine, as you call it, was the thing that made a free election possible—and even now it's all that holds Koslo's old organization in check."

"John—" Her hand gripped his arm. "With that—thing—always at your beck and call, you can control anyone, anything on Earth! No opposition can stand before you!"

She looked directly at him. "It isn't right for anyone to have such power, John. Not even you. No human being should be put to such a test!"

His face tightened. "Have I misused it?"

"Not yet. That's why . . ."

"You imply that I will?"

"You're a man, with the failings of a man."

"I propose only what's good for the people of Earth," he said sharply. "Would you have me voluntarily throw away the one weapon that can protect our hard-won freedom?"

"But, John—who are you to be the sole arbiter of what's good for the people of Earth?"

"I'm Chairman of the Republic—"

"You're still human. Stop—while you're still human!"

He studied her face. "You resent my success, don't you? What would you have me do? Resign?"

"I want you to send the machine away—back to wherever it came from."

He laughed shortly. "Are you out of your mind? I haven't begun to extract the technological secrets the Ree ship represents."

"We're not ready for those secrets, John. The race isn't ready. It's already changed you. In the end it can only destroy you as a man."

"Nonsense. I control it utterly. It's like an extension of my own mind—"

"John—please. If not for my sake or your own, for Dian's."

"What's the child got to do with this?"

"She's your daughter. She hardly sees you once a week."

"That's the price she has to pay for being the heir

to the greatest man— I mean—damn it, Monica, my responsibilities don't permit me to indulge in all the suburban customs."

"John—" Her voice was a whisper, painful in its intensity. "Send it away."

"No. I won't send it away."

Her face was pale. "Very well, John. As you wish."

"Yes. As I wish."

After she left the room, Mallory stood for a long time staring out through the high window at the tiny craft, hovering in the blue air fifty feet away, silent, ready.

Then: *Ree mind*, he sent out the call. *Probe the apartments of the woman, Monica. I have reason to suspect she plots treason against the state. . . .*

AFTERWORD

The process of writing a story is often as enlightening for me as, hopefully, for the reader.

I began with the concept of submitting a human being to an ultimate trial in the same way that an engineer will load a beam until it collapses, testing it to destruction. It is in emotional situations that we meet our severest tests: fear, love, anger, drive us to our highest efforts. Thus, the framework of the story suggested itself.

As the tale evolved, it became apparent that any power setting out to put mankind to the test as did Koslo and the Ree—places its own fate in the balance.

In the end, Mallory revealed the true strength of man by using the power of his enemies against them.

He wins not only his freedom and sanity—but also immense new powers over other men.

Not until then did the danger in such total victory become apparent. The ultimate test of man is his ability to master himself.

It is a test which we have so far failed.

In the Queue

The old man fell just as Farn Hestler's power wheel was passing his Place in Line, on his way back from the Comfort Station. Hestler, braking, stared down at the twisted face, a mask of soft, pale leather in which the mouth writhed as if trying to tear itself free of the dying body. Then he jumped from the wheel, bent over the victim. Quick as he was, a lean woman with fingers like gnarled roots was before him, clutching at the old man's fleshless shoulders.

"Tell them *me*, Millicent Dredgewicke Klunt," she was shrilling into the vacant face. "Oh, if you only knew what I've been through, how I *deserve* the help—"

Hestler sent her reeling with a deft shove of his foot. He knelt beside the old man, lifted his head.

"Vultures," he said. "Greedy, snapping at a man. Now, I *care*. And you were getting so close to the Head of the Line. The tales you could tell, I'll bet. An Old-timer. Not like these Line, er, jumpers," he diverted the obscenity. "I say a man deserves a little dignity at a moment like this—"

"Wasting your time, Jack," a meaty voice said. Hestler glanced up into the hippopotamine features of the man he always thought of as Twentieth Back. "The old coot's dead."

Hestler shook the corpse. "Tell them Argall F. Hestler!" he yelled into the dead ear. "Argall, that's A-R-G-A-L-L—"

"Break it up," the brassy voice of a Line Policeman sliced through the babble. "You, get back." A sharp prod lent urgency to the command. Hestler rose reluctantly, his eyes on the waxy face slackening into an expression of horrified astonishment.

"Ghoul," the lean woman he had kicked snarled. "Line—!" She mouthed the unmentionable word.

"I wasn't thinking of myself," Hestler countered hotly. "But my boy Argall, through no fault of his own—"

"All right, quiet!" the cop snarled. He jerked a thumb at the dead man. "This guy make any disposition?"

"Yes!" the lean woman cried. "He said, to Millicent Dredgewicke Klunt, that's M-I-L—"

"She's lying," Hestler cut in. "I happened to catch the name Argall Hestler—right, sir?" He looked brightly at a slack-jawed lad who was staring down at the corpse.

The boy swallowed and looked Hestler in the face. "Hell, he never said a word," he said, and spat, just missing Hestler's shoe.

"Died intestate," the cop intoned, and wrote a note in his book. He gestured and a clean-up squad moved in, lifted the corpse onto a cart, covered it, trundled it away.

"Close it up," the cop ordered.

"Intestate," somebody grumbled. "Crap!"

"A rotten shame. The slot goes back to the government. Nobody profits. Goddamn!" the fat man who had spoken looked around at the others. "In a case like this we ought to get together, have some equitable plan worked out and agreed to in advance—"

"Hey," the slack-jawed boy said. "That's conspiracy!"

"I meant to suggest nothing illegal." The fat man faded back to his Place in Line. As if by common consent, the small crowd dissipated, sliding into their Places with deft footwork. Hestler shrugged and remounted his wheel, put-putted forward, aware of the envious eyes that followed him. He passed the same backs he always passed, some standing, some sitting on canvas camp stools under sun-faded umbrellas, here and there a nylon queuebana, high and square, some shabby, some ornate, owned by the more fortunate. Like himself: he was a lucky man, he had never been a Standee, sweating the Line exposed to the sun and prying eyes.

It was a bright afternoon. The sun shone down on the vast concrete ramp across which the Line snaked from a point lost in distance across the plain. Ahead—not far ahead now, and getting closer every day—was the blank white wall perforated only by the Window, the terminal point of the Line. Hestler slowed as he approached the Hestler queuebana; his mouth went dry as he saw how close it was to the Head of the Line now. One, two, three, four slots back! Ye Gods, that meant six people had been processed in the past twelve hours—an unprecedented number. And it meant—Hestler caught his breath—he might reach the Window himself, this shift. For a moment, he felt a panicky urge to flee, to trade places with First Back, and then with Second, work his way back to a safe distance, give himself a chance to think about it, get ready. . . .

"Say, Farn," the head of his proxy, Cousin Galpert, poked from the curtains of the three foot square, five foot high nylon-walled queuebana. "Guess what? I moved up a spot while you were gone."

Hestler folded the wheel and leaned it against the weathered cloth. He waited until Galpert had emerged, then surreptitiously twitched the curtains wide open. The place always smelled fudgy and stale after his cousin had spent half an hour in it while he was away for his Comfort Break.

"We're getting close to the Head," Galpert said excitedly, handing over the lockbox that contained the Papers. "I have a feeling—" He broke off as sharp voices were suddenly raised a few Spaces behind. A small, pale-haired man with bulging blue eyes was attempting to force himself into Line between Third Back and Fifth Back.

"Say, isn't that Four Back?" Hestler asked.

"You don't understand," the little man was whimpering. "I had to go answer an unscheduled call of nature. . . ." His weak eyes fixed on Fifth Back, a large, coarse-featured man in a loud shirt and sunglasses. "You said you'd watch my Place . . . !"

"So whattaya think ya got a Comfort Break for, ya bum! Beat it!"

Lots of people were shouting at the little man now:

"Line-ine-ucker-bucker—Line bucker, Line bucker. . . ."

The little man fell back, covering his ears. The obscene chant gained in volume as other voices took it up.

"But it's my *Place,*" the evictee wailed. "Father

left it to me when he died, you all remember him. . . ." His voice was drowned in the uproar.

"Serves him right," Galpert said, embarrassed by the chant. "A man with no more regard for his inheritance than to walk off and leave it. . . ."

They watched the former Fourth Back turn and flee, his hands still over his ears.

After Galpert left on the wheel, Hestler aired the queuebana for another ten minutes, standing stony-faced, arms folded, staring at the back of One Up. His father had told him some stories about One Up, back in the old days, when they'd both been young fellows, near the end of the Line. Seemed he'd been quite a cutup in those days, always joking around with the women close to him in Line, offering to trade Places for a certain consideration. You didn't see many signs of that now: just a dumpy old man in burst-out shoe-leather, sweating out the Line. But he himself was lucky, Hestler reflected. He'd taken over from Father when the latter had had his stroke, a twenty-one thousand two hundred and ninety-four slot jump. Not many young fellows did that well. Not that he was all that young, he'd put in his time in the Line, it wasn't as if he didn't deserve the break.

And now, in a few hours maybe, he'd hit the Head of the Line. He touched the lockbox that contained the old man's Papers—and of course his own, and Cluster's and the kids'—everything. In a few hours, if the Line kept moving, he could relax, retire, let the kids, with their own Places in Line, carry on. Let them do as well as their dad had done, making Head of the Line at under forty-five!

Inside the queuebana it was hot, airless. Hestler pulled off his coat and squatted in the crouch-hammock—not the most comfortable position in the world, maybe, but in full compliance with the Q-law requirement that at least one foot be on the ground at all times, and the head higher than the waist. Hestler remembered an incident years before, when some poor devil without a queuebana had gone to sleep standing up. He'd stood with his eyes closed and his knees bent, and slowly sunk down to a squat; then bobbed slowly up and blinked and went back to sleep. Up and down, they'd watched him for an hour before he finally let his head drop lower than his belt. They'd pitched him out of Line then, and closed ranks. Ah, there'd been some wild times in the queue in the old days, not like now. There was too much at stake now, this near the Head. No time for horseplay.

Just before dusk, the Line moved up. Three to go! Hestler's heart thumped.

It was dark when he heard the voice whisper: "*Four Up!*"

Hestler jerked wide awake. He blinked, wondering if he'd dreamed the urgent tone.

"Four Up!" the voice hissed again. Hestler twitched the curtain open, saw nothing, pulled his head back in. Then he saw the pale, pinched face, the bulging eyes of Four Back, peering through the vent slot at the rear of the tent.

"You have to help me," the little man said. "You saw what happened, you can make a deposition that I was cheated, that— "

"Look here, what are you doing out of Line?" Hestler cut in. "I know you're on-shift, why aren't you holding down a new slot?"

"I . . . I couldn't face it," Four Back said brokenly. "My wife, my children—they're all counting on me."

"You should have thought of that sooner."

"I swear I couldn't help it. It just hit me so suddenly. And— "

"You lost your Place. There's nothing I can do."

"If I have to start over now—I'll be over seventy when I get to the Window!"

"That's not my lookout—"

". . . but if you'll just tell the Line Police what happened, explain about my special case—"

"You're crazy, I can't do that!"

"But you . . . I always thought you looked like a decent sort— "

"You'd better go. Suppose someone sees me talking to you?"

"I had to speak to you here, I don't know your name, but after all we've been four Spaces apart in Line for nine years—"

"Go away! Before I call a Line cop!"

Hestler had a hard time getting comfortable again after Four Back left. There was a fly inside the queuebana. It was a hot night. The Line moved up again, and Hestler had to emerge and roll the queuebana forward. Two Spaces to go! The feeling of excitement was so intense that it made Hestler feel a little sick. Two more moves up, and he'd be at the Window. He'd open the lockbox, and present the Papers, taking his time, one at a time, getting it all correct, all in order, With a sudden pang of panic he wondered if anyone had goofed, anywhere back along the line, failed to sign anything, missed a Notary's seal or a witness' signature. But they couldn't have. Nothing as dumb as that. For that you could get bounced out of Line, lose your Place, have to go all the way back—

Hestler shook off the morbid fancies. He was just nervous, that was all. Well, who wouldn't be? After tonight, his whole life would be different; his days of standing in Line would be over. He'd have time—all the time in the world to do all the things he hadn't been able to think about all these years. . . .

Someone shouted, near at hand. Hestler stumbled out of the queuebana to see Two Up—at the Head of the Line now—raise his fist and shake it under the nose of the small, black-moustached face in the green eye-shade framed in the Window, bathed in harsh white light.

"Idiot! Dumbbell! Jackass!" Two Up yelled. "What do you mean take it back home and have my wife spell out her middle name!"

Two burly Line police appeared, shone lights in Two Up's wild face, grabbed his arms, took him away. Hestler trembled as he pushed the queuebana forward a Space on its roller skate wheels. Only one man ahead of him now. He'd be next. But no reason to get all upset; the Line had been moving like greased lightning, but it would take a few hours to process the man ahead. He had time to relax, get his nerves soothed down, get ready to answer questions. . . .

"I don't understand, sir," the reedy voice of One Up was saying to the small black moustache behind the Window. "My Papers are all in order, I swear it—"

"You said yourself your father is dead," the small, dry voice of Black Moustache said. "That means you'll have to reexecute Form 56839847565342-B in sextuplicate, with an endorsement from the medical doctor, the Residential Police, and waivers from Department A, B, C, and so on. You'll find it all, right in the Regulations."

"But—but he only died two hours ago: I just received word— "

"Two hours, two years; he's just as dead."

"But—I'll lose my Place! If I hadn't mentioned it to you—"

"Then I wouldn't have known about it. But you did mention it, quite right, too."

"Couldn't you just pretend I didn't say anything? That the messenger never reached me?"

"Are you suggesting I commit fraud?"

"No . . . no . . . ." One Up turned and tottered away, his invalidated Papers clutched in his hand. Hestler swallowed hard.

"Next," Black Moustache said.

It was almost dawn six hours later when the clerk stamped the last Paper, licked the last stamp, thrust the stack of processed documents into a slot and looked past Hestler at the next man in Line.

Hestler hesitated, holding the empty lockbox in nerveless fingers. It felt abnormally light, like a cast husk.

"That's all," the clerk said. "Next."

One Down jostled Hestler getting to the Window. He was a small, bandy-legged Standee with large, loose lips and long ears. Hestler had never really looked at him before. He felt an urge to tell him all about how it had been, give him a few friendly tips, as an old Window veteran to a newcomer. But the man didn't give him a glance.

Moving off, Hestler noticed the queuebana. It looked abandoned, functionless. He thought of all the hours, the days, the years he had spent in it, crouched in the sling. . . .

"You can have it," he said on impulse to Two Down, who, he noted with surprise, was a woman, dumpy, slack-jowled. He gestured toward the queue-bana. She made a snorting sound and ignored him. He wandered off down the Line, staring curiously at the people in it, at the varied faces and figures, tall, wide, narrow, old, young—not so many of those—dressed in used clothing, with hair combed or uncombed, some with facial hair, some with paint on their lips, all unattractive in their own individual ways.

He encountered Galpert whizzing toward him on the powerwheel. Galpert slowed, gaping, came to a halt. Hestler noticed that his cousin had thin, bony ankles in maroon socks, one of which suffered from perished elastic so that the sock drooped, exposing clay-white skin.

"Farn—what . . . ?"

"All done." Hestler held up the empty lockbox.

"All done . . . ?" Galpert looked across toward the distant Window in a bewildered way.

"All done. Not much to it, really."

"Then . . . I . . . I guess I don't need to . . ." Galpert's voice died away.

"No, no need, never again, Galpert."

"Yes, but what . . . ?" Galpert looked at Hestler, looked at the Line, back at Hestler. "You coming, Farn?"

"I . . . I think I'll just take a walk for a while. Savor it, you know."

"Well," Galpert said. He started up the wheel and rode slowly off across the ramp.

Suddenly, Hestler was thinking about time—all that time stretching ahead, like an abyss. What would he do with it . . . ? He almost called after Galpert, but instead turned and continued his walk along the Line. Faces stared past him, over him, through him.

Noon came and went. Hestler obtained a dry hot dog and a paper cup of warm milk from a vendor on a three-wheeler with a big umbrella and a pet chicken perched on the back. He walked on, searching the faces. They were all so ugly. He pitied them, so far from the Window. He looked back; it was barely visible, a tiny dark point toward which the Line dwindled. What did they think about, standing in Line? How they must envy him!

But no one seemed to notice him. Toward sunset he began to feel lonely. He wanted to talk to someone; but none of the faces he passed seemed sympathetic.

It was almost dark when he reached the End of the Line. Beyond, the empty plain stretched toward the dark horizon. It looked cold out there, lonely.

"It looks cold out there," he heard himself say to the oatmeal-faced lad who huddled at the tail of the Line, hands in pockets. "And lonely."

"You in Line, or what?" the boy asked.

Hestler looked again at the bleak horizon. He came over and stood behind the youth.

"Certainly," he said.

Here is an excerpt from Book I of THE KING OF YS, Poul and Karen Anderson's epic new fantasy, coming from Baen Books in December 1986:

THE KING OF YS: ROMA MATER

POUL AND KAREN ANDERSON

The parties met nearer the shaw than the city. They halted a few feet apart. For a space there was stillness, save for the wind.

The man in front was a Gaul, Gratillonius judged. He was huge, would stand a head above the centurion when they were both on the ground, with a breadth of shoulder and thickness of chest that made him look squat. His paunch simply added to the sense of bear strength. His face was broad, ruddy, veins broken in the flattish nose, a scar zigzagging across the brow ridges that shelved small ice-blue eyes. Hair knotted into a queue, beard abristle to the shaggy breast, were brown, and had not been washed for a long while. His loose-fitting shirt and close-fitting breeches were equally soiled. At his hip he kept a knife, and slung across his back was a sword more than a yard in length. A fine golden chain hung around his neck, but what it bore lay hidden beneath the shirt.

"Romans," he rumbled in Osismian. "What the pox brings you mucking around here?"

The centurion replied carefully, as best he was able in the same language: "Greeting. I hight Gaius Valerius Gratillonius, come in peace and good will as the new prefect of Rome in Ys. Fain would I meet with your leaders."

Meanwhile he surveyed those behind. Half a dozen were men of varying ages, in neat and clean versions of the same garb, unarmed. Nearest the Gaul stood one who differed. He was ponderous of body and countenance. Black beard and receding hair were flecked with white, though he did not seem old. He wore a crimson robe patterned with gold thread, a miter of the same stuff, a talisman hanging on his bosom that was in the form of a wheel, cast in precious metal and set with jewels. Rings sparkled on both hands. In his right he bore a staff as high as himself, topped by a silver representation of a boar's head.

The woman numbered three. They were in ankle-length gowns with loose sleeves to the wrists, of rich material and subtle hues, ornately belted at the waist.

The Gaul's voice yanked him from his inspection: "What? You'd strut in out of nowhere and fart your orders at *me*—you who can talk no better than a frog? Go back before I step on the lot of you."

"I think you are drunk," Gratillonius said truthfully.

"Not too full of wine to piss you out, Roman!" the other bawled.

Gratillonius forced coolness upon himself. "Who here is civilized?" he asked in Latin.

The man in the red robe stepped forward. "Sir, we request you to kindly overlook the mood of the King," he responded in the same tongue, accented but fairly fluent. "His vigil ended at dawn today, but these his Queens sent word for us to wait. I formally attended him to and from the Wood, you see. Only in this past hour was I bidden to come."

The man shrugged and smiled. My name is Soren Cartagi, Speaker for Taranis."

The Gaul turned on him, grabbed him by his garment and shook him. "You'd undercut me, plotting in Roman, would you?" he grated. A fist drew back. "Well, I've not forgotten all of it. I know when a scheme's afoot against me. And I know you think Colconor is stupid, but you've a nasty surprise coming to you, potgut!"

The male attendants showed horror. One of the woman hurried forth. "Are you possessed, Colconor?" she demanded. "Soren's person when he speaks for the God is sacred. Let him go ere Taranis blasts you to a cinder!"

The language she used was neither Latin nor Osismian. Melodious, it seemed essentially Celtic, but full of words and constructions Gratillonius had never encountered before. It must be the language of Ys. By listening hard and straining his wits, he got the drift if not the full meaning.

The Gaul released the Speaker, who stumbled back, and rounded on the woman. She stood defiant— tall, lean, her hatchet features haggard but her eyes like great, lustrous pools of darkness. The cowl, fallen down in her hasty movement, revealed a mane of black hair, loosely gathered under a fillet, through the middle of which ran a white streak. Gratillonius sensed implacable hatred as she went on: "Five years have we endured you, Colconor, and weary years they were. If now you'd fain bring your doom on yourself, oh, be very welcome."

Rage reddened him the more. "Ah, so that's your game, Vindilis, my pet?" His own Ysan was easier for Gratillonius to follow, being heavily Osismianized. " 'Twas sweet enough you were this threenight agone, and today. But inwardly—Ah, I should have known. You were ever more man than woman, Vindilis, and hex more than either."

He swung on Gratillonius. "Go, Roman!" he roared. "I am the King! By the iron rod of Taranis, I'll not take Roman orders! Go or stay; but if you stay, 'twill be on the dungheap where I'll toss your carcass!"

Gratillonius fought for self-control. Despite Colconor's behavior, he was dimly surprised at his instant, lightning-sharp hatred for the man. "I have prior orders," he answered, as steadily as he could. To Soren, in Latin: "Sir, can't you stay this madman so we can talk in quiet?"

Colconor understood. "Madman, be I?" he shrieked. "Why, *you* were shit out of your harlot mother's arse, where your donkey father begot you ere they gelded him. Back to your swinesty of a Rome!"

It flared in Gratillonius. His vinestaff was tucked at his saddlebow. He snatched it forth, leaned down, and gave Colconor a cut across the lips. Blood jumped from the wound.

Colconor leaped back and grabbed at his sword. The Ysan men flung themselves around him. Gratillonius heard Soren's resonant voice: "Nay, not here. It must be in the Wood, the Wood." He sounded almost happy. The women stood aside. Vindilis put hands on hips, threw back her head, and laughed aloud.

Eppillus stepped to his centurion's shin, glanced up, and said anxiously, "Looks like a brawl, sir. We can handle it. Give the word, and we'll make sausage meat of that bastard."

Gratillonius shook his head. A presentiment was eldritch upon him. "No," he replied softly. "I think this is something I must do myself, or else lose the respect we'll need in Ys."

Colconor stopped struggling, left the group of men, and spat on the horse. "Well, will you challenge me?" he said. "I'll enjoy letting out your white blood."

"You'd fight me next!" yelled Adminius. He too had been quick in picking up something of the Gallic languages.

Colconor grinned. "Aye, aye. The lot of you. One at a time, though. Your chieftain first. And afterward I've a right to rest between bouts." He stared at the woman. "I'll spend those whiles with you three bitches, and you'll not like it, what I'll make you do." Turning, he swaggered back toward the grove.

Soren approached. "We are deeply sorry about

this," he said in Latin. "Far better that you be received as befits the envoy of Rome." A smile of sorts passed through his beard. "Well, later you shall be. I think Taranis wearies at last of this incarnation of His, and—the King of the Wood has powers, if he chooses to exercise them, beyond those of even a Roman prefect."

"I am to fight Colconor, then?" Gratillonius asked slowly.

Soren nodded. "In the Wood. To the death. On foot, though you may choose your weapons. There is an arsenal at the Lodge."

"I'm well supplied already." Gratillonius felt no fear. He had a task before him which he would carry out, or die; he did not expect to die.

He glanced back at the troubled faces of his men, briefly explained what was happening, and finished: "Keep discipline, boys. But don't worry. We'll still sleep in Ys tonight. Forward march!"...

It was but a few minutes to the site. A slate-flagged courtyard stood open along the road, flanked by three buildings. They were clearly ancient, long and low, of squared timbers and with shingle roofs. The two on the sides were painted black, one a stable, the other a storehouse. The third, at the end, was larger, and blood-red. It had a porch with intricately carven pillars.

In the middle of the court grew a giant oak. From the lowest of its newly leafing branches hung a brazen circular shield and a sledgehammer. Though the shield was much too big and heavy for combat, dents surrounded the boss, which showed a wildly bearded and maned human face. Behind the house, more oaks made a grove about seven hundred feet across and equally deep.

"Behold the Sacred Precinct," Soren intoned. "Dismount, stranger, and ring your challenge." After a moment he added quietly, "We need not lose time waiting for the marines and hounds. Neither of you will flee, nor let his opponent escape."

Gratillonius comprehended. He sprang to earth,

took hold of the hammer, smote the shield with his full strength. It rang, a bass note which sent echoes flying. Mute now, Eppillus gave him his military shield and took his cloak and crest before marshalling the soldiers in a meadow across the road.

Vindilis laid a hand on Gratillonius's arm. Never had he met so intense a gaze, out of such pallor, as from her. In a voice that shook, she whispered, "Avenge us, man. Set us free. Oh, rich shall be your reward."

It came to him, like a chill from the wind that soughed among the oaks, that his coming had been awaited. Yet how could she have known?

Here is an excerpt from the newest novel by Martin Caidin, to be published in September 1986 by Baen Books:

The senior officer on duty on the flight line of Guantanamo Air Base on the southern coastline of Cuba checked the time, made a notation on his clipboard, and lifted his head as a buzzer affixed to his ear rattled his skull. He turned. They were right on time. Captain Jeff Baumbach moved his hand more by reflex than directed thought to check the .357 Magnum on his hip. He gestured at the armored vehicle slowing at the gate, its every movement covered by heavy automatic cannon.

"Check 'em *all* out!" Baumbach called. Military Police motioned the truck in between heavy barricades until it was secured. They checked the identity passes of every man, went through, atop and beneath the vehicle, finally sent it through the final barricade to the flight line where two machine gun-armed jeeps rolled alongside as escort. The armored truck stopped by an old Convair 440 twin-engined transport with bright lettering on each side of its fuselage. The cargo doors of the transport of ST. THOMAS ORCHARD FARMS opened wide. The crew wore Air Force fatigues and all carried sidearms.

A master sergeant studied the truck and the men. "Move it, move it," he said impatiently. "Load 'em up. We're behind schedule."

Four cases moved with exquisite care from the truck to the loading conveyor to the aircraft. Each case carried the same identifying line but differing serial numbers. It didn't really matter. NUCLEAR WEAPON MARK 62 is enough of a grabber without any silly serial number.

The bombs were loaded and secured with steel cabling and heavy webbing tiedowns, men signed their names and exchanged papers, doors slammed closed, and the right engine of the Convair whined as the pilots brought power to the metal bird. . . .

In central Florida, horses moved through the tall morning-wet grass of a remote field. It is an ordinary scene of an ordinary Florida ranch . . . until the trees and the fences begin to move.

Tractors pulled the trees, tugging with steel cables to move the wheeled dollies from the soft ground. Pickup trucks and jeeps latched on to fence ends and moved slowly to swing the fences at enormous hinges. Within minutes a clear path seven thousand feet from north to south had been created, and the whine of machinery sounded over the staccato beating of equine hooves. Men kept the animals clear of field center, where high grass moved as if by magic to reveal an asphalted airstrip beneath. Still invisible to any eye, powerful jet engines rose from a deep-throated whine to ear-twisting shrieks and the cry of acetylene torches. Shouting male voices diminish to feeble cries in the rising crescendo of power, and workers move hastily aside as the front of a hill disappears into the ground and two jet fighters roll forward slowly, bobbing on their nose gear.

"Sir, they're loading now," the controller tells the lead pilot, knowing the second man also listens. "Are you ready to copy? I have their time hack for takeoff and the stages for their route."

The man in the lead jet fighter responds in flawless Arabic. "Quickly; I copy. And do not speak English again." . . .

"Orchard One, you're clear to the active and clear for takeoff. Over."

Captain Jim Mattson pressed his yoke transmit button. "Ah, roger Gitmo Control. Orchard One clear for the active and rolling takeoff. Over."

"Orchard One, it's all yours. Over."

"Roger that, Gitmo. Orchard One is rolling." Mattson advanced the throttles steadily, his copilot, John Latimer, placing his left hand securely atop the knuckles of his pilot. The convair sped toward the ocean, lifted smoothly and began its long climbing turn over open water. . . .

The horses shied nervously with the relentless howl of the jet fighter engines. Everyone on the field waited for the right words to pass between the controller in his underground bunker on the side of the runway and the two men in the fighter cockpits. A headset in the lead fighter hummed.

"Control here."

"Go ahead."

"Your quarry is in the air. Confirm ready."

The pilots glanced at one another. "Allah One ready."

"Allah Two waits."

"Very good, sirs. Three minutes, sirs." . . .

They came out of the sun, silvery streaks trailing the unsuspecting shape of Orchard One. Their presence remained unknown until the instant a powerful electronic jammer in the rear cockpit of the lead T-33 broadcast its signal to overpower any electronics aboard the Convair. The shriek pierced the eardrums of the Convair's radioman and he ripped off his headset. In the cockpit, Captain John Latimer, flying right seat, mirrored the reaction to the icepick scream in their ears. Instinct brought Captain Jim Mattson's hands to the yoke. But the automatic pilot held true, and the Convair did not wave or tremble. Only the radio and electronics systems had seemingly gone mad. The flight engineer rushed to the cockpit, squeezed Mattson's shoulder, and shouted to him. "Sir! To our left! There!"

They looked out to see the all-black fighter with Arabic lettering on the fuselage and tail. The pilot's face was concealed behind an oxygen mask and goldfilm visor. "Who the hell is that?" Mattson wondered aloud, and in the same breath turned to Latimer. "You all right?"

Latimer sat back, shaking his head to clear the battering echoes in his brain. He nodded. "Yeah, sure; fine. What the hell was that?"

The radioman wailed painfully into the flight deck with them, his face furrowed in pain. "Jamming . . . somehow they're jamming us. They must have, God, I don't know . . . but I can't get out on anything."

They exchanged glances. Not a single word was needed to confirm that they were in deep shit. Nobody shows up in a black T-33 jet fighter with Arabic markings and knocks out all radio frequencies unless they're a nasty crowd with killing on their minds. Mattson instantly became the professional military pilot.

"Emergency beacon?"

"No joy, sir. Blocked."

"Anybody see more than one fighter out—"

The answer came in a hammering vibration that blurred their sight. The Convair yawed sharply to the right as metal exploded far out on the right wing. "There's another one out there, all right!" Latimer shouted. "He just shot the hell out of the wing! He's coming alongside—"

They watched the black fighter slide into perfect formation to their right and just above their mangled wingtip. His dive brake extended. The pilot pointed down with his forefinger and then his landing gear extended.

"Jesus Christ!" Latimer exclaimed. "He's ordered us to land!"

"Screw that," Mattson snarled. "Sparks! Get Patrick Control and tell them we're under attack. We need—"

"Sir, goddamnit! I can't get out on any frequency!"

Glowing tracers lashed the air before the Convair. The T-33 on their left had eased back and above to give them another warning burst. They looked out at the fighter to their right. The pilot tapped his left wrist to signify his watch, then drew a finger across his throat.

SEPTEMBER 1986 • 65588-4 • 448 pp. • $3.50